BRIGHTON

BRIGHTON

MICHAEL HARVEY

An Imprint of HarperCollinsPublishers

This book is a work of fiction. The characters, incidents, and dialogue are drawn from the author's imagination and are not to be construed as real. Any resemblance to actual events or persons, living or dead, is entirely coincidental.

HarperCollins books may be purchased for educational, business, or sales promotional use. For information please e-mail the Special Markets Department at SPsales@harpercollins.com.

FIRST EDITION

Designed by Ashley Tucker
Title page art ©Miloje/Shutterstock

Library of Congress Cataloging-in-Publication Data has been applied for.

ISBN 978-0-06-244297-0

16 17 18 19 20 OV/RRD 10 9 8 7 6 5 4 3 2 1

In memory of
Brian "the Cat" Ward
Boston through and through

How often have I lain beneath rain on a strange roof, thinking of home.

—William Faulkner, *As I Lay Dying*

———

PROLOGUE

1971

HE FIRST met Bobby Scales along the banks of the Charles River. Kevin wasn't doing much, skipping rocks across the gray-green water and watching light dance along the skin of oil that floated on top. He turned just in time to see Bobby clear a crook in the path. He was older, maybe twelve or thirteen, with coal black hair and features bleached white against the sun. He walked with his head down, kicking at the ground as he went, and carried a burlap bag over his shoulder. The bag was moving.

"Hey," Kevin said. He'd seen Bobby around and knew enough to know no one fucked with him. It wasn't that Bobby was big. He wasn't. Or that he carried a gun or a knife. He might, but Kevin had never heard of it. Bobby didn't have any parents. That might make a kid seem tougher, but it was mostly the way he locked on to you with that quiet, pitiless gaze. Everyone in Brighton knew Bobby Scales wasn't messing. And he wasn't anyone to fuck with.

"What are you doing down here?" Bobby said.

Kevin tried hard not to look at the bag, still twitching at the older boy's feet. "Just throwing rocks. What's in the bag?"

Bobby squatted on his heels and opened it. A dog's head

popped out, yellow teeth flashing. Bobby put a hand on the dog's muzzle and calmed it. "I got his legs tied up so he can't stand. He isn't very strong anyway."

"What happened to him?"

"You know Fat Frank?"

Everyone knew Fat Frank Tessio. He drove a green Barracuda and liked to sit by himself on a bench in the park, watching the ball games and smoking cigars in the cool, blue moonlight. One afternoon he pulled up to a curb Kevin was sitting on, short eyes buzzing and thick lips spread in a smile. Kevin was gone before Fat Frank could lean across the seat and pop the door open.

"Fucker keeps the dog tied up in his cellar," Bobby said. "Beats hell out of him with a cut-down piece of pipe. So I took him."

Kevin counted the ribs down one side of the dog's flank and stopped at a half dozen. He had the lean face of a mutt, with white flecking across the neck and shoulders. His eyes were clouded and rimmed in red. When Kevin came close, the dog snapped his jaws and tried to get up.

"Better stay back."

Kevin sat against a tree and didn't move. "What are you gonna do?"

Bobby scratched the dog behind his ears, stubby and curled like a couple pieces of dried leather. Kevin listened to the labored breathing and watched the dog's tongue pulse in and out.

"Going down to the riv." Bobby pointed to a screen of trees. "You hear someone coming, you give a yell. Okay?"

Kevin nodded. He didn't know why he nodded. Didn't know why he didn't run like hell. But he didn't. Bobby carried the dog, bag and all, down the slope. Kevin shifted so he could see the silhouettes of boy and dog against the sun rubbing off the river.

Bobby leaned low and pressed his head against the mutt's for what seemed like three or four lifetimes. Then he sat back, stroking the dog's muzzle and staring out over the water. After a bit, he started to pull rocks out of the bag, flat and heavy. He pushed the dog's head down, closed up the bag, and tied it tight with a length of rope. Then he leaned close again and began to whisper. Kevin thought of his stint as an altar boy and the prayers the priests kept to themselves as they stood behind the altar and laid their hands over the chalice. Bobby picked up the biggest rock in his fist, raised it high, and brought it down hard. Once, twice, three times. The bag never moved. The dog never made a sound. Bobby put the rock and three others like it into a smaller satchel and tied it to the other end of the rope. He waded into the Charles until the water covered his thighs. Then he pushed the bag down and made the sign of the cross as it sank. When he came back, Kevin was still there, arms around his ribs, crying like a baby and not caring a damn bit either. Bobby sat beside him and picked up a stone, black on one side and white on the other, smooth as glass.

"I pulled him out of Fat Frank's cellar three different times, but he just kept going back." Bobby skimmed the stone, four skips before it caught an edge and sank. "Then I figured it out. Some things are just better off dead. And there ain't no use fighting it."

Kevin stared across the infinite void of space and watched the world spin and tumble in the pale orbits of Bobby Scales's eyes. Life, death, and everything in between. After ten minutes, the bag hadn't surfaced. Bobby stood, Kevin in his shadow, and the two of them left.

PART ONE

1975

1

HITTING'S ALL about hips and hands. Unless you thought about it too much. Then it was impossible. But Kevin was fifteen and the world was still pretty simple. See the ball. Hit the ball. Hips and hands.

The kid from Charlestown stood behind the mound and rubbed up a new baseball. Just like Catfish. Kevin stepped out and picked up a handful of dirt. Just like Pudge. The pitcher climbed back up on the mound. Kevin let him wait. The backstop behind him was packed with hard, white faces. Someone told him to get the fuck back in the box. Kevin told him to piss off without looking back. Then the catcher mumbled something and the umpire took off his mask and yelled at everyone to shut the fuck up. Kevin leveled the bat back and forth, testing its weight and feel. His eyes were on the pitcher now. Watching him watch. Kevin stepped back in the box, dragging his spikes through the loose gravel. He was in an 0-2 hole and shortened up an inch or so on the bat. Tommy Doucette danced off second. Someone yelled from down the third base line. Kevin pointed his bat once, twice, at the mound. The pitcher wound up and threw. An inside fastball, but not inside enough. Kevin opened up his hips and let his hands fly. The moment he hit it, he knew the third baseman had no chance. The only question was whether it would stay fair. Kevin snuck a look as he ran. The ball caught a lick of chalk and skittered into a pack of locals who scattered in a flurry of Styrofoam and beer bottles. The umpire screamed fair as Kevin hit first and dug for second. He slid out of habit, but the shortstop already had his glove on his head. Tommy Doucette was on the bottom of a half-dozen teammates at the plate. Brighton was in the other guy's park but had been designated home team for the city semifinal. And now they'd won, 3–2.

Kevin stood on second and felt his heart thump in his chest. His teammates turned and began to run toward him—a series of grass-stained images framed forever in his mind. He pulled off his helmet, never knowing where it landed as they fell upon him, crumpling under their weight on the hard infield while a couple hundred Townies watched and cursed. At fifteen, the game was easy, a world unto itself. That time, however, was drawing to a close. And somewhere inside Kevin knew it would never be like this again.

———

They drove out of Charlestown in a daze. Kevin sat in the backseat of Teddy Boyle's rusted-out convertible. Teddy was an assistant coach for the team. His claim to fame was that he'd been arrested after his wife was found dead in her bed by a neighbor. Teddy swore up and down he'd slept in the same bed with the corpse for two nights and never noticed a thing. Teddy told the police his wife had always been a sound sleeper and the couple never talked much anyway. When the coroner's report came back as a massive cerebral hemorrhage, the cops let Teddy go. And he had a great story for his buddies at the Grill.

Teddy had given each of the kids a bat before they left the parking lot, just in case they had trouble getting out of Charlestown. Teddy wore a porkpie Budweiser hat sideways and had a cold bottle of the stuff tucked in his crotch as he tooled through Thompson Square, laying on the horn and flipping off the locals. Once they hit Storrow Drive, he told the kids to put away the bats and gave them each a beer, sharp and wonderful at the back of their throats. Teddy did seventy-five on Storrow, leading the car in chants of Brighton and city champs as they cruised past Harvard and its clock tower, gleaming crimson and white on the far side of the river. By the time they rolled through Oak Square, streams of people were bubbling out of various bars and into the street. Charlestown had been city champs three years running and a heavy favorite to make it four. No one gave Brighton a chance. They circled Tar Park, Teddy laying on the horn, then pulled into the Grill's parking lot as Kevin's coach, Jimmy Fitz, blessed the car in beer. Kids piled out. Fitz grabbed Kevin by the back of the neck and raked his face with a bristle of beard.

"What did I tell you? What did I tell you?"

Fitz let Kevin go and began to dance a jig in the gutter. Kevin tried to explain they still had one more game to play, but his coach wasn't having it. Someone yelled Fitz's name and he wandered off, stopping once to tip his head back, spread his arms wide, and howl a toothless howl at a starless sky. Then Kevin was alone again. He picked his way through the crowd clogging the street, taking all the hugs and pats on the back in stride until he'd broken free. In the middle of Oak Square was a traffic rotary with a spit of grass surrounded by park benches. Everyone in Brighton called it the Circle. Bobby Scales sat on one of the benches, watching the festivities and drinking a Brigham's frappe.

"You won?"

"Yeah." Kevin sat down beside him.

"How did you do?"

"Two for three. Single and a double."

"Who do you play next?"

"City championship against Dorchester. I think it's downtown. At the Boston Common or something."

Bobby finished his frappe and threw the cup in a barrel. "I played there. Nice field. No rocks, real grass. They got a P.A. system."

"No kidding."

"Sure. They announce the name of every hitter." Bobby was the best baseball player Brighton had ever seen. Kevin remembered standing behind the backstop one night as he hit three over the right-field fence and into Friendly's parking lot. Brighton lost to Medford 6–5, but all anyone talked about afterward was Bobby and the sweet, left-handed stroke.

"Dot's always tough," Bobby said. "Lot of hockey players."

Kevin shrugged like he didn't give a fuck, which was a lie. Bobby studied him.

"You wanna grab a slice?" Kevin said.

They walked across Washington Street to Imperial Pizza. The owner, a small, neat Italian everyone called Joe, sat at a table, folding delivery boxes and reading a soccer magazine.

"You win?" Joe said.

Kevin nodded.

"Good boy. Slice?"

Bobby held up two fingers. They ate sitting on the curb. Hot tomato and cheese, crisped slices of pepperoni sitting in puddles of grease, pillow soft crust. Kevin noticed for the first time that his pants were ripped and stained with blood. He peeled back his uniform at the knee and cleaned out the rocks and dirt as best he could.

"You working tomorrow?" Bobby said.

Kevin worked weekends at his grandmother's cab office. Bobby lived in a spare room above the office. He'd gone through a string of foster homes growing up, finally landing in a house run by some priests in Cambridge when he was thirteen. Then Kevin's grandmother took him in. Kevin remembered the day she came home with Bobby. She swore up and down she'd never go to mass again, then stayed up all night with Kevin's mom, whispering over cigarettes and tea and saying decades of the rosary. When he was sixteen, Bobby quit high school. He wasn't dumb, far from it, but he'd decided that was how it was gonna be and started driving cabs the next day.

"I was gonna go in about nine," Kevin said.

"Come in at seven. We'll go behind the Jeff. Get you a little time behind the wheel."

"I don't even have my permit."

"Fuck it. We ain't going nowhere except around an empty lot. Besides, your grandmother won't mind." Bobby slapped Kevin on the brim of his hat. "Congrats on the game. Now go kick the shit out of Dot."

Kevin watched Bobby walk back to the Circle and take the same seat on the same bench. He stretched his legs out in front of him and draped his arms along the back, content to survey the world as it spun past. Kevin mimicked the pose, leaning back on the pavement with his elbows and letting his sneakers trail into the gutter. A car hit the Circle and slowed. A kid stuck his head out the rear window, but Bobby waved them on. Across the Square, Teddy Boyle was standing on the hood of his car, singing a song Kevin couldn't hear while someone pounded the horn. Tomorrow they'd climb out of their three-deckers and head to the job. Punching tickets on the T. Banging nails into drywall for some rich lady's house in Newton. Fixing carburetors and flat tires in Allston. Drinking a ball and a beer for lunch. Boiling in their own rage and drowning in a puddle of sorrows. But that was tomorrow. Tonight they'd celebrate.

———

He walked up Champney Street alone, the crooked line of two-families and three-deckers lit up for the evening, a dull yellow smear running uphill and into the night. A shade jerked to Kevin's right, and Mrs. Chin's face gleamed from a second-floor window. She and her husband ran a Laundromat, living above it with their girls in a three-room apartment. Kevin had been scared of Mrs. Chin when he was a kid and wouldn't look at her face cuz it was covered in peeling patches of white. His grandmother explained that she'd lived in Hiroshima when "they'd dropped the bomb" and had her skin cooked by the blast. Kevin asked his grandmother why she'd said "they" dropped the bomb when it was really "us." She'd told him that was a good point and when did he get so goddamn smart. Kevin hesitated, then raised his hand to wave at Mrs. Chin, who tracked him with her eyes, looking like an animal who'd been tied to a tree and would never trust another human being again. He continued up the hill to number eight. A single light burned in a bay window that sagged out over the street. That would be the old man, sitting in his chair, drinking whiskey by the glassful, smoking cigars and humming tunelessly to himself. Somehow he'd already know about the game. And Kevin's winning hit. And that would kill him.

Kevin cut down a hidden path that burrowed along the far side of the three-decker. Light from the porch cast wispy shadows over the weeded lot that served as his backyard. A scrub of trees ran a dark curtain down one side of the property. The other side was bordered by Indian Rock, two acres of woods, granite, and grass growing wild. Indian Rock was owned by the church and favored by every kid within five miles who was looking to get drunk, laid, or, in that best of all possible worlds, both. At the very back of the lot was a chain-link fence and two-story building with a peaked roof and five or six dark shapes surrounding it. His grandmother's cab company. Kevin thought about going over and crashing on a couch in the office. There was a blanket and some pillows there and a TV he could wheel out and watch in the dark. In the end, Kevin scooted up the back steps of the three-decker and slipped into the first-floor apartment.

He slept on a mattress laid out on the floor of a converted pantry. Down the hall, his sisters slept in one of the two real bedrooms. Kevin eased their door open, an ear tuned to the Sox game blaring on the TV in the living room. A pair of single beds filled the narrow room from wall to wall. Plastered above one bed were posters from movies. *Bambi, Dumbo, The Wizard of Oz*, anything with Julie Andrews in it. Kevin's baby sister, Colleen, was nine and already hooked on make-believe. All things considered, he couldn't blame her. On a shelf above the other bed was a thick medical dictionary and a lumpy copy of *Gray's Anatomy*. Those belonged to Bridget. She was three years younger than Kevin and liked to take things apart to see what made them tick. Except instead of a toaster, Bridget picked the legs off spiders she caught in the yard. More than anything, however, she liked to dissect her little sister. And then watch her squirm. Kevin was about to back out of the room when Colleen lifted her head, shook out her long, rumpled locks, and yawned.

"What time is it?"

"Almost ten. Go back to sleep."

She yawned again and stretched her legs under the covers. Colleen still slept the sleep of a child and Kevin envied her without really understanding why.

"Did you win?" she said.

"Sure."

She held out her hand. He deposited a baseball in it. It was a ritual they'd started at the beginning of the summer. She dated each ball and kept them in a cardboard box under the bed. Kevin played it off like he was doing a favor for his kid sister but was secretly thrilled, feeling a little bit like a big-leaguer signing autographs every time he handed over a ball. Colleen was studying the latest addition to her collection when a hand snaked out from under a lump of blankets and ripped it from her fingers. Colleen looked up at Kevin, enormous eyes already beginning to fill.

"Cut it out," he whispered.

Bridget peeked out from beneath the bedding, a lurid smile slumming on the twelve-year-old's lips. "Let her cry."

Colleen was about to burst and Kevin could hear movement in the living room. "Here." He had another ball in his glove and gave it to Colleen. "This is the one that won the game anyway."

She immediately brightened. "Really?"

"He's lying," Bridget said. "This is the real one. That's why he gave it to you."

An image shot through Kevin's head. His mom, fingers greased with Dippity-Do, fashioning thick rings of curls in Colleen's hair, then oohing and aahing as they cascaded down her back. Bridget, sitting in the corner and watching in the mirror, hating everything and everyone she saw reflected there. Nothing and no one more than herself. Kevin felt a pinch of sorrow and plucked the ball from Bridget's hand in the smooth, easy motion of an older brother. "Both of you go to bed. Colleen, keep that one for now and we'll figure it out later."

There was another creak in the hallway—someone walking to the front door and back into the living room.

"Better get out of here before he comes down." Bridget's tone screamed *coward,* and Kevin felt her eyes drilling into his spine as he walked back down the hall toward the pantry. He lay in the bed he'd made under a high window, watching the world turn in long beams of moonlight, listening for footsteps until he fell asleep.

2

KATIE PEARCE drew hard on her cigarette, letting the smoke soak into her lungs before exhaling into the sharp morning air. HE would be up soon. She needed to get Kevin out of the house, get going on breakfast. Her eyes traveled across the brooding presence of Indian Rock. Her mind climbed the hill that lived behind it. At the top of that hill was Saint Andrew's Academy, an all-girls high school. Twenty years ago, her high school. Class of 1955. Katie took another suck on her cigarette and poured out the memories in twisted ribbons of smoke. Old men, long-nosed and rawboned, yellow teeth and whiskers, perched on thin wooden chairs, cheeks coarse and ruddy under cold, black eyes. Boston. Brahmin. Blue bloods. She conjured up her opponents as well. Four other students, all boys, sizing up one another as they waited. Two whispered in a corner. One looked like he wanted to talk, but she froze him out. Fear curdled her stomach. They were from Latin School, BC High, Exeter, Groton. Crème de la crème. Goliath to her David. Finalists for the state oratory medal. St. A's had never hosted the event, never won it either. Katie would be the first. The nuns were certain of it, and so they'd heaped everything on her seventeen-year-old shoulders. The Smart One.

And she'd loved them fiercely for it. Until now. Now that the moment was here. It wasn't like practice, standing at one end of the gleaming third-floor hallway while Sister Ellen stood at the other, snapping a wooden clicker and telling her to enunciate. Not like the prelims where they'd arrived as a team, the Academy girls, smart as whips, quiet, modest, confident. Feared. That was then. This was different. They trotted out the finalists one at a time. The first speaker was a senior from Groton. He rested his hands lightly on the lectern and leaned forward, every gesture polished and easy, his speech little more than a private chat between two generations of New England privilege and power. When he was finished, the boy took his time, gliding past Katie with barely a glance. Then her name was announced, and a tiny trickle of piss leaked down her leg.

Stupid Irish cow. Dumb cunt. Whore.

Her father's whispers hissed and snapped all around her as she walked on wooden legs to the lectern. He'd noticed the attention his daughter was getting. Fuck yes, he'd noticed. His attention. His spotlight. And that could never be. So he'd taken her for a drive two nights before the final and explained the pecking order—where she stood, what she was, what she'd always be.

Stupid Irish cow, dumb cunt, whore.

Katie looked out at her audience. One of the judges, the oldest with white hair and purple lips, took a handkerchief out of his pocket and waved at her to begin. She opened her mouth and a dry croak hopped out. The patrician wiped his lips clean and leaned to his left for a whisper, then a delicious smile. Katie felt the shame well in her chest as a chair scraped and her head emptied. She turned and fled, running from her stillborn future, hiding somewhere in its cooling past. Eventually, one of the nuns found her in a bathroom stall. She told Katie it was all right. She'd do better next time. But Sister Ellen never spoke to her again, not like she had before. No one at the Academy did. And the only foothold she'd ever had in the world was scrubbed away in a flush of tears and fear and cunning. And she slid back down the hill, back into the valley of soot and ash where she belonged, where they all waited with their eager, misshapen smiles and sharp, shining teeth. And the bulb that had burned so brightly, so briefly, popped inside her head, the filament glowing red for the briefest of moments before her mind went dark forever.

Stupid Irish cow. Dumb cunt. Whore.

Katie Pearce flicked her cigarette into the morning breeze and watched it catch in the grass before winking out. There was more movement inside the house. HE would be up soon. She had to start the breakfast. And she had to get her only son out before they ate him alive as well.

3

KEVIN WOKE to the rough burn of tobacco and squinted at the smell in his sheets and on his clothes. His mom was awake, standing on the back porch with the kitchen door open, enjoying a smoke in the cold. He pulled the blanket up to his chin, relishing the warmth of his bed for another moment or two. In the concrete distance, he could hear the early morning rounds of the ragman. He haunted the neighborhood at five miles an hour, hanging his head out the window of an ancient pickup, beating a spoon against a tin pan dropped on a rope over the driver's-side door and sawing away in a singsong voice.

Any old rags, any old rags, any old raaaags . . .

Kevin listened to the wax and wane until the ragman's call had faded down the hill. Then it was quiet again. His mother came back inside, slippers scraping across the cracked linoleum as she went back and forth. Kevin waited until the kettle began to whistle, then got dressed and crept into the kitchen.

It was cold for early September. The radiator heat wasn't up, so his mom had lit the stove and left the oven door open. Kevin pulled a chair next to the heat and drank from the cup of Barry's she'd fixed.

"Want me to make some?" She held up a package of Jiffy corn muffin mix. Kevin loved corn muffins and his mom thought it made up for everything else. At nineteen cents a package, it was a cheap fix.

"Sure, Ma. Corn muffins would be great."

That was all the absolution she needed. Ten minutes later, they were ready—thin, gritty meal, but hot with a dollop of butter. Kevin ate two of them with tea. His mom sat with him and stared into some blank space only she could visit. After a few minutes, she stiffened in her chair, eyes moving to the hallway.

"Your father's up."

Kevin heard the hollow fear in her voice and felt it balloon in his belly. He scooped up another muffin, wrapped it in a paper napkin, and made his way to the back door. She helped him slip on his coat.

"Ma." He pulled away, but she still managed a kiss on the cheek.

"Got you." She wiped at the spot with the flat of her thumb and pushed back the hair from his forehead. "I love you, Kevin."

"I gotta go."

She took him by the chin and forced his eyes onto hers. "I do, Kevin. You know that."

"Yeah." There was the sound of water now from the bathroom. "I gotta go."

She rolled her eyes to the ceiling. "Stop upstairs and see her."

"I'm running late."

"Stop up and see her. It'll only take a minute."

Kevin grabbed his glove and slipped onto the landing, his mom snapping the lock behind him. He listened to the scrape of a kitchen chair and the cut of voices through the thin wooden door. Then he turned and took the stairs, two at a time.

———

The big cat slouched in a shadow, easy in his skin, watching as the boy ran up the stairs, Indian quiet, a baseball glove slapping off his thigh as he went. The boy disappeared into the third-floor apartment and the cat waited, almond eyes tick-tocking back and forth between the front windows of the cab office and the top floor where the old lady lived. Leaves chattered in the breeze. The cat flared his nostrils and squinted against the sun, dipped in fifty shades of cold heat and rising fast, its nascent rays caught in a stray pane of white glass. He thought about the boy. Then the old lady. It would be another hour before she made her way across the yard. The big cat shrank back into the scrub and settled in to wait.

4

MARY BURKE sipped at her tea and thought about her shorties. She had them stashed all over the apartment, waiting for a late night or early morning when Horrigan's was closed and she needed one. She got up from the kitchen table and walked into the living room, playing bent fingers among the dust bunnies that lived on the ledge over the door. Her cigarette butt was crouched in the corner just where she'd left it. Mary took it back to the kitchen and lit up, pulling the velvet smoke down into her lungs. At night she could sometimes feel the phlegm, thick and hard and brown, and the pump as her heart skipped and struggled. Mary would hack and cough until she'd cleared a passageway and her heart had settled back into its normal rhythm. Then she'd light up again, just to show her lungs who was boss. She'd lie in bed and listen to Larry Glick on the radio, blowing smoke rings at the ceiling and thinking about cycles within cycles—dreamless days that blended, one into another.

She'd been born sixty years ago at the same table where she took her breakfast. The sixth of seven, Mary grew up silent and smart. Her mother died when she was thirteen. They told the neighbors she'd fallen down a flight of stairs, but Mary knew better. When her father fell down the same flight six months later, Mary and Shuks (one of her five brothers and Mary's favorite) stared down at his body from the landing and thought that was just about right. She married in the winter when she was seventeen. Today they'd probably call it rape, but once her future husband took her cherry she didn't really have much choice. And thinking about anything else just wore her out. Mary churned out six kids in eight years—a regular hump machine, staring at cracks in the wall as he rutted over her. Her husband was her father in every respect. Only this one knew better. He feared Mary. And so the beatings were that much worse.

She'd set up the closet when her oldest was twelve. It had a sliding black bolt on it, some pillows, and a blanket. The kids would hear him on the stairs late at night and show up at the bedroom door, eyes lit by a cold, vacant light. She'd walk them down the hall and stuff them all in the closet. She'd go in last and slide the bolt across. Then they'd sit. The first time he clubbed his fists against the door. The old boards shuddered and paint cracked and fell off in thin, curling pieces. But the door held. One of the middle girls started to cry and Mary put an arm around her and wiped the tears dry with the back of her hand. On the other side of the door, her husband pulled up a chair and talked to his family. Each, in turn. The girls were whores. The boys, faggots and fairies. Their mother? She'd sucked his dick the first night they'd met. In an alley just off Oak Square. She'd sucked and he'd watched her suck. And now her children knew and how did that feel? Mary could have told him it didn't feel like anything at all. But he already knew that. And one day it would kill him.

She took a final drag and crushed out the cigarette with her thumb, watching memories fade and die in the coal red ash.

There was a tread on the stairs outside. She got up slowly and shuffled to the back door just as it opened. Her grandson, Kevin, was there, gray eyes catching hers in sketches of early morning light.

"Hi, Gram."

"You want some tea?"

"I gotta get going."

"Sit down for a minute."

The boy took a seat at the kitchen table. She could already feel the sadness in him. It rippled through the generations. Some seemed immune, the stony ground of their souls reflected in the hard, flat planes of their faces. And then there were ones like him. Mary felt the familiar tightening in her chest, a squirming bag of fears in her gut. A new generation would be served. And she was powerless to stop it.

"Are you working today?" she said.

"I was gonna ride with Bobby."

"Let me guess, you want to drive?"

"Bobby said you wouldn't mind."

"Is that what he said?" Her chuckle turned into a hacking cough. They both waited while it ran its course.

"Is it okay, Gram?"

"Take one of the old cabs. And for cripes sake, don't hit anything." She got up to fill the kettle.

"Are you going over?" he said.

"I'll probably go in for the morning and see how I do."

"What's the matter?"

"Nothing. Just don't get old." She pulled out a box of wooden matches, struck one, and lit a burner on the stove. "You win last night?"

"Yep. We're in the city final." He held up his glove. "Got practice at eleven."

The water was still hot and the kettle began to whistle almost immediately. Mary pulled out a box of Red Rose tea and dropped a bag in a mug. Tea was her constant companion—a cure-all for whatever brand of heartache came traipsing through the door. Everything about it, from the ritual of boiling the water to fixing the accompanying toast, calmed and soothed her. She knew it was crazy, but the world always seemed to make a little more sense when you considered things over a cup of tea. At least that was her opinion and the hell with anyone who disagreed. The water spit as she poured from the kettle, and she set the tea in front of her grandson. Then she poured a cup for herself. He stirred in milk and sugar. She got out the butter and began to fix the toast.

"Mom made corn muffins." Kevin pulled a white napkin from his pocket and unwrapped it.

"Oh, all right." She sat down again and picked at the muffin, tapping the side of her foot against the table in an urgent, anxious rhythm. "How's your mother?" Katie Pearce was Mary Burke's third youngest, the smartest of the lot, and the one who'd stayed close.

"She's fine."

"Tell her I went to the store yesterday. Never mind, I'll tell her myself."

Even with the milk and sugar, the tea was strong and brown and rich. They sat and sipped.

"Your father home last night?" she said.

"He watched the game in the living room."

"That's it?"

"That's it."

She caught the boy's tone and let it go, opting for a pen and the *Globe*'s crossword. Kevin reached for the front page. He'd been weaned on Watergate, following every twist and turn, living and dying with Woodward and Bernstein as they took down a presidency. She'd watched from across the kitchen table, arguing the finer points with the boy, forcing him to defend his beliefs, challenging at every opportunity. Along the way she'd witnessed the blossoming of a mind. No one had ever been to college in their family. He'd be the first. And so much more.

"What's the headline?" she said.

The *Globe* was running a retrospective on Watergate, with a focus on Nixon and what he'd do with the rest of his life. She took one look at the former president's face on the front page and pushed it away. "Crook."

"All Nixon ever had to do was tell the truth," Kevin said.

"You don't know Republicans."

"That's all he had to do, Gram. Just tell the truth about the robbery."

"And why would he do that?"

"Two reasons. First, Americans would have forgiven him. Second, the *Washington Post* was gonna get him."

"The Republicans told JFK they'd kill him if he came to Dallas and they did."

"What's that got to do with Watergate?"

"They're Republicans. That's what." She broke off a piece of muffin, soaking it in her tea until it was soft. "Did you hear about Brackett Street?"

"What about it?"

"Some black bastard from Fidelis Way broke into an apartment and nearly killed a woman."

"I heard there was no one home."

"He had a knife with him. What do you think he was looking to do?"

"How do you know he had a knife? And how do you know he was black?"

Mary Burke got up and began to pace, the fear now screwed up tight and spinning in her belly. "Goddamn niggers."

"I hate that word, Gram."

"I'm not talking about all of them."

"I don't care."

"I saw one in the backyard yesterday." Her words came out in a quick rush of air.

"Saw what? A black kid?"

She nodded. It was just three in the afternoon. He'd caught her peeking at him from behind a shade in her kitchen and hightailed it down the alley. But she'd seen him. And that was enough.

"Maybe he knew someone who lives around here," Kevin said.

"He ran like hell when he saw me."

"I cut through backyards all the time, Gram."

She grunted. The boy drained his cup and pulled on his coat. "Bobby's gonna be waiting."

"Come here." She gave him a kiss on the cheek and ran rough fingers through his hair. "You're right, Kev. It's an awful word."

"Then why use it?"

"Cuz I'm an old woman and I'm scared. And I should know better."

The boy's face flushed. "You don't have to apologize to me, Gram."

"Like hell I don't." She slid her hands under the collar of his coat and felt the weight of it between her finger and thumb. "You sure you're gonna be warm enough in this?"

"I'm fine."

She let go of the collar, smoothing it flat. "Ask Bobby why he didn't stop in this morning."

"I don't like asking him that."

"Ask anyway."

The boy fidgeted in his sneakers.

"You like Bobby a lot, don't you, Kev?"

A shrug. "Bobby's cool."

"You think so?"

"Heck, yeah."

"Look at me."

He did.

"You know I'm not always gonna be around."

"Don't."

"I'm not in the grave yet. I'm just saying, someday."

"All right, someday. Way in the future."

"When it does happen, things will change."

"What kind of things?"

"I don't know for sure, but there'll be a void and it's just human nature to want to fill it. The point is I think you've got 'special' written all over you."

"Gram . . ."

"That doesn't mean it'll be easy. There might still come a time when the whole thing could tip one way or the other. And you won't know which way to push. Or even if you should push at all."

"I'll know."

He was always so certain. Late at night, it's the thing that scared her most. "You won't know, Kevin. You'll think you know, but you won't. I want you to promise me you'll trust Bobby. He'll know. And he'll do what it takes. All right?"

"Sure."

"Bobby. No one else."

"I got it."

"Good. Now, give me a kiss."

He leaned in. She searched his face the way she always did. Then she let him go and the boy was gone.

———

Mary Burke watched her grandson pick his way across the back-yard toward the cab office. When he was halfway there, she drew the shade and pulled down a strongbox she kept on the top shelf of her china cabinet. Inside was a stack of cash held together by a thick rubber band and a thirty-eight-caliber revolver with winds of gray tape wrapped around the grip. She picked up the gun and felt the weight of it in her hand. Then she shook her head and put it back up on the shelf, a hard, dark lump alongside the box of money.

5

FIVE BLACK taxis stood sentry outside the cab office. Massive
Detroit machines, with bumpers made of iron and headlights as
big as hubcaps, doors heavy enough to knock you over when they
swung open and engines that shook the ground under your feet
when they turned over. Each of them had OLD TOWNE TAXI stenciled
on the side. Kevin found the key to the back door of the office
under a rock and let himself in. His grandmother's wooden desk
sat silently by the window, looking back at the three-decker sunk
down in the yard. On the desk was a stack of papers and an enormous phone with a silver rotary dial. Kevin picked up the hand-
set and stared at the cab company's number, ST2-6400, stamped
in thick red letters on the receiver. Kevin's grandmother owned
the cab company outright. Her five brothers drove. Usually they
made it to their destination. Sometimes they found a drink and
hit a tree instead. Kevin hung up the phone and wandered out of
the main office, headed toward the second floor.

"Who's that?"

Kevin jumped and looked down at his feet. The voice came
from what his grandmother called the mouse hole—a half circle cut into the wall near the floor. The mouse hole was usually

sealed up. This morning, however, it was wide open, a shaft of white light streaming through.

"Hey, Aggie. It's just me."

Aggie was Kevin's great-aunt and his grandmother's only sister. She lived in a one-room apartment that shared a common wall with the office. Aggie never came out of her apartment and no one ever went in except Kevin's grandmother. All of Kevin's conversations with Aggie took place on his hands and knees, staring at a slice of her face through the mouse hole.

"Hi, Kevin. Take this, will you?" An empty plate with some crumbs on it and a teacup came sliding through. Kevin hated it but bent down so his face was nearly flat against the floor. A large blue eye rolled his way.

"You working today?"

"Yeah, Aggie."

The eye drifted. Now Kevin was looking at a piece of inflamed ear fringed by white hair and a stretch of moving red lip.

"I took my goofballs when I woke up. Four of 'em."

"Are you supposed to take that many?"

"Doctor says I should, but they make me crazy." The blue marble rolled back into its wooden socket. Kevin blinked and believed every inch of the power of the goofball.

"Where's Mary?" Aggie said.

"She's not in yet."

Every afternoon, Aggie and her sister sat in Aggie's apartment, watching *Candlepins for Cash* and eating bowls of ice cream. Something went wrong once and they rushed Aggie to the hospital with tubes up her nose and eyes gone back in her head. For three weeks after that, Kevin's grandmother ate ice cream alone, just her and the sound of pins falling on the black-and-white in a small kitchen at the back of the office. Kevin watched once from the dark hallway but left without saying a word.

"Tell Mary I got peach today," Aggie said.

"Peach?"

"Ice cream. She knows cuz she bought it. Make sure you tell her."

"You got it."

"Gotta go. Bye, Kevin."

The mouse hole snapped shut and Kevin was left on his hands and knees. He got up from the floor and took Aggie's cup and plate into the kitchen. His great-uncle, Shuks, sat at the table. He had the *Herald* laid out in front of him and a large black coffee beside it.

"Hey, Shuks."

"Hey, kid. What did Aggie want?"

"Nothing. She just gave me her stuff." Kevin dumped cup and plate in the sink. "Bobby up?"

"Haven't seen him."

"He's gonna let me drive one of the cabs."

"Good for you."

Kevin could have said he was gonna drink a case and a half of beer and piss off down the Mass Pike blindfolded and Shuks would have been all in. Dukie was the youngest and most naturally Irish of the five brothers, with curly hair of iron gray, long, sharp features, and a nose you wouldn't forget. He was also probably the best-looking, which wasn't saying a whole lot unless you said it to him. Shuks, on the other hand, wasn't pretty. His face was lumpy like soft potatoes. His hands were huge, with doorknobs for knuckles and thick, coarse fingers stained with nicotine. Still, he was Kevin's favorite. Shuks had been a wild man

back in the day—boozing and brawling his way through most of
the Irish joints in Boston until he finally decided to let his fists
earn him a living. Kevin had seen one of the old boxing posters,
so he knew it wasn't the usual family bullshit. Shuks at twenty-
three, crouched in front of the camera, tight blue eyes stitched
above a set of black gloves. Underneath, the script read NEW ENG-
LAND JUNIOR WELTERWEIGHT CHAMP, 1937. Most of Shuks's fights were
at places like the Taunton Civic Center or the Allston VFW. Twice
Shuks fought in Filene's window. He told Kevin those were the
best-paying bouts. They'd set up a ring in the big window on
Washington Street and people would stand on the corner and
watch. Shuks wasn't the type to brag, but Kevin liked to hear
about the fights. And he thought Shuks liked to talk about them.
Why the hell not? Kevin slapped his glove on the table and pulled
out a chair.

"Sox win?"

"Three to two. Lynn hit a home run in the eighth. Goin' all
the way this year, kid."

"They always blow it."

"Not this year."

"You think?"

"I got a feeling." Shuks reached for a pack of Lucky Strikes on
the table, shaking out a cigarette and pointing the business end
at Kevin. "Don't start. Cuts down on your wind." He always said
that before he lit up. And Kevin always nodded.

"You got practice today?"

"Yeah."

"What time?"

"Eleven. We play Dorchester for the title next week."

Blue streams of smoke issued from the tunnels his great-uncle called nostrils. "I'll be there." Shuks lived by himself in a cheap studio across from Tar Park and never missed a game. Rarely missed a practice. He didn't say much. Just sat on one of the benches drinking tallboy cans of Schlitz. Drank and smoked. Smoked and watched.

"It's down at the Commons," Kevin said. "Bobby told me they announce your name over a speaker."

"You gonna be nervous?"

"Probably."

"You don't look it out there."

"No?"

Shuks shook his head and pulled again on the Lucky. Kevin could hear the tobacco crackle and burn.

"When I played baseball, I was a wreck," Shuks said.

"Come on."

"Ask your grandmother. I'd shake like a leaf with that bat in my hands, praying to Christ they didn't hit the ball my way in the field. Course they always did."

"You were a professional boxer, Shuks."

"Boxing's nothing but a fistfight. No time to think about what can go wrong. Baseball's different." He tapped his temple with a knobby finger. "Gotta have it up here. Grace under pressure."

"You think I got that?"

"I know you do. Now, don't be getting a big head or nothing."

"I won't."

Shuks's chuckle was full of love and smoke and whiskey. "I know. I'm just giving you a hard time." He licked the side of ham he called a thumb and turned a page to the racing section. "Now, let me see if I can't make us a few shekels."

Kevin watched him mark up the page with a black pen, hesitant to say anything more because it was quiet and peaceful and safe with Shuks and it wasn't always that way. He took a final drag on the Lucky, crushing it in a tin ashtray and blowing out twin engines of smoke, then stretching his arms over his head and cracking his jaw in a ferocious yawn. Shuks had black rocks for teeth and precious few of those. Kevin remembered the night he'd seen one pulled. It happened at the same table where they were sitting now. Kevin was eight and had snuck into the back of the low-lit room. His great-uncle was slumped in a chair, rag stuffed in his jaw and a bottle of Paddy's on the table. Three of his brothers sat in a shiftless row along the wall. Kevin's gram stood over Shuks, a long, red-handled plumber's wrench in one hand. Shuks pulled out the rag and took a belt of whiskey. Then he nodded and Kevin's grandmother didn't wait. One of the brothers turned away as she worked the pliers. The other two watched and winced. She slipped once, ran her upper teeth over her lower lip, and got a better grip. Shuks's huge blue eye never left her, big man's hands twitching by his side, left foot tapping out a beat. Kevin remembered the god-awful crack and belly moan. Then the pliers were back on the table—rotting tooth, horned roots and all, in their gory maw. Shuks spit blood and went hard for the bottle. Kevin's grandmother sat down in a chair, slightly out of breath, and reached for her cigarettes. That was when she noticed Kevin. His eyes must have been as wide as the world because she hustled him out of the room, swearing he'd go to a dentist when the time came and to forget what he'd seen. Fat chance. Kevin's first trip to Dr. Foster ended when he gave the dentist a busted lip. Kevin's mom was mortified. Shuks had been proud as all hell and told him he had a good right hand. Kevin studied the creases in his great-uncle's face, suddenly desperate to commit them to memory for some reason he couldn't quite fathom. Shuks turned another page in his *Herald* and made some more notes.

"Got a nice one today, kid. Three fifteen at Suffolk."

"Oh, yeah?" Kevin crowded closer.

"Name's Gun Hill. He's been out for a couple of months with an injury. Dropping down into the claimers for the first time."

"Horse belongs in the fucking glue factory."

Shuks and Kevin looked up as one. Bobby was slouched in the doorway, wearing faded jeans and a Sox sweatshirt, black hair curling and still wet from the shower. He came over to the table and picked up the pack of cigarettes. Bobby shook one out and stuck it behind his ear.

"What do you know about Gun Hill?" Shuks said, grabbing his smokes off the table.

"Stay away from him, Shuks." Bobby winked at Kevin, turned around one of the chairs, and sat down. "You already owe Fingers a hundred for the piece of shit you bet on last week." In addition to driving cabs, Bobby hustled part-time for a local bookie named Fingers. "On top of that, you owe another twenty for the nigger pool from last week."

"Speaking of which . . ." Shuks pulled off an enormous lump of black boot and fished out a slip of paper he'd stuck in the heel. "Here's the number for this week. Twenty bucks."

"Forget it."

"How much was the payout last week?"

"Five fifty."

"I missed by one number."

"Everyone misses by one number, Shuks."

The nigger pool was a neighborhood lottery run by the local bookies. The winning numbers were taken from the last three digits of Saturday's take at Suffolk Downs printed in the Sunday paper. Shuks played every week. So did all his brothers and Kevin's grandmother. She hit the number once, and it was the only time Kevin had ever heard her laugh without any strings attached.

"Just put the bet in. I'll have Fingers's money tonight." Shuks flipped on the TV. A reporter stood in front of Charlestown High, talking about the new school year and the first full week of busing. The news report cut to videotape of a white kid wearing a Barracuda jacket inside out and throwing a bottle at a school bus stopped at a red light. Three more white kids pulled a kid with a yarmulke off the bus and beat him to the pavement. One of the kids started toward the camera with a bat, then everyone ran across the street. Two black faces peered out of a dry cleaners. The kid in the 'Cuda lobbed a brick through the front window and they poured in. A couple of cops on motorcycles rolled up as they cut back to the reporter still in front of the high school and talking a blue streak. Shuks turned down the sound.

"Fucking assholes," Bobby said.

Shuks twitched a thumb and blinked. "How'd you like to get bused through Dudley Square every morning?"

"Half those kids aren't even in school. They just want to crack some skulls. And if the skulls are black, so much the better."

Shuks rolled an eye toward Kevin. "You expecting trouble?"

Kevin went to Boston Latin School. Latin was the oldest public school in the country and offered its own entrance exam for prospective students. If you got in, it was free, at least until you flunked out. Every fall, eight hundred kids of every color and creed enrolled in Latin's seventh-grade class. Six years later, about a hundred graduated. Kevin didn't tell anyone when he applied to Latin. Didn't tell anyone when he was accepted. A month before school started, his mother found the letter in a drawer. She sat him down in the kitchen and asked what it was all about. When he told her, something stirred in her eyes, something fierce and young and bright and proud. Then his father banged through the front door and the spark was snuffed. She jammed the letter in one of Kevin's pockets and started hunting around in the cabinets for a box of mac and cheese. Two flights up, his grandmother taped the letter to her fridge and took it off every time anyone visited so they could read it and marvel.

"I go to Latin, Shuks."

"It's on the other side of the city and you take a bus."

"I'm fine."

Shuks glanced at Bobby, who shrugged and dangled a set of keys. "I'm gonna get him some time behind the wheel."

"Donnie Campbell needs a pickup at nine."

"Where's he headed?"

"Logan. Said he'd be waiting on the porch."

"Got it." Bobby turned to Kevin. "You ready?"

There was a sound outside in the lot. Three sets of eyes looked to the door. Kevin's grandmother wasn't expected into work for at least another fifteen minutes. But sometimes you never knew.

6

BRIDGET PEARCE sat in the kitchen, chin six inches off the table, shoveling Sugar Pops into her mouth as fast as she could. Her father sat across from her, fingers black under the nails from working on carburetors all week. Her mother was in between, clasping and unclasping her hands, a sure sign she was getting ready to speak. *Shut up,* Bridget thought. *Just shut up.*

"It's only up the hill, Jack."

"Up the hill. My ass, up the goddamn hill." Bridget's father picked up the blue-and-white ceramic shaker and tapped a sprinkle of salt over his eggs. Her mother moved the butter dish closer so he could reach it. They watched while he buttered, then dipped a corner of his toast in the yolk and took a bite, licking at a smear of yellow on his lip and taking a suffering sip of coffee before setting the cup back in its saucer.

"She has friends in Newton, Jack. She plays up there all summer."

"What's wrong with her friends down here?" The old man salted his eggs a second time and chewed noisily on a piece of bacon wrapped in a fold of yolky toast. Bridget could see the remains of breakfast in his teeth as he spoke. "Maybe Brighton's not good enough for her?"

"No one said that."

He beckoned without looking. "Come here."

Colleen was silhouetted in the doorway, shifting her weight from one foot to the other.

"I said come here, goddammit."

Bridget's mother gave the slightest of nods, and Colleen edged into the room. He swept her between his legs and pulled her close to his body, turning her around so she was staring at her mother.

"You'd love to go up the hill with her, wouldn't you, Kate?"

Bridget's mother's eyes ran on tracks in her head, from husband to daughter, hunting for an escape where there was none. "It's got nothing to do with that."

Lie. It had everything to do with that. And she damn well knew it. Bridget remembered the day last summer when she left, cheap clothes on wire hangers slung over her shoulder, Kevin's dry whispers in her ear, Colleen's screams taking the paint off the walls as she scraped at her mother's skirts, Bridget dead-eyed and blinking, watching her father in the flat heat as his wife went out the front door. She was gone three days, the old man sitting sentry in the living room the whole time. Bridget snuck out of bed on the first night just to see if he was still there. She watched the glow of his cigar pulse in purple clouds of darkness, counting ten pulls before she allowed herself to slip back into bed.

Her mother came home on the afternoon of the third day. Bridget was on the roof of their building as the car slalomed down the hill, a freshly washed Caddy with gleaming chrome bumpers winking in the sunlight as it pulled to the curb. There was a man behind the wheel. Bridget watched them fall into a clinch by the side of the car, her mother pressing against him, then hanging on even as he tried to pull away. Bridget hated her for that last bit as much as anything. She trudged up Champney, her clothes still on hangers but all wrinkled now and stuffed under an arm. Bridget scrambled off the roof and sat alone in the kitchen, listening as her mother shuffled down the hall and closed the door to the bedroom. The old man cracked the seal on a fresh bottle of whiskey that night and drank most of it, still chain-smoking cigars and never moving from the living room. The next morning Bridget's mother was back in the kitchen, making breakfast. And he was at the table, eating whatever she put in front of him. No one ever spoke about any of it. What was there to say? Until there was.

"Apple didn't fall far from the tree, did it?" He twisted a curl of Colleen's satin locks around one of his fingers.

"Keep them out of it, Jack."

He grabbed a fistful of his daughter's hair and buried his nose in it. "She even smells like you."

Colleen let out a tiny whimper. Bridget rose up from her chair, kicking at the book bag she'd stashed by her feet. "Leave her alone."

His eyes swept across the table. "Who the Christ was talking to you?"

"Bridget . . ."

"Shut up, Ma. Just leave her alone."

Colleen suddenly found some spine, struggling in vain to work herself free.

"Relax," Bridget said. "He's not gonna hurt you."

"Hurt her? Why would I hurt her?" He turned Colleen around

and studied her like she was a doll he'd won at a carnival. "Who would hurt something like this?" He traced the fine bones of her face, running a thumb along a cheek until he found the hollow spot beneath her eye, then pressing in until Colleen squealed and her knees buckled.

Bridget leaned forward. Her father narrowed the gap between them with his eyes, pink tongue shooting between his lips.

"You gonna stick me with that, little pup?"

She looked down at the black-handled kitchen knife gripped in her fist, then back up at his face flushed with a complex of emotions. Anger, fear, anticipation? Maybe all three.

"Let her go," Bridget said, the words even and thick and solid in her mouth. She'd do what it took, even at the breakfast table on a Saturday morning. And so there it was, fully conceived and freshly birthed, ugly in all its wrinkles and all its greed, licking its lips and gnashing its teeth, squalling and looking to feed. And everything else crumbled before it and raised itself up again, except it wasn't the same in that house and never would be. Her father could see that, plain as day. So he let Colleen go, his face spasming with some private pain as she ran from the room. Then he tucked back into breakfast, salting his eggs a third time and asking his wife if it wasn't too much trouble for him to get a look at the goddamn, fucking *Globe*. She shuffled off to puzzle together whatever pieces she could find. Bridget slung her bag over her shoulder and followed her baby sister out.

———

They snuck up the back stairs and climbed a wooden ladder onto the roof. Bridget led the way—scrambling over a loose pile of bricks and ducking underneath a forked TV antenna. At the front of the building they perched like a couple of skinned birds, staring down at Oak Square and the tangled web of streets spinning off it. The wind had turned raw and raked across the roof in cold, clean sheets. Bridget still had the book bag with her and held it against her chest. Colleen shivered.

"I'm freezing."

"Come on."

The back of the roof looked out over their yard and offered shelter in the form of a sooted chimney. Bridget sat cross-legged. Colleen huddled against a wall of rough brick, stick arms wrapped around her ribs, hands tucked under her armpits.

"Thanks." Her voice rode just under the wind, but Bridget heard it well enough.

"He wasn't gonna hurt you."

"He scares me."

"Everything scares you. That's why you're a target."

"I don't want to be a target."

"Then you need to toughen up."

Colleen wrinkled her nose and blinked. They looked alike, she and Colleen, except Colleen was a more finished product—features sanded and chiseled to finer proportions. Bridget, on the other hand, looked like she'd been taken out of the oven a half hour early. Dull, muddy, a little lopsided, not quite done.

"Why do you come up here so much?" Colleen said.

"It's called privacy. You wouldn't know anything about that."

"I know more than you think."

Bridget cut her eyes to her sister, who trembled under the weight of her secret.

"You don't know nothing," Bridget said.

"I know you've got a crush on Bobby."

"Who?"

"Bobby who lives above the cab office. I saw you watching him."

"I wasn't watching him."

"Yes, you were. Right here from the roof."

Bridget pulled her bag onto her lap and opened it. "No wonder they hate you."

"No one hates me."

"Everyone hates you. Mom, Dad. Everyone."

"You're wrong."

"They hate me, too. Think I care? I can look after myself."

"Dad used to give me his Communion water."

Before Colleen made her First Communion, their father would come home from church every Sunday and wordlessly fill a glass with water. He'd take a sip and then let Colleen have some. Their mom said it was his way of giving her the body of Christ.

"Big deal."

"It is."

Bridget could read the desperation in her little sister's voice and brushed at her cheek. The outline of his thumbprint was tattooed there in tiny threads of purple and red.

"You bruise too easy, Col."

A fat tear trickled down Colleen's nose and dripped off the curl of her lip. Bridget opened her arms and let her sister snuggle in, burying herself in the sleeve of Bridget's coat. The sun moved out from behind the clouds and walked shadows across the roof.

"You were a beautiful baby," Bridget whispered. "Mom said you could be in commercials."

Colleen's head popped up. "You're lying."

Bridget shooed away the notion.

"Mom really said that?"

"Of course she did."

Colleen sat up against the wall again, sniffling and wiping her nose, still upset but unavoidably pleased.

"Feeling better?" Bridget said.

Colleen nodded. "I'm glad you're my sister."

"Yeah?"

"You're tough and you take care of me. Are you glad you're my sister?"

"Do I have a choice? Sure, I'm glad."

"I'm sorry I teased you about Bobby."

"Forget it. You wanna see something?"

"What?"

Bridget pulled a big, blue medical dictionary out of her bag.

"Why do you carry that thing around?"

"I like it." Bridget loved all things flesh and blood. The walls inside her head were covered with maps of arteries and organs, coils of intestinal tract, cross sections of bowels and brains. She was fascinated with the idea of a heart and wondered why it beat at all.

"You won't start crying?" she said, flipping open the dictionary to a page she'd marked.

"No."

"You sure?"

Colleen nodded, all bright and eager. Bridget pointed to an entry. "You know what this word means?"

Colleen leaned over the word and squinted. " 'Pre' something."

"Preeclampsia. It's another name for high blood pressure. It happens sometimes when women have babies."

"Babies?"

Something primal flickered in the deepest black of Bridget's eyes. "Yes, babies. You know what they are."

Colleen scooched closer, like they were around a campfire or in the library or something.

"Preeclampsia." Bridget pointed at the entry again. Colleen repeated the word.

"Good. Now, you know why it's important?"

Colleen shook her curls, not so much to say no but just because they were rich and full and everyone loved the sound of them. And because Bridget hated every shake.

"It's important cuz Mom had it."

A shadow crossed Colleen's brow. A wrinkle creased her smooth forehead. "Mom?"

"She got it when she had you. Preeclampsia." Bridget stretched out each syllable. "You didn't you know any of this?"

"No."

Bridget flipped the dictionary shut. "It's what made her go blind. For six months after you were born, Mom couldn't see a thing."

"Mom wasn't blind."

"That's why she never held you when you were a baby."

"She held me." An eyebrow jerked, followed by another tremor in Colleen's perfect upper lip.

"You promised you wouldn't cry."

"I'm sorry."

"Come here." Bridget opened her arms a second time and Colleen fell into them, coiling into the embrace of her older sister, who kissed the top of her forehead, cooing and fussing, explaining and apologizing until Colleen grew calm again. And then they sat together, huddled against the morning chill, staring out over flat rooftops and empty streets. Colleen had gotten all the looks and loved to play her games, but she didn't understand pain. Not like she needed to. She'd learn. They'd all have to learn. Even at twelve, Bridget could feel that certainty bleaching her bones and knew there couldn't be any other way.

7

THEY TOOK cab number four, Bobby behind the wheel, adjusting the radio, lighting a cigarette, and downshifting as they bumped down a long, potholed driveway. They turned onto Hunnewell Avenue, climbed up Burton Street, then coasted back down Washington, past Sammy's corner store and the cobbler, a Greek pizza joint, Patty's Donuts, and the Catholic grammar school Kevin's sisters attended. After that came the march of bars: the Irish Village, the Last Drop, Castlebar, Jimmy's Nineteenth Hole, and the Oak Square Grill. They drove around the Circle, three locals on full display, rolled up in the grass and sleeping off Friday night. A fourth lay across one of the benches, vomit on his clothes, more puddled at his feet.

The bell inside Saint Andrew's Church had just struck seven when Bobby goosed the car up a broken runt of a street called Nonantum. About halfway up sat the Thomas Jefferson Middle School. The "Jeff" was a public school and offered the usual city education, which was to say crap. It did, however, have a large back lot. When Kevin was in grammar school, he and his buddies would spray-paint a strike zone on one of the brick walls and play baseball all day in the flat, summer heat. Kevin would pretend he was Sonny Siebert or Luis Tiant. It didn't matter what anyone else pretended, because in Kevin's head he was playing the entire game before a packed house at Fenway. When they hit thirteen or so, the neighborhood found other uses for the back of the Jeff—nighttime uses, like drinking beer and smoking dope. Kevin did enough of both so as not to be an outcast, but never enough that he forgot the best thing about the Jeff—throwing a Ray Culp screwball and watching someone swing and miss. Sure there were no seams to grip on a sponge ball, but who gave a shit? He swung and missed, didn't he?

Bobby hit the turn signal with a flick of his finger, navigating a narrow path that emptied into the Jeff's back lot. Kevin felt the wheels bump and watched the flag on the cab's meter bounce with every lurch in the road. Bobby pushed on the brakes as the cab creaked to a stop and settled into a rough idle. Kevin rolled down the window. A couple of kids were sitting on a low wall. One was wearing a long, black leather coat, the other a satin green Celtics jacket. They were drinking tall cans of early morning Bud and passing around what was left of a joint pinched in a roach clip.

"Coreys," Kevin said.

"Go on out."

"Where you going?"

"Gotta gas up. I'll be right back."

Kevin climbed out and watched Bobby head back down the alley, tailpipe hanging a few inches off the ground and trailing gray smoke. Kevin scuffed his sneakers as he made his way across the lot. "DIE NIGGA DIE" was spray-painted in black letters on one of the school's brick walls—three words reflecting the crudest understanding of a conflict that feasted on fear and swept like a plague through the narrow neighborhoods of Boston. Kevin barely registered the message as he walked past.

"Kevin boy, what's up?" David Corey was a year older than Kevin. He'd dropped out of Brighton High after his freshman year and got hired as an apprentice electrician, making sixteen bucks an hour, six days a week, on one of the high-rises going up downtown. He was too young to be an apprentice, but David looked old for his age and paid off some guy at the union hall to get the gig. He took a sip of beer and banged his boots against the wall in pointless, nervous energy.

Sitting beside him was his older brother, Paul. His specialty had always been huffing airplane glue and stealing cars. One night when he was thirteen, he boosted a half dozen and lined them up behind the Jeff with their headlights on and engines running. Then he and his pals burned rubber around the lot until dawn. Just for the fuck of it. These days he made a living selling drugs out of the basement of his uncle's building. Dope, speed, blotter acid, angel dust—you name it and Paulie C. could hook you up. He pried what was left of the joint out of the roach clip and brought it to his lips, one eye stuck on Kevin the whole time.

"What's up, shithead?" Paulie spoke with the smoke still down in his lungs so the words came out in gasps of air.

"Fuck you."

Paulie reared up from his perch and cuffed Kevin across the side of the head. Kevin countered with a sneaky fast right that surprised the older boy almost as much as Kevin when it grazed his chin.

"Motherfucker." Paulie tossed the roach and came at Kevin with both hands, bouncing him off a brick wall and doubling him over with a knee to the stomach. He got Kevin in a headlock and flipped him to the ground. Kevin could smell weed and beer and the leather of Paulie's coat in his nose and reached up to claw at whatever he could find. Paulie snickered and squeezed down with his biceps, the muscle flexing and crushing Kevin's windpipe. He could hear himself gurgling, hungry for a sip of air. Threads of darkness crowded the edges of his vision. His hand slipped, scratching feebly at the older boy's shoulder. Then the hold was broken. Kevin fell forward, retching and coughing. Bobby stood over him, holding Paulie by a twist of his jacket.

"You all right?"

Kevin spit on the hardtop and rubbed his throat. "I'm good."

Paul Corey wasn't the kind of guy you could really take a lot of shit from. Some guys you could. Let them mess around because they didn't really mean anything by it. Not Paulie. He was always jabbing with the needle, testing to see who might be a bit of a pussy. If he found one, then he'd just keep pushing. Better to push back and be done with it. Or be like Bobby. He threw Paulie onto the wall beside his brother. "Take a fucking seat."

"Kid needs to learn some manners," Paulie said, eyes already scouting the ground for the scrap of dope he'd dropped. His brother pulled a tallboy off a plastic ring and offered it to Bobby, who shook his head.

"I'm driving."

"You still wasting your time with that? Look at the cake I'm making." Paulie gestured to his ride, a Camaro, shiny and blue and looking pretty nice sitting beside Old Towne Taxi's beat-to-hell-and-back cab number four.

"It's a fucking car," Bobby said. "Besides, I'm not interested in dealing."

Paulie crushed an empty beer can and tossed it toward a

crooked tangle of weeds that grew out of a seam where the wall met the blacktop.

"You hear about the break-in over on Brackett?" David said.

"When?"

"Couple days ago. Some smoke broke in and cleaned out an old lady's house while she was shopping."

"How do you know it was a black kid?" Kevin said.

"Brendan Higgins lives next door." Paulie popped another tallboy and took a sip. "His sister saw the bonehead leaving. Said he was from Fidelis."

"She tell the police?" Bobby said.

"Cops don't give a fuck. We gotta take care of this shit ourselves." Paulie glanced at his younger brother, who nodded his support.

"You just gonna grab any black kid you see, then?"

Paulie furrowed his brow and dropped his voice a notch. "You some kind of nigger lover, Bobby?"

"Piss off."

Paulie eyed Bobby, but thought better of it. Bobby stayed with both brothers until he was sure they understood how things were. Then he turned to Kevin.

"Come on. We gotta go."

They were halfway to the cab when David hopped off the wall and pointed. Thirty yards away, outlined in quick charcoal strokes, was a skinny black kid, twelve, thirteen years old, perched atop a fence that separated the Jeff from the houses behind it. The Coreys took off at a silent run. The kid on the fence slipped down the other side, and was gone.

"No chance," Kevin said as one of the Coreys shinnied up and over the fence.

"No shit," Bobby said and they started to walk again.

"What would they do if they caught him?" Kevin said.

"Fuck him up, big time. Paulie's a mean prick. You don't want to be messing with him."

"I can take care of myself."

Bobby gave him a look. "You talking about the kid from Rosie?"

Bobby had taught Kevin how to hit last summer in his room above the cab office. They'd wrapped towels around their fists and boxed, Bobby popping Kevin in the face every time he tried to throw a punch. Kevin bled all over himself, stuffed his nose with toilet paper, and kept coming. After a couple of weeks, he got better. Bobby even let him land a few, just to feel what it was like. Then Kevin kicked the shit out of a kid from Roslindale who'd called one of his classmates a "Latin fag." The kid from Rosie walked into two straight rights, went down, and didn't move. The whole thing happened in a handful of seconds outside Rourke's, a hamburger joint a couple blocks from school. Kevin stood over the kid, blood pounding in his ears, terrified at what he'd done and hoping against hope the kid would get up so he could hit him again. That night he stared at his clenched fist in the bathroom mirror and wondered what he had there. According to Bobby, not very much.

"That kid weighed even less than you."

"I weigh a hundred and three."

"Jesus Christ, do they feed you in that house?"

Kevin pulled a napkin full of crumbs from his pocket. "I like corn muffins."

"Listen, the kid didn't weigh much more than you. Besides, I know his older brother and he's a pussy. Paul Corey isn't. You know he busted some kid's jaw from Smith Park last weekend?"

Kevin shook his head.

"Said he didn't like the way he looked at him. Busted his jaw, then went at him with a baseball bat. Took three cops from Fourteen to pull him off."

"I didn't hear about that."

"Yeah, well, you're hearing it now."

They stopped near the front of the cab. Bobby put a foot up on the fender. Kevin sat on the hood, then leaned back across the windshield so he was looking at the bruised and broken sky when he spoke.

"You don't like Paulie, do you?"

"He's a loser."

"How about what he said about you?"

"You mean when he called me a nigger lover?" Bobby picked up a rock and fired it at a NO LOITERING sign fixed to the side of the building. He missed. "I don't hate people cuz of their color if that's what you're asking. And I don't really give a fuck who knows it. The truth is half these jag-offs don't care what color you are. They just want to mess someone up."

"I guess."

"You guess?" Bobby threw another rock. This time he hit the sign. The metal ping rippled across the lot. "This place likes to eat its own. And it's always looking to be fed. Remember that."

Kevin sat up again. "I'm not like you, Bobby. I can't just look at someone and they walk away."

"Then you walk away."

"You mean be a pussy."

"I mean stay alive long enough to fucking stay alive. You wanna go to college or what?"

The great dream. Getting out of Brighton. Getting anywhere

but where you were. Some people hated Kevin cuz he had a clean shot. Others lived for it, pushing in all their chips on the teenager, knitting his future out of the cloth of their own fears and failures. Kevin could feel it, too. Something out there, alive and electric. All he needed to do was plug in. But first, he had to get out.

"Sure, I wanna go."

"All right, then," Bobby said. "Keep your nose clean. And don't mess with guys like Corey."

"And if I can't?"

"If you got no choice . . . I mean no choice at all . . . then you go hard-core. Kill-or-be-killed sort of shit. But you walk away first. Or you find me. Got it?"

"Yeah."

"Good. You ever drive a stick?"

"I was born for the stick."

Bobby chuckled. "Come on."

Kevin climbed in the driver's side of the cab, hands running over the steering wheel and sliding down to touch the round knobs and thick buttons. Bobby slipped into the passenger's seat and pointed to the floor. "That pedal there is the clutch. You put the car in first, let the clutch out slow, and feed it some gas at the same time."

"Piece of cake."

"Yeah, right. Clutch is loose as hell on this tank so that'll make it easier. All right, Mario, give it a go."

Kevin stomped on the clutch with his left foot, touched the gas with his right, and jammed the shift lever into first. The car never moved. Bobby swung a set of keys off his finger. "Be nice if you turned the thing on." He thought that was funny as all hell and stuck a key in the ignition.

The first three times the car bucked and died. The fourth time it went five feet. After six tries, Kevin got the sense of it. Pretty soon, he was rolling across the lot, shifting from first to second to third, then back to second.

"Good. You can downshift instead of using your brakes. Watch the fucking wall."

Kevin hit the brakes five feet from the redbrick side of the school. The car sputtered and stalled. "I saw it."

"Sure you did. That's enough for today."

"Let me drive home."

"Next time. Now, get out." Bobby slid behind the wheel as Kevin ran around to the passenger's side. Bobby reached forward to turn over the engine, then stopped. They both heard the hard thump of rubber on brick.

"Finn," Bobby said.

"You think?"

"Who else?"

They walked around the corner to a smaller lot on the far side of the school. Finn McDermott tossed a tennis ball high in the air, arched his back, and rocketed a serve against the brick wall fifty feet away.

"What's up, boys?" Finn had a wiffle cut and a hard, square chin. He wore blue sweats, a long-sleeved gray shirt, and white Adidas tennis shoes. At his feet was a half-empty wire bucket of green tennis balls and maybe fifteen more rolling around on the blacktop. Pushed up against the wall was a shopping cart, filled with three more buckets of balls, another racket, a jacket, an extra pair of suede Cons, and a full tennis net with the hard wire needed to hook it up to the posts down at the park.

Finn bounced a palm off the face of his racket and nodded toward the back lot. "Having a liquid breakfast with the Coreys?"

"They back there every day?" Bobby said.

"Sure." Finn picked up a ball that had rolled to his feet. "They'll be there until they head to AA, or the graveyard." Finn held the ball tight to the strings of his racket, stared down an imaginary opponent, coiled his body, and unleashed another serve. "What's up, Kevin?"

"Nothing, Finn. How you doing?"

Finn lifted up his shirt and pulled at a quarter inch of skin at his waist. "Look at this."

"What?" Kevin's eyes searched for a scar or a bruise or something.

"Love handles. I'm seventeen years old and I have love handles."

Kevin had never heard of love handles and didn't know what to say. Turns out he didn't have to say anything because Finn wasn't half done.

"Five hundred serves a day. That's what I do, Bobby. Just like Borg." Finn looked over to see if Bobby was listening, which was impossible to tell. "See this board I got?" Finn went over to his cart and pulled out a long piece of plywood about one-third the height of a hockey net. "I tie this to the fence down at the park."

"Why?" Kevin said.

"When I serve, the ball bounces right back. And see here."

Finn pointed to a couple of squares marked on the board in black Magic Marker. "I read about this in *SI*. These are my hot zones. I hit them and know the serve will be good when I get on the court."

"So you can practice your serve anywhere," Kevin said.

"With this board, I'm golden. Course I'm still down here every morning. Pounding the brick. That's the only way I get to Florida."

"Florida?" Kevin said.

"I'll be down there for six months of training next winter and then on to the pro circuit. Right, Bobby?"

"Right, Finn."

"You gonna come down with me?"

"I told you I'd visit."

"Two years, we'll be sipping champagne and eating strawberries at Wimbledon. That's what they serve at Wimbledon. Strawberries and cream. Right, Bobby?"

"Right, Finn."

"Gotta be in shape. Eat good. See that?" Finn pointed his racket at the shopping cart. In the compartment where they put the kids was a carton of milk and a box of powdered doughnuts. "Quart of milk for breakfast. No fucking around. Meanwhile, they're back there. Who drinks a six-pack at eight in the morning?"

Kevin shrugged. "The Coreys do."

Finn took out the doughnuts and offered them around. Bobby and Kevin passed. Finn ate two in four bites, then washed the powdered sugar off his lips with some milk. After that, he began to pick up tennis balls and put them in the bucket.

"Where you going?" Bobby said.

"Cunt from the YMCA has classes at the park on Saturdays. Takes all the courts unless I get there early."

"Why don't you play her for the court?" Bobby said, a gentle needle in his voice. Finn was oblivious.

"Wouldn't waste my time on the bitch. See you boys around."
He scarfed the last doughnut and threw the box in a barrel.
Then he pushed his overloaded cart across the lot, back left
wheel in a steady wobble as he went.

"Soft as puppy shit," Bobby said.

"You think he'll make it to Florida?"

"He'll be lucky if he makes it to the park."

"He's a pretty good tennis player."

"Pretty good ain't gonna cut it."

"He's out here practicing every morning."

"Hitting balls off a brick wall. And in between eating a box of
doughnuts. Finn's going nowhere and he knows it. We all know
it."

"We?"

"The Coreys, Shuks, your old man. Me. We were all born here
and we'll all die here. Scares the fuck out of us even though no
one will admit it. Why do you think everyone's always strut-
ting around, looking for a beef?" Bobby flicked his wrist, sting-
ing Kevin in the arm with a jab. "Cheer up, fuckhead. I told you,
you're not one of us."

"I live here."

"And you're getting out."

"How can you be so sure?"

"Cuz your grandmother says so. And she's not a person to
mess with. Come on, you gotta get back and I have a fare to pick
up."

They climbed into cab number four. Bobby slammed the stick
into first and rumbled out of the lot. They listened to the radio on the way back and talked about the Red Sox and whether
they'd win the pennant.

8

BRIDGET WATCHED her little sister walk over to the ladder and climb down off the roof. She listened for Colleen's footsteps on the back steps and, finally, the slam of the door to their apartment. Then she was alone. Bridget crept over to a low parapet wall that ran along the back and sides of the roof, dangling her legs over the drop and staring hard at the cab office. Her grandmother was silhouetted at her desk, talking on the phone and rolling back and forth in her chair. Bridget watched for a while, then padded along the roofline to the far end of the building. She moved a couple of loose bricks and pulled out a notebook. It was dirty brown and had "Saint Andrew's Grammar School" written in Old English script across the cover. Bridget sat up against the chipped facing of the chimney and read through the last few pages. Then she took out a pen she kept clipped to the front cover and wrote down everything that happened at breakfast, followed by her conversation on the roof with Colleen. When she was done, she sealed up the notebook again behind the bricks and walked over to the ladder. She lay flat on her stomach, staring down the hole at the third-floor landing and the back door to her grandmother's apartment. The wind was still up and the building smelled like wood and coal and soot. Bridget picked herself up, slung her book bag over her shoulder, and started to climb down.

———

It had been nearly an hour since he'd seen the outline of the old lady, standing on the back porch like an inky scarecrow, then making her way across the yard and disappearing inside the office. Earlier, the kid had sloped out of the same door with the other one. Older, taller, lean and strong, skin sculpted white in a bloom of random light. Even safe in his hide, the cat had felt the older one's eyes as he scanned the tree line, stopped, then scanned again. They'd climbed into one of the black cabs, engine roaring to life, and left. Now, it was quiet. The air felt wet and gray and hugged the big cat's skin. He pulled out a knife and ran a finger along its edge. She was sitting at her desk, a cardboard cutout hanging in the window, smoking a cigarette like a scene out of a painting about a diner he'd seen once in a book. *Nighthawks.* Back in the day his teacher had gone on about it, but he'd never bothered to listen. At least not to his teacher. The painting was another story. It spoke to him, more like a movie than a painting, and he wondered, in the remaining hours he had left on this earth, as he sat in the bushes and waited until the time was right, if there would be other things that would speak to him. He hoped so but didn't count on it. The cutout tipped her chin up and blew a soft line of smoke toward light that collected near the ceiling. And then the cat moved. His name was Curtis Jordan. He was a part-time thief and full-time drug dealer. One profession fed the other, clients providing him with information on easy marks in return for an extra bit of blow or bag of weed. That was how Curtis knew the old lady lived alone. Worked Saturday mornings in the office. And kept a strongbox full of cash in her apartment. He flattened himself against the side of the three-decker. All it took was one white face peering out a window. And finding a black one looking back. Jordan flared his nostrils and filled his lungs. Then he ran up the first flight of stairs, turned on the landing, and bounded up the next.

9

KEVIN WALKED up the short, sharp hill with his head down. Bobby hadn't wanted to talk anymore about Brighton, about getting out. If it had been anyone else, there'd have been more talk. But that was Bobby. And so his future cut its own throat. And no one was there to raise a hand in protest. Or even an eyebrow to record its passing. A breeze brushed past, prickling the skin on Kevin's scalp and causing him to lift his eyes off the pavement. Thirty feet up the road, a blurry sketch of arms and legs was crouched at the corner of his grandmother's building. The sketch turned, head on a swivel, eyes locking on Kevin's. Then he scuttled away, flitting across Champney Street and ducking into the backyard of a two-family the thirteen Santoro kids lived in with their mother.

Kevin rocked hard in his tracks, staring at the spot where the black man had disappeared, feeling the urge to chase while wondering where that lust came from and if he wasn't destined to be a racist like all the others. Then he heard the scream, high and pure, chilling his blood and stopping his heart in midbeat. Kevin's legs carried him down the alley and into the yard behind his house. He could see lights in his grandmother's cab office, bright smudges against a smoky pall that suddenly hung in the air. Fresh light flared as the office door swung open and a small, dark figure wavered on the threshold. Another scream, long and winding, ribboning through the trees, coming from his grandmother's apartment. The figure on the threshold began to move across the yard. Short, clumsy strides. Kevin turned and took the back steps, up and around one landing, then a second. Somewhere below he heard people yelling and windows slamming open. A third corner and Bridget was there, lying on the steps, legs splayed, one hand clutching her side as blood wept between her fingers.

"Bridget."

Kevin fell to his knees and put a hand to her wound. She pushed him away and pointed. In the fine grain of light, he could see a trail of blood running up the stairs. Behind him, he heard footsteps, heavy breathing, a muttered prayer doubling as a curse. Kevin turned and found his mother at his elbow, pale eyes on stalks, staring at her children, both of them smeared and torn. Bridget clawed at his arm and dragged him close.

"Upstairs, go." His sister's eyes were as full and rich as any he'd ever seen, glittering with the same light he remembered in his father's, late at night when he was filled with drink and doubt and fury and regret.

Kevin's mother dropped to her knees beside him. "Oh, Jesus, Mary, and Joseph. Oh, Jesus, Mary, and Joseph." She pressed her hands into Bridget's side, trying to stop the flow of blood and only making it worse.

"I'm fine," Bridget whispered, never letting her brother look away. "Go."

———

He found her in the narrow hallway that led to the living room. She was curled over on her side, legs pulled toward her body like she was trying to hug herself, face floating in a perfect pool of light. Years later, Kevin would wonder where the light had come from. At the time, all he could wonder about were her features, peaceful and unmarked. For a wild moment, he thought she was sleeping, perhaps hit her head and merely unconscious. He touched her shoulder and whispered *Gram* for the last time in his life. On cue, she rolled onto her back so he could see the belly laid open, a coil of something wet and grayish-blue leaking onto the floor. Kevin ran for the back door and vomited on the scarred boards of the porch. His mother was halfway up the stairs. She saw death cast in his eyes and howled. Then she ran past him and fell to the floor beside the body. Kevin got sick again as his mother screamed and wept and cried and called out for a divine presence she'd never know nor understand. She screamed until the sirens drowned her out and they took her away. The last thing Kevin saw was his baseball glove. Someone had picked it up off the landing where he'd found Bridget. It was sticky with blood.

10

ONE NIGHT when he was nine, Kevin asked about his grand-father and she started talking about McNamara's. Everyone in Brighton got their turn at McNamara's, his grandmother told him, the big white funeral home perched up on a hill. "What does that have to do with my grandfather?" Kevin said. She glared across the table and asked if he wanted to hear the story. Kevin shut up and she continued. His grandfather had worked at McNamara's when he was a kid. Back then they didn't embalm bodies like they do now. "What's embalming?" Kevin said and got another baleful blue eye for his trouble. One of his grand-father's jobs involved "tying down the body." This usually oc-curred when someone died sitting up in a chair. If rigor mortis set in before they could straighten out the limbs, the folks at McNamara's would have to stretch the body flat and tie it to the table for the wake. So it happened one day that Kevin's grandfa-ther had finished tying down one of McNamara's clients when he took it in his head to remain under the table as the family was led in for the final viewing. It was at the height of the pro-ceedings that he pulled out a knife and cut the ropes, allowing the recently deceased to sit up and give his loved ones a final, unforgettable good-bye. "Everyone was screaming and fainting," Kevin's grandmother said between teary gasps of laughter. "Your grandfather was no older than you. He ran like hell and didn't set foot inside McNamara's again until the day they laid him out. And, to their credit, they did a lovely job."

Kevin remembered thinking his grandfather must have been a heck of a guy. His grandmother let him think it until he didn't. And now she was here. Her turn in the basement at McNamara's. And his turn to mourn. Except he didn't know how. And didn't have anyone to teach him. She'd been his world, his beginning and end, his sense of who he was and who he might become. And no one had ever told him it could end so soon.

He forced himself to look at her face. It was all wrong. Lips stretched tight, cheeks too red and sunk into pockets of bone. He waited for her to open her stitched eyes and tell him it was a bad dream. They'd laugh at the job the hacks had done, cancel the wake, and head home for a cup of Barry's and toast. He noticed the way they'd arranged her hands on her chest. When he was eleven, he'd saved up money and gotten her a Madonna pendant made from mother of pearl and matching earrings. They'd ripped the pendant off her neck when they killed her. Taken it along with the cash in the strongbox. But they didn't get the earrings. Now she'd wear them for eternity and Kevin couldn't fathom it. There was the sound of footsteps on the stairs that wound down from the public areas of the funeral home, then, a voice.

"How the fuck did you get in here?"

Kevin looked up at Bobby filling the doorway.

"I told them it was my grandmother. They made me sit upstairs for a while, then let me down."

Bobby moved closer before circling away. Kevin hadn't talked to him since that morning, another face lost in the blurred rush of images—cops and neighbors standing on the sidewalk in front of the house in small circles; his father sitting in the hushed darkness of their living room, phlegmatic eyes shining white and watching him as he crept in, then pushing him back down the hallway; his mother collapsed on the bed, weeping uncontrollably and caving in on herself until there was nothing left but rubble and tears and dust; Colleen in the kitchen, holding his left hand with her fingers and asking if she could have cereal for dinner; Bridget, alone in her room with a wound in her side and the door closed tight. Bobby took a seat on the other side of the body and picked up the cold, stiff fingers. Something passed there that was alive and breathing and Kevin felt his soul move in its too young, too hard shell. Then Bobby released the hand, and the corpse again became a corpse. He looked at Kevin with eyes gone soft around the edges.

"I'm sorry, pal."

And then the dam burst and Kevin started to cry for what felt like the first time in his life, wrenching sobs that came from a place he never knew existed, a place that had no bottom and no dimension other than pain and pity and the insatiable greed of loathing. Bobby pulled his chair around and held him in his arms and Kevin told him about the apartment, her face in the awful God-light, silent eyes and thin line of lips, the blood and vomit and dripping blue gray of the entrails, and all the rest. Bobby held him until he'd finished. And then he held him some more.

"I don't know what to do," Kevin said, his head buried in the thick knot of Bobby's shoulder, words all blurred and messy.

"You don't have to do nothing, bud. Don't have to do nothing at all." Bobby spoke in a hushed, even cadence, like the hum of a prayer in church. Kevin pulled back, wiping his nose on his sleeve. Bobby gave him some space, and they sat with her in the basement.

"How's everyone?" Bobby finally said, turning toward Kevin and at an angle to the body.

"What do you think? Fucked up as usual."

"Your old man bothering you?"

"He's fine."

"Your mom?"

Kevin just shook his head. Bobby leaned in.

"You gotta step up, Kev. Be there for her and your sisters. You know what I mean?"

"I think so."

"Listen, the fucking old man is what he is. Nothing you can do and there's no point getting into it. But your mom and your sisters, they're gonna need you to be there. Nothing heroic or anything like that. Just be there."

"I got it, Bobby."

"Do you?"

Kevin glanced past him to a small window set at ground level and looking out at an alley that ran alongside McNamara's. A clock ticked somewhere, and there was the murmur of movement upstairs. McNamara's ghouls pushing around wax flowers and frozen corpses.

"She thought the world of you, Kev. Talked about your future all the time, the things you were gonna do. None of that's changed. Not a fucking bit."

Kevin studied the flat, white wall that ran underneath the window and felt himself nod.

"All right, bud. You wanna get out of here?"

"Think I'm gonna hang for a bit."

There was the scrape of wood as Bobby stood, his presence looming over Kevin and the body on the table. "Don't stay too long." He squeezed Kevin's shoulder, then leaned in and touched her powdered cheek with the back of his hand, whispering something close before disappearing back upstairs.

Kevin waited until the footsteps had died off and he was alone again. He stared at a twist of plastic rosary beads they'd wound between his grandmother's fingers and thought about her prediction. There'd be a void, she'd said. And it was human nature to want to fill it. Kevin traced the hard outline of the gun in his pocket and conjured up the face he'd seen running from the three-decker, the person who'd killed his grandmother. He touched the trigger and began to mumble a Hail Mary. The words tasted like ash in his mouth and his tongue was cast into stone.

11

IT HAD taken Bobby Scales less than twenty-four hours to dis-
cover the name of the man who'd run out of Mary Burke's apartment. Curtis Jordan was black and lived somewhere in Fidelis
Way. Bobby didn't know the exact address, but Fidelis wasn't that
big of a place. He parked across the street from the projects and
walked down the block until he found an empty doorway with
a view.

The wake was this afternoon. Funeral, tomorrow morning.
Bobby wouldn't be there. He'd already said his good-byes to the
closest thing he'd ever had to a mother. Now, it was all about
protecting her grandson. Bobby had talked to Mary Burke many
times about what would happen after she died. Neither of them
expected this. But Bobby was ready to hold up his end.

He leaned a shoulder against the jamb, arms folded across
his chest, and considered his options. If he knew about Jordan,
Kevin probably did as well. Even if he didn't know, someone,
someday, would whisper the name in his ear. And then what?
Bobby felt a cold flutter in his chest. All things being equal, he'd
be happy turning Jordan over to the cops. But where would that
lead? Bobby had a friend inside Station Fourteen, a mick cop

named Quigley. He could see Quigley's face now, a long stretch of pale marble, studded with black eyes and cracked in all the places you'd expect. *Take care of it yourself, Bobby,* Quigley would say. *That's the way you handle these sorts of things. We understand it. The D.A. understands. Everyone understands.* Quigley had a point. If Bobby didn't take care of it, who would? Kevin would. And that could never be. Still, it was a bridge to cross. A turn in the road. A running jump off a fucking cliff. Bobby looked up. A streetcar rumbled past, and he caught a flash of brown hair. Bobby knew that head, the angular features and slouched walk. He hustled across Commonwealth Avenue and up a short hill. Kevin was maybe twenty yards ahead, moving quickly, eyes on the pavement, right hand in his jacket pocket. Bobby was about to yell when Kevin turned a corner and disappeared into the projects. Bobby began to run.

———

Curtis Jordan was sitting behind a long wooden desk when Kevin pushed in the door. Jordan's eyes swiveled left, right, then reached behind Kevin before relaxing.

"You a long way from home, white bread."

Kevin inhaled the room in huge, heaving gulps. A stack of money on the table. A gun beside it. Jordan's fingertips humming, but not yet moving for the piece. There was a scattering of other objects on the table, but they all faded to black once he saw it, a pale gleam caught in a slash of light from the window. Kevin pulled out the shiny twenty-two and watched the barrel shake as he raised it. Until the very end, he thought he'd just talk. Ask why. Try to understand. Then he saw his grandmother's pendant on the desk and his world went red. Curtis Jordan swung his piece up as Kevin started to squeeze back on the trigger. The gun flew out of his hands and there was a blast in his ears, followed by a second. Jordan was jerked from his seat, like a puppet being lifted by some huge invisible hand, except this puppet fell back to earth in a bloody, boneless heap. Kevin got a glimpse of blank eyes peeking back at him from under the desk. Then he was being dragged down the hallway, feet skipping across the ground as he went. It was Bobby, a black revolver in his fist, sticky gray tape wrapped around the grip and the muzzle pointed to the ceiling. He pulled Kevin through a set of fire doors and glanced up and down the stairwell. Kevin twisted free and sprinted back down the hall, Bobby hissing at him to stop.

A slick of blood was already creeping across the tiled floor of the apartment. Kevin almost slipped as he scrambled behind the desk. It was layered with the cash, a set of keys, and two bottles of pills. The pendant had rolled off the desk and into a corner. Kevin grabbed it, wiping off a tiny necklace of blood with his thumb. Then he picked up the gun he'd dropped.

Curtis Jordan's body was all twisted up under the desk, one arm flung over the top of his head like he was trying to scratch his opposite ear. Kevin rolled the body onto its back and took a good look, carving the image onto the surface of his brain in quick, deft strokes. Then he dropped to a knee, pressed the gun against Jordan's forehead, and pulled the trigger. The twenty-two barely made a sound and left behind a dry, puckered hole. Kevin stuck the gun in his pocket and ran out of the apartment, straight into the hollow gaze of a black girl. She was standing stock-still in the middle of the hallway, a finger in her mouth and pink and white bows in her hair. Their eyes locked for a moment before Kevin sprinted for the fire doors. Bobby pulled him down two flights and into the basement of the building. The hallway smelled like stale piss, and a dark slick of grease ran along the base of the walls where rats had rubbed themselves against the yellow brick. Bobby pointed to what looked like a janitor's closet.

"There's probably a sink in there."

"I had to get the gun." Kevin pulled out the twenty-two. Bobby stashed it inside his jacket.

"We can't be here when the cops arrive. Now, go wash up."

Kevin looked down at his hands. They were smeared with blood. He also had some rimming the soles of his shoes.

"Now, Kevin. Go."

He walked into the janitor's room and turned on the faucet. The pipes groaned and the water ran like rust. Kevin waited a few seconds and it began to clear. Somewhere in the distance, a police siren howled. All told, they'd been in the building less than seven minutes. In other words, a lifetime.

PART TWO

2002

12

AT LEAST he wasn't taking a leak. Kevin had read somewhere that's what Mike Royko was doing when they told him he'd won the Pulitzer Prize. True or not, it's one of those stories print reporters love to tell. Kevin's moment wasn't nearly as memorable. Just standing in line at the Registry of Motor Vehicles. The woman in front of him was eating an Egg McMuffin and talking on her cell phone, telling her friend that no, she hadn't slept with Joey DeTucci and that Cindy was a fucking bitch who was going to get her ass kicked across Chelsea if she didn't shut her fucking mouth. The guy behind him was thumbing through the *Herald*, breathing garlic and peppers down Kevin's neck and pushing up against his shoulder every chance he got. That's where he was when he got the call from his boss at the *Globe*.

"Done deal," Jimmy Edwards said, laughing his fat man's laugh. "Done fucking deal."

Edwards was a member of "The Cabal," a group of newspaper editors who made it their business to sniff out the Pulitzer's annual list of nominees. This year Edwards had done one better. It wouldn't be official for another few days, but he'd gotten the word from a source Edwards called "bulletproof." Kevin turned off his phone just as it buzzed again. He'd moved somehow, at least two feet out of line. The ranks had already closed, Mr. *Herald*'s newspaper firmly tucked up against the sloping back and greasy hair of the girl from Chelsea. People in line stole quick glances Kevin's way, anticipating his counterattack. After all, he'd put in his time, shuffling forward a foot or two every couple of minutes for the better part of an hour. And yet he felt none of the unarticulated and consuming rage that was the province of Boston and its proud inhabitants. Instead, he wandered ten more feet, then twenty, past the end of the line and out the door. So what if he didn't have a valid driver's license from the Commonwealth? He was the Pulitzer Prize winner for best investigative piece of the year, 2001. That would be the first line in his bio. The first sentence in his obituary. His career would never be the same. His life, forever changed. At least that was the hype. Why, then, didn't he feel any different? Or, for that matter, anything at all?

13

HE DROVE west on Soldiers Field Road, the Charles River twisting and turning alongside, afternoon sun glancing daggers off his windshield. Kevin exited at Market Street and climbed the long hill toward Brighton Center. He'd avoided driving through the center for more than two decades and wasn't sure why he was making the detour now. The storefronts of his youth had mostly disappeared, Woolworth's and Brigham's gone, five or six bars and half as many packies history. There were still plenty of places to get lit, but they looked cleaner now, safer, gentrified. And probably not nearly as much fun. Kevin drove past Daniel's Bakery, where his sisters had spent their youth frosting cakes for minimum wage. Next to it was an Indian take-out place that had once been the Blue Bayou. Kevin had been a month shy of eleven and hanging around outside the Bayou one Sunday afternoon when Shakey Callahan walked in and fired a gun between Sean Bryant's legs. Bryant pissed himself and fainted dead away off his bar stool. Shakey rifled Sean's pockets, left a few dollars on the bar for the tab, and walked out whistling. After the cops left, Kevin and his pals snuck into the bar and took turns sticking their fingers in the bullet hole Shakey had left in the stool's green padding. All in all, not bad for a Sunday. Just past the Indian joint was Mandy and Joe's deli, Fleet Bank, and a CVS. Kevin pulled into the bank's parking lot, slid a MEDIA placard onto the dashboard, and walked into the CVS for a pack of gum. He listened from the next aisle as an old man explained to a female clerk how he had to put a two-by-four under the toilet seat to prevent his balls from taking a bath. He was unbuckling his pants to show off the low-hangers when Kevin left. Outside, traffic was snarled for a block and a half. People leaned on their horns and hollered at anyone who'd listen while no one went anywhere. Kevin walked over to the cause of the tie-up—a homeless man wrapped in a long rubber fireman's coat and lying on his side in the middle of the street. A woman came out of the CVS, took one look, and crossed at the light. More people walked past as Kevin rolled the man over. He was wearing leather suspenders with no shirt under the coat, and his eyes were nailed wide open.

"You okay?" Kevin said.

"I don't know." The man blinked once and looked at Kevin as if to say "What next?" Just then a siren whooped, traffic cleared, and a squad car pulled up. A cop with a meaty Irish face got out, took one look at the man on the ground, and started cursing. Kevin was pushed to the periphery of the crowd and watched as an ambulance arrived. The homeless man departed on a stretcher, waving at his fans and trying to shake hands with the cop. There was a pleasant buzz now, everyone happy to have another person's misfortune to talk about. That much, at least, hadn't changed. Kevin walked back to his car and drove down Parsons Street, headed toward Electric Avenue. Already he had a headache.

———

Electric Avenue bellied up to the Mass Pike before curling off into a dead end that was more of a mercy killing. Kevin parked in front of the main office for L&G Radiator and listened to the cars whistle overhead. He walked past two boarded-up buildings, three cats, and a rat that looked like it could eat the cats for breakfast, lunch, and dinner. Kevin stopped in front of a skinny three-decker, shoehorned between a factory that made screen doors and an abutment for the highway. A Puerto Rican leaned his head out of a second-floor window and asked if Kevin wanted to buy some rum. Kevin said no. The Puerto Rican told him to come back on Sunday when the packies were closed and he'd give him a deal. Kevin walked up three steps of poured concrete and knocked on the door to the first-floor apartment. She opened it on the chain and stared out at him.

"Yeah?"

"Gemele, it's Kevin. Kevin Pearce."

A child yelled for mom from somewhere behind her. Gemele Harper unchained the door and left it open. Kevin followed her in. Gemele was small but sturdy. And she needed to be. She lived with her four kids, aged twelve down to six, in a one-room apartment with a kitchenette and table in one corner and a foldout bed in the middle. Three of the kids were sitting around the table, watching Kevin from under sleepy eyelids. The youngest, a girl named Natalie, sat on the far side of the bed, scribbling with crayons on the wall.

"I got to be somewhere at five." Gemele sat down heavily.

"Who takes care of them?"

Gemele nodded at the oldest girl. "Tasha handles it."

The apartment smelled like burnt grease and smoke. A length

of electrical cord ran from a space heater at the foot of the bed, up and under the covers.

"That's dangerous as hell, Gemele."

"It's unplugged."

"But you use it in the winter?"

She pushed a look toward the radiator, a cold lump of steel squatting in the corner. "No heat coming up most nights. You rather they freeze to death? What do you want, Kevin?" He hadn't seen her in a while, but her voice was already stretched thin, nearly transparent.

"Is there somewhere we can talk?"

"Here's fine."

Kevin hesitated.

"They know about their daddy. Know what he did. Know what he didn't do." Gemele nodded again at the oldest. "Tell him about your daddy."

Tasha stood up like she'd been asked to recite in school, feet shuffling and fingers scratching her palms in nervous energy. "My daddy's name was James Harper. He was sent to prison for killing a woman named Rosie Tallent. He was in prison for . . ." Tasha squinted hard and looked at the ceiling as she counted on one hand. " . . . two or three years, I think. Then they killed him."

"Stuck him in the neck with a screwdriver," Gemele said and waited for Tasha to continue.

"My daddy was innocent. He was framed because he was a black man. And that's just how it was."

Kevin looked at Gemele and back to Tasha. Then at Gemele again.

"You got a problem with that?" she said.

"What do you think?"

"Not a word that's not true."

"And you think it helps?"

"You know why?"

"Because otherwise James never lived at all?"

"For a white boy, you get it. A little bit, anyway."

"Thanks."

"You know how I feel, Kevin."

"Yeah."

"So why did you come here? Not to hear my girl recite her family history."

He sat down on the bed.

"Kevin?"

"What?"

"Lift up your goddamn head."

He did.

"You're one of the finest men I know, and the only reason my James ever got a bit of justice from this state. Didn't save him, but it might save them." She glanced again at the circle of eyes staring back at her from around the table. "So whatever you have to say, you can say it here. And it's all right."

"Thanks, Gemele. This isn't bad."

She waited.

"I won a prize today."

"That's what you want to tell me?"

"I won the Pulitzer Prize. I won it for James's story."

She smiled—a crooked, broken thing that always caused a tightness in his chest even though he never knew why.

"Your family must be proud."

"I guess."

"Congratulations on your prize, Kevin. You deserve it."

"Thanks. Listen, when they announce this, there might be more publicity. They might revisit the case. Want to interview you." Kevin's voice dropped. "Maybe the kids."

"We live in peace with it all, don't we?" Varying degrees of nods from around the table.

"All right."

"What else you got to tell me, Kevin?"

"How do you know?"

"It ain't hard. Now, what else?"

"When I get the prize—I think it's a certificate. When I get it, I'd like you to have it."

Gemele moved her lips, but didn't speak. She drifted that way sometimes, a lot like his mom when he was a kid. Kevin had always thought of it as damage. Or maybe just damage control.

"If you don't want all the trouble," he said, "that's cool. I just thought . . ."

She laid her hand flat on his. It felt warm and fine and strong. "Come here." She led him to a small pantry off the kitchen. Up on the shelf were a few boxes of mac and cheese, some canned goods with white labels, and a massive jar of peanut butter. She reached behind them and pulled out a red scrapbook with MEMO-RIES in peeling gold script across the front.

"I keep this back here. Figure I'll give it to Tasha when she gets a little older." Gemele opened the book. Inside was a couple of old snapshots of her and James and a sheaf of newspaper clippings. Kevin picked one up. The headline read:

HOW DID SUFFOLK COUNTY CONVICT AN INNOCENT MAN OF MURDER? SLOPPY POLICE WORK AND A WEAK DEFENSE CONSPIRE TO SEAL ONE MAN'S FATE.

Kevin's story followed. A Sunday piece, longer, stitching together the entire case—from the time James Harper was arrested,
through his trial, conviction, and, finally, the morning he was
shanked inside a segregation unit at Walpole state prison.

"If you want to give me your prize, I'll put it in here. Kids will
have it long after I'm gone."

"That'd be great." He slipped the clipping back into its place
and pressed the pages shut. "I'll call you about the media and
stuff."

"Be happy, Kevin. You saved a man's life."

"I wish that were true."

"You saved James." She picked up the scrapbook. "And you
gave him back to us. Come on, say good-bye to the kids."

———

Kevin stepped out of the airless flat and blinked against the late-
afternoon sun. It was April and the wind blew up out of nowhere,
collecting in the high pockets of the trees, then descending like
a hawk, talons stretched, raking his face with the final, frozen
lashes of a New England winter. Kevin jammed his hands in his
pockets and wrapped his coat around his ribs. They'd found Rosie
Tallent's body in a cardboard box in Allston, about a mile from
where Kevin was standing. She was eighteen but had lived a lot
longer than that. Her hands and feet were bound with rope. There
was a gag stuffed in her mouth and a length of thin packing wire
wrapped around her neck. The wire, however, wasn't what killed
her. It was the three stab wounds to her chest and side. To make
sure, the killer popped her once in the head with a thirty-eight.
He'd taken her purse, including cash totaling less than a hundred

dollars, as well as a few small articles of clothing. In 1997, the investigation wasn't much. The cops focused on James Harper almost from the start. He was estranged from Gemele at the time, knew Rosie, and had a record, mostly minor drug offenses and two convictions for assault. They were both barroom fights, but the D.A. didn't care. James was a violent offender. He was black and, according to the prosecution, had no alibi for the night of the murder. So James got his half-day trial and pulled a life sentence. That is, until he caught a screwdriver in the neck. Kevin met with James seven times before he died. Twenty-three hours of interviews. Kevin also talked to three of James's friends. They claimed they were with James at a Dorchester bar called the Pony Room on the night of the murder. None of them had ever been interviewed by the police or called to testify by James's lawyer. When Kevin asked why, the defense attorney said they all had criminal records and would have done more harm than good. What the defense attorney didn't know was that the Pony Room had a security tape no one had ever asked for and no one had ever seen. Kevin finally got hold of it six months after James died. The tape was time-stamped on the night of the murder and showed James Harper drinking in the bar from six P.M. until close. According to the court transcript, Rosie Tallent was killed around ten P.M. that night, her body found a little after midnight. Kevin published his stories less than a year after the funeral. Too late for James, but they gave Kevin the Pulitzer anyway.

He drove back up the hill into Brighton Center and bought beer at Dorr's liquors. The old man behind the counter used to let him buy there when he was thirteen. Back then, a six-pack was an adventure. They'd drink in the muffled depths of December, three or four of them huddled against the elements, listening to Led Zep and sharing a single pair of gloves to keep the cans from freezing to their hands, talking about girls and sports, boasting, arguing, laughing, bullshitting. They drank fiercely, shooting beers and swilling hard stuff whenever they could get it, instinctively understanding the escape offered, first to their fathers and grandfathers and now to them. Kevin put the six-pack on the seat beside him, drove past McNamara's funeral home, and dropped into Oak Square. He'd played a childhood's worth of games at Tar Park, but it was nothing he recognized. The rocks and weeds were gone, replaced by a green carpet of grass and smooth brown dirt. A clean white rubber crowned the pitcher's mound. Kevin left the beers on a bench and walked onto the field. The batter's box was lined in chalk, the clay red and yielding. He dug in, right foot first, then left, and looked down at home plate.

"Let's go. Infield." Jimmy Fitz wandered out from the shadow of the batting cage, a ball in one hand and a fungo bat on his shoulder. "Tarpey, first base. Doucette, second." Their coach waved at the empty diamond. "You all know where you're going. Get out there."

Kevin slapped his glove against his leg as he ran out to short. Fitz stood at the plate, Brighton's catcher, Gerry Sullivan, beside him.

"Once around," Fitz said and lashed a ball down the third-base line. Joey Nagle backhanded it and fired a strike to first.

"Nice," Kevin yelled, even as a second ball rocketed toward him. Kevin took three steps to his right, angling back as he ran. He caught the ball deep in the hole, planted his right foot, and threw in one motion. Their first baseman, Brian Tarpey, dug out the ball on a short hop, pointed his glove at Kevin, and fired the ball back to Sully.

"Get two," Fitz grumbled, tossing another ball in the air and *driving it between first and second. Kevin knew his coach's infield routine and was already on the move. Tommy Doucette caught the ball on what should have been the outfield grass (if Tar Park had any grass) and pivoted. The second baseman knew not to wait on Kevin and fired a strike to the bag. For an instant, it looked like the ball was headed to left field. Then Kevin glided across, catching it with a backhanded sweep of his glove and rifling a throw to first. The ball ping-ponged back to Sully, who threw down to Kevin at second. Kevin turned and fired the ball to third, over to first and back to home. Jimmy Fitz had another ball in his hand and tapped out a grounder to first. And so it went. The ballet of baseball. Kevin followed with hands, feet, and mind—his world reduced to the breath in his ears, the blur of a batted ball, and five kids in an infield, sharing one heartbeat.*

Kevin stepped out of the box and stared at the ghosts manning his empty infield. To grow up in Brighton was to be tethered to the past. Some tethers swung tight and fast, a vicious, self-destructive arc that took the measure of anyone who got in the way. Others wheeled far and wide, sweeping up new friends and family, money, power, even infamy. But all held this place at their center. A tangled, grasping place. A place of dark and light. Kevin walked back down the first base line, took a seat on the bench, and cracked a beer. Maybe he thought he'd broken his tether, maybe he was a goddamn fool.

A couple drifted into the park, a pair of bulldogs on leash. They let the dogs ramble and settled in the outfield grass, bundled close together, bodies mingling one into the other. Kevin's eyes crossed the street and found the darkened windows of his great-uncle's old apartment. Shuks had driven Kevin to New York that afternoon, then kept tabs on him growing up, all the way through college and even when he'd moved back to Boston. They'd meet up here and there over the years, a beer, coffee, the newspaper—just like their mornings at the cab office when Kevin was a kid except now his grandmother hung over every word in every conversation and they never laughed when they were together. Not once. Kevin had noticed the weight loss and graying, first around Shuks's eyes then the touches in his cheeks. At the end, the boxer's hands shook as he sipped his coffee and made scratch marks in his racing form, Kevin at his elbow, always and forever the acolyte-in-training. The call came a year after Kevin's parents passed. Shuks had gone to the doctor in the morning about an x-ray. It was a hot summer day and the Sox were playing a rare double-header against the Indians. After his appointment, Shuks packed up a ham and cheese sandwich and Salinger's *Catcher in the Rye*. He sat on the bank of the Charles and smoked a Lucky. Then he took off his socks and shoes, filled up his pockets with rocks, and walked into the water. On the day of his funeral, Kevin sat alone at the back of a church in Newton and watched McNamara's boys wheel the coffin past. He cried that day for the first time since his grandmother. He cried because he'd loved the old man in a simple, spare way that was impossible to measure in the fashion people liked to measure such things. He cried at the passing of a generation and because already he couldn't hardly remember what Shuks looked like. And he always thought he would.

A car door slammed in the lot behind him. Kevin glanced over as a black man pulled a bat and bag of balls out of the trunk. His kid, maybe ten and wearing a Red Sox warm-up jacket, was already running toward the diamond in loose, loping strides. The dad set up his kid on the mound. The two of them talked for a while, dad showing the kid all the good stuff—how to grip the ball, push off the rubber, arm angle. Dad trotted back behind home plate and crouched. The kid tugged at his hat, pounded the ball twice in his glove, and leaned in for an imaginary sign. Kevin leaned in with him, watching quietly. The kid wound up and threw, the ball skipping in on two hops, dad fielding it cleanly. Kevin smiled softly without hardly realizing it.

"Am I fucking dreaming?"

Kevin jumped in his skin and turned. He hadn't seen Finn McDermott since that Saturday morning behind the Jeff. As is usually the case with guys, decades didn't seem to matter.

"Finn, what's up?"

"Kevin Pearce, as I live and fucking breathe. You thinking about pulling out the glove?"

"Sox could use it."

"Tell me about it." Finn took a seat on the bench. "What in Christ brings you back here?" The kid who used to worry about love handles now had a full bay window hanging out over his belt. Too many draft beers and bowls of chowder thick with pepper and cream. Too many cheap cigars. Too many nights on the couch. Too many fucking doughnuts.

"I was in the area. Figured I'd stop by the park."

"Memories, right?" Finn crossed his legs at the ankle and leaned back, folding his hands over his swollen belly like it was an unborn child. "Somebody told me you work for the *Globe*?"

Kevin was surprised Finn knew what he did for a living. Hell, Kevin was surprised Finn was still alive. "Yeah."

"You cover sports?"

"Nah, I do mostly investigative stuff."

"No shit. Anything I heard of?"

"I won the Pulitzer Prize for a story I did in Brighton. That's why I'm back." Kevin felt his cheeks flush as he mentioned the prize. Finn took no notice.

"I scalp tickets and sell T-shirts down at Fenway. Had to put my time in, but I got a primo spot in front of the Cask. Right next to the sausage and peppers guy."

"Nice."

Finn uncrossed and recrossed his feet. "Yeah, it's pretty sweet."

Kevin picked up the six-pack by an empty plastic ring. "Beer?"

Finn waved him off, then took one anyway, draining half of it in one go and finishing with a wet belch. "You seen Bobby?"

"Is he around?"

"Bobby's always around." Finn stuck out his lower lip and creased his eyes into twin folds of fat. "Why you asking?"

"Asking what?"

"'Bout Bobby?"

"I don't know. Like to see him, I guess."

"Bobby and I are tight, you know."

"Sure."

"He runs Fingers's book. I help him out."

Bobby the bookie. Kevin knew about it. Still, it was a hard thing to hear. When they were kids, Bobby was the guy who held the world in his hands. And Kevin never thought it could be any other way. The black kid was done with the mound. Now he was at the plate, a bat on his shoulder. Dad was tossing balls in the air and the kid was whacking them into the backstop.

"Fucking hey." Finn shook his head. "Never see that back in the day. Not at Tar Park." He waited for a grunt of assent, but none was forthcoming so he finished his beer, tossed the can, and climbed to his feet. "Well, I gotta hit it. Swing by my spot. Give you a deal on a jersey."

"By the Cask?"

"Right."

"Tell Bobby I said 'hey.'"

"You know it's funny I saw you."

"Why's that?"

"I was going through some old shit last night and came across something." Finn pulled out a wrinkled photo. It was a picture of Finn, Bobby, and Kevin in the bleachers at Fenway.

"Yankees," Kevin said. "We sat three rows off the bullpen."

"Bobby almost got a ball."

"Yeah." Kevin went to give back the picture. Finn refused.

"Keep it. I got a ton of them old shots."

"You sure?"

"Why not? You don't get back much." Finn leaned in and touched Kevin lightly on the shoulder. "And, hey, I'm sorry about your grandmother."

"Long time ago, Finn."

"Still, I never got to see you or nothing." He produced a business card from another pocket, turning it over once or twice in his hands before passing it along. "Bobby works construction during the days. Call 'em and they can usually tell you what job he's on. And congratulations on that prize."

"Thanks. I'll catch you later."

Finn nodded, both men acting as if they saw each other every day, instead of every other decade. Kevin watched him shamble across the park, then sipped at his beer and studied the old photo, wondering what he was doing here and why Brighton still held him in its grip.

14

BOBBY SCALES parked across the street and stared at the church, gray stone washed white in the flecked and fading light. Inside, the air was heavy and still, like someone was holding his breath and hoping for the best. Bobby walked past a cold row of votive candles and knelt in the last pew. He prayed for three people—a decade of the rosary for each—then made the sign of the cross and sat back. Bobby had a small Bible in his pocket and opened it to a random page. He believed in the power of the unknown—fate, instinct, Jesus, Buddha, karma—he bought it all, thought it wove together into a seamless garment that wrapped you up head to toe and cradle to grave. Some people understood what they wore . . . and who they were. Most never had a clue.

Scratches on stone, footsteps. Bobby watched as Father Lenihan came out of the sacristy and began to light candles behind the altar. The old priest performed the same ritual every afternoon at quarter to five. And never knew about the solemn watchman who sat in the shadows. Bobby waited until the priest had finished and the altar was empty. In a city full of Catholics, no one went to mass anymore. Instead, there was talk of churches being shuttered and sold—the money earmarked to pay off the ones who'd been ruined. Bobby had read all the stories in the *Globe*. Fifty, sixty, seventy priests. Unlike the rest of Brighton, Bobby wasn't surprised. Not a fucking bit. What he did wonder about were the ones who'd never touched a kid but were branded pedophiles all the same. Did the collar ever burn their throat? Or was it just part of the gig? Cross to bear and all that? Bobby closed up his Bible and walked to the back of the church where he lit a candle, slipped a twenty in the box, and left.

———

By the time Father Lenihan welcomed the four people who showed up for five o'clock mass, Bobby was back in his Jeep. He parked in front of Brighton Hardware, where they kept faded pictures of old Little League teams in the front window, including one of Bobby's team when he was eleven. First baseman and pitcher for the Brighton Yankees. Bobby had never seen the picture, but people told him it was there so he took it on faith. Next to the hardware store was the Palace Spa. A long stretch of a man walked out of the Palace, an old dog shuffling behind. The man had a thick shock of black hair with a white streak that ran parallel to the part in his scalp. Bobby knew the face, a miserable strand of Irishman who laid bricks for a living and did his drinking in the Corrib. He loved to get starched on Bushmills and talk about how America was full of cunts and how fucking wonderful it was back in Galway. Of course, he was a Golden Gloves champion back in the old sod . . . weren't they all . . . until one day when a kid from Allston knocked out three of his teeth and used the toe of his boot to turn the Irishman's left eye into jelly. Seamus something or other turned his head away from Bobby as he ducked into a parking lot. Bobby smiled at the eye patch. Golden Gloves, my ass. The fucker owed Bobby fifteen hundred from a Man U soccer match. At least another three K from the week before.

The Irishman drove a pickup with a tricolor plastered across the bumper. He opened the door and booted the dog in the ribs just for the hell of it as he jumped in. Bobby watched from across the street as the pickup rolled out of the lot, then slammed his Jeep into gear and followed.

They climbed out of Brighton Center and navigated up and over a humpbacked street called Mount Vernon. The Irishman pulled down a cramped driveway to a cluster of single-story shacks backed up to a fence and a vacant lot. Bobby came up fast, boxing in the pickup. Irish climbed out with a string of oaths. Bobby hit him with a short left and heavy right. The Irishman had his fists up now on either side of his face. There was a small wedged cut breathing at his temple that was a perfect replica of the thick ring Bobby wore on his finger. The Irishman threw a jab or two, for the old sod no doubt, but there was nothing in them. Bobby cracked him once more with a left, then ran his head into the driver's-side window. Irish grabbed at a mirror and broke it off. Otherwise, the driveway was quiet.

"Fucking cunt," the Irishman breathed.

"You owe me money."

"I paid your man three thousand last week."

Bobby still held a handful of black hair and pulled the Irishman's face close. "You think I got time for this shit?"

A head peeked from behind a shade in a house to Bobby's right. The Irishman smiled, a rope of red saliva linking two gray nuggets of teeth. The patch had slipped, and Bobby could see a piece of scarred and scaled flesh underneath. He drove his thumb into the pink pulp at the corner of the Irishman's good eye. The pupil bulged in its socket.

"How about I take the other one, Seamus O'Toole, or whatever the fuck your name is?"

The Irishman whimpered back in his throat, but otherwise kept his yap shut. Not easy for that breed of folk, but when you're already down an eye . . . Bobby spied a nail gun in the back of the pickup and pulled it out, kneeling on the Irishman's arm and forcing his hand flat on the pavement.

"You ain't got the stones for it," the Irishman said in that half-proud, half-scared-shit voice the paddies had perfected over the centuries.

Bobby punched two nails through the back of his hand and watched him scream as he rolled down the driveway. Bobby followed to the gutter and pulled his wallet, thick and green, from a back pocket. He took out five hundred dollars, leaving fifty behind.

The Irishman struggled to his knees, hand held close to his chest, pinkie finger bent at an odd angle and quivering. "Take the whole fucking thing . . ." The rest of the sentence dissolved into curses delivered between frothy bursts of spittle. Bobby walked back up the incline and swung open the door to the pickup. The old dog jumped out and rubbed up against Bobby's legs, looking for food. Bobby nudged him away and watched as he picked his way across the driveway, past his owner, and down the street. He went about ten yards, pissed on a telephone pole, then retraced his steps and jumped back into the pickup.

"You need to smarten up."

The dog just looked at him, and Bobby realized what he already knew—some things were just born to get beat the fuck over the head. He slammed the door shut and cranked down the window, just in case the dog came to his senses. Then he walked back down to the Irishman.

"Don't bet with me again. And if I see you touch that dog, the next nail goes through your fucking eye."

"Piss off."

Bobby walked back to his Jeep and backed out of the driveway. The last thing he saw in his rearview mirror was the Irishman flipping him off with his crippled hand and wiping blood off his face with the other. Bobby smiled. His pulse had never risen above sixty.

———

He drove back down Washington and parked across from the Palace Spa. The owner, a Jew named Max, was behind the counter, selling scratch tickets to a ferret-faced old lady in a red cloth coat with long bags under her eyes.

"Bobby, what's up?"

"The *Herald* and a pack of Marlboros," the lady said. "Soft pack."

Max had already pulled the smokes from a slot above his head. The old lady shoved across some bills and a pile of coins. Max threw the money in the register without counting it. The lady grabbed her paper from a stack and slammed the door on her way out.

"Orders the same thing three times a week. Two scratch tickets, a *Herald,* and the cigs. Thirteen dollars and twenty-seven cents, exact change, right down to the penny." Max pushed his stomach up against the register and screamed at the closed door. "Fucking bitch."

"Jesus, Max."

"Sorry, Bobby. It's the job. The pressure, you know?"

Bobby took a look around. Three aisles jammed with staples such as coffee, tea, bread, cereal. Another aisle with pharmacy items—toothpaste, shaving cream, shampoo, soap, a rack of condoms. A cooler with milk, eggs, butter, and cheese. A couple of lonely-looking potatoes beside a bunch of brown bananas and three dried-up tomatoes. A coffee machine. And, of course, the lottery in all its varied forms. No one did the lottery like Massachusetts. A hundred thousand ways to lose your money on scratch tickets and if that wasn't enough, there was Keno going off every twelve minutes. Fucking assholes might as well put slot machines in the statehouse.

"You want a coffee?" Max had the pot in his hand, a ribbon of steam curling out of the top. Bobby nodded. Max poured him one with cream and a half teaspoon of sugar. Then Max poured one for himself, cream and five sugars.

"How's business?"

"Ragheads opened up down the street."

"They taking your customers?"

"Fuck, no. You ever go in there?"

"Didn't even know it existed."

"Place smells like camel shit." Max took a sip from his coffee and added two more sugars. "They gotta bring in a fucking goat just to use as an air freshener. You want a doughnut or something?"

"Nah. Is he here?"

Max smiled, revealing a row of teeth stained anywhere from pack-a-day yellow to lung-cancer brown. "What do you think? Been waiting ten minutes."

Bobby walked toward the back of the store. Finn was stalking back and forth in front of a Keno screen hanging from the ceiling. Yellow balls were tumbling, and numbers were dropping into place.

"Give me an eighty. Give me a *fucking* eighty."

A sixty-four popped up, followed by a seven, a twelve, and a forty-three. Finn welcomed each number with its very own expletive. Then the game was done.

"Cock*SUCKER*." He tore up his ticket and threw it on the floor with the rest of the Keno confetti.

"What are you playing?"

Finn's head whipped around. "Hey, B. I didn't see you there. Same four numbers all week. First three come in, but I can't hit the fucking eighty."

"Go with a different number."

"Yeah, then the eighty comes in all day long. Fucking ballbreaker, right?" Finn slipped onto a stool. Bobby sat on a long wooden table that ran the length of one wall and let his legs dangle.

"Was reading an article in *SI* about Michael Jordan," Finn said. "Did you know he has a brother?"

Bobby shook his head.

"Dude's five eight. Imagine that. You're Michael Jordan's brother and you're five fucking eight."

"You think it bothers him?"

"Sure as shit would bother me." Finn had a folded *Herald* in front of him and a white paper bag. Bobby ignored the newspaper and opened the bag. He took out a blueberry muffin and broke off a piece.

"Thanks."

Finn nodded at the *Herald*. Bobby sighed and pulled it across. Inside the fold was a stack of twenties.

"Three forty. All paid up."

"You don't have to do it this way, Finn."

"It's smart."

"It's fucking stupid. Who's watching us? Max?"

"You want to go in the bathroom and count it."

"Shut up." Bobby took out the money and stuffed it in his pocket. It had been their ritual for the last five years. Once a week, they'd meet at the Palace. They saw each other every day, but this meeting always took place at the Palace. Finn would bring a blueberry muffin and a *Herald*. If he owed money (the usual case), he'd stick it in the paper. If Bobby owed him (the unusual case), Finn would wait while Bobby tucked his winnings in the paper. Bat-shit crazy? Sure. But it was Finn.

"You work today?" he said.

Bobby hung drywall most mornings starting around six until two in the afternoon. He didn't need the cash, not with the book operation and everything, but Bobby liked the physical labor. In fact, it was one of the best things in his life.

"Yeah." Bobby tossed the remains of his muffin in the trash. "I just saw the Irishman outside. The tall one with the white streak and eye patch."

"Slattery?"

"Is that his name? What's he owe us?"

"I don't know. Four, maybe five K."

"He said he paid in three thousand last week."

"He's a liar. Check with Bridget. She'll tell you."

"Fuck it. I just went Wayne Cashman on his ass."

"So what's he still owe us?"

"Get what you can out of him. Then tell him to take his business elsewhere. If he gives you any trouble . . ."

"I can handle that prick."

Bobby considered Finn—jowls and belly balanced on a spindly set of grandpa legs. He could handle the weekend bettors from Newton and Brookline. Scare the crap out of most college kids. That was about it. Bobby still paid him like he was a tough guy just because he did. It gave Finn something to talk about on those nights when the Sox sucked and he was sitting outside Fenway with his buddies trying to move a half-dozen grandstand for something close to face.

"I know you can handle him, Finn, but if he gives you any problems, I want to know. Okay?"

"Sure."

"What?"

"Nothing."

"Fuck you, nothing. What is it?"

Finn hitched his shoulders. Bobby knew he scared people. He was the guy who'd put a bullet in Curtis Jordan. And that bought a lifetime of respect among the locals. Not to mention a healthy dose of piss-pounding fear. All of which Bobby put to good use. "You still drink in the Corrib?" he said.

"Place sucks."

"What's the matter?"

"They started putting butter and chives on the baked potato they give you with the steak tips. I like to do that shit myself."

"You still drink there, Finn?"

"A little bit. Why?"

"Just watch yourself and let me know if they give you any problems."

"Fine."

"You wanna grab a beer?"

"Supposed to work the game tonight."

"All right." Bobby jumped to his feet.

Finn licked his lips like a nervous spaniel. "Fuck it, I'm already late. You wanna smoke a joint first?"

"When was the last time you seen me smoke a joint?"

"Wanna wait for me?"

Bobby looked his friend up and down. "How you doing with the blow?"

"You know I'm off that shit."

"Yeah?"

"Yeah." Finn's eyes were turning to water, his lower lip starting to crumble.

"What's the matter?"

"Nothing. Why you fucking with me today?"

Bobby glanced around, then leaned close. "Cuz if you're on the blow again, I got no choice but to hurt you. Before you hurt me. You understand what I'm saying?"

"Of course."

"Come on then."

They walked to the front of the store. Max was drinking his coffee and reading the paper.

"Where'd you get them?" Bobby said, nodding at a chorus line of roasted hens sitting under a yellow light behind the counter.

"People gettin' sick of the subs and all that crap. Fucking things are delicious."

"Delicious, huh?"

"Sold out yesterday. You want one?"

Bobby looked at Finn. "Hungry?"

"Thirsty."

Bobby pulled out a roll of bills. "Wrap one up."

Ten minutes later, they were sitting in a Market Street dive called Joey's. The bartender put down two Buds and went back to his perch on the cooler, eyes fixed on a muted TV slotted over the men's room. *Family Feud* was on. Bobby tipped his beer so it clinked against Finn's. Then they sat in the quiet, the only sound Finn cracking bones and tearing hen flesh.

"How's your mom?" Bobby said.

Finn's mom lived by herself in a subsidized housing complex off Faneuil Street. Finn visited the old woman every day, and every day she left a twenty-dollar bill for her only son under a cookie jar in the kitchen. Bobby knew about the double sawbuck but never hassled Finn about it. Bobby also made sure the old woman's rent was paid up and kicked in a little extra so the building manager didn't fuck with her like they did with some of the old-timers in those places. Finn didn't know about that, either.

"Doc told her she's got maybe a year or two," Finn said.

"They said that five years ago."

"Yeah, well . . ."

"Don't worry about it, Finn."

"I don't."

Bobby could already hear the cracks in his voice and knew he'd be a fucking basket case when his mom finally went.

"Thanks for asking, B."

"No big deal."

"Yeah, it is. No one else really gives a fuck, you know?"

The bartender swung by to see if they needed another. Finn was ready. The bartender set him up and drifted away again.

"I'm gonna be putting something on the C's this weekend. They got the Knicks at home." Finn began to run through the different permutations of how he might lose his money. Bobby listened to the drone and stared at himself in a clouded mirror that ran behind the bar. He noticed the sag under his chin. A little puffiness around the eyes.

"So what do you think? Bobby?"

"Yeah?"

"What do you think? About Florida?"

Bobby pulled his eyes off the mirror. He had no idea how they'd gotten from Finn's basketball bets to the Sunshine State, but there they were. "You wanna go next winter?"

"I know. I say it every year."

"Yeah, you do. Right here, at this bar, sitting on that stool."

"This time I got the money. It's all tucked away and not a penny's going to the gambling. None of that shit."

"That's good, Finn."

"I know I'm too old to play on the circuit."

"You can still go down and watch."

"I'm thinking I can coach."

"Coach?"

"Sure. You ever seen those New York guineas sitting in the stands at the U.S. Open? All I need is to go down there and find a prospect. I was thinking about a girl. Fifteen, sixteen years old. I'll teach her the game. How to really hit. Not gonna bang her or nothing like that. Just coach."

"Sounds like a plan."

"You think so?"

"Why not?"

Finn wiped chicken grease off his fingers with a bar napkin and sucked down half his beer in a long, greedy swallow. "Fuck, yeah. Why not?" The thought seemed to warm him. "You'll come down and visit?"

"Try to keep me away."

"I was thinking I'd get one of those condos in a marina. We could keep a boat. Go out and tuna fish in the gulf."

"You ever been fishing, Finn?"

"Caught a catfish once up at Chandler's Pond."

"Good enough, brother."

They laughed and drank to Finn's make-believe future.

"Did I tell you who I saw?" Finn said.

"Who's that?"

"Kevin Pearce."

Bobby stopped the bottle of beer halfway to his lips and returned it to the bar. "Where did you see him?"

"Over at Tar Park this afternoon. He was asking about you."

"What did you say?"

"Nothing. He told me he won the Pulitzer Prize or something."

Bobby whistled. "No kidding."

"That a big deal?"

"Jesus Christ."

"I read the sports page. And that's mostly to see what time the games start."

Bobby's gaze traveled out the window and down Market Street.

"B?"

"Yeah."

"You haven't seen him in twenty, thirty years."

"He's like a brother, Finn."

"Like you and me?"

"That's right. Just like you and me."

Finn grunted and polished off his beer. "I should get going."

"Have a good night." Bobby touched his nose with a finger. "And remember what I told you about that shit."

Finn tossed what was left of the chicken in the trash. Bobby watched him go, then walked behind the bar.

"You see some black broad got killed in Brighton," the bartender said without taking his eyes off the set. Bobby looked up at the news banner. A reporter stood on a street corner talking.

"Why should I care?"

The bartender shrugged. "I know. It's a fucking smoke, right?" He smiled. Not so much at what he'd said, but just because he could say it. "You want company down there?" The bartender poked his eyes toward a door next to the reach-in cooler.

"She's coming in with the books."

"Anyone else?"

"No. And give a yell down fifteen minutes after she gets here. Tell me I got a call or something." Bobby grabbed another beer out of the cooler and walked down a sagging set of wooden steps to a cold basement. He flicked on an overhead light and took a seat behind a large metal desk. To the left of the desk was a couch, a refrigerator, and a couple of old filing cabinets. Beside the cabinets were three TVs, a dry-erase board drilled into the wall, a Nerf basketball hoop, and a small, free-standing safe. Bobby turned on a computer and began to go through the baseball lines. A phone on the desk rang three times. Bobby ignored it. He felt his cell phone buzz in his pocket and ignored that. It was going to be a heavy night. Fourteen baseball games, four on the West Coast. Plus basketball and hockey. Bobby needed to focus, but all he could think about was Kevin. There was a creak on the stairs. Bobby looked up. She stepped into a circle of light, a blue binder under her arm.

"Hey," Bobby said.

"I heard he's back." Her eyes were bright and liquid and measuring.

"That's what Finn says."

"I'm not surprised. You want to go over the numbers first?"

Bobby kicked out a chair. Bridget Pearce took a seat

15

SITTING IN the privileged shadow of the Boston Public Garden, the Bull and Finch Pub used to be a classic watering hole, so classic that they made it into a TV show called *Cheers* and, of course, ruined it. Walk around the corner, however, and you'll find the closest thing to what the old place used to be. Perched along Charles Street, on the hallowed cobbles of Beacon Hill, the Sevens isn't much to look at: long bar, a rough collection of tables, dartboard, and jukebox. The beer, however, is cold, the roast beef sandwiches are cut fresh behind the counter, and a few heads at the bar still talk about the day Luis Aparicio cost the Red Sox a division title when he tripped over third base. Still hate him for it, too.

Kevin found an empty stool and ordered a pint of Heineken. The beer had just hit the back of his throat when the pub's front door swung open. Lisa Mignot was there, hand on a hip, powdery motes of sunlight fighting to fill the space around her. Kevin smiled. She slipped off the threshold and drifted in, brushing his cheek with her lips and running her nails across the back of his neck.

"Hey, Kev."

Lisa was a prosecutor for the Suffolk County district attorney's office She'd grown up in Roxbury, graduated with honors from Harvard Law School, and decided to spend a couple of years putting bad guys in jail before moving on to attorney general, the governor's office, senator, president of the United States. That kind of thing. Most people wondered why she'd ever decided to talk to Kevin, never mind date him. It's not that supremely intelligent, decidedly hot women of Caribbean and French ancestry don't cotton to pale, white, scrawny Irish-Catholics from Boston. Kevin was certain it happened all the time. He'd just never heard of it.

"What are you drinking?" he said.

A man with skin the color of wet cement surfaced from somewhere beneath the taps. He was wearing black hi-tops, black shorts, and a shapeless Celtics T-shirt. There was an unlit cigarette stuck between his lips, a pen and scratch paper at the ready. Lisa lit him up with a smile and the bartender danced a little in his Cons.

"Maybe just a glass of OJ? With a straw?"

Kevin figured the barkeep might squeeze the oranges himself. After he planted a tree in the back of the place. Three minutes later, Lisa had her OJ. First time Kevin ever saw it delivered in a frosted mug, but there you go.

"How was your day?" he said.

"Pretty good." Lisa took a sip and settled herself on her stool. They'd been together almost a year. Some days, it seemed like they hardly needed to speak—the connection so strong words just got in the way. Other days, Kevin barely managed to scratch the surface. Maybe it was just women. For him, they'd always been akin to Russian nesting dolls, one secret wrapped inside another, both container and contained. Inscrutable. Irresistible. Life.

Lisa pulled a soft, black briefcase onto the bar and began to unpack it. "Actually, I've got this work thing I wanted to talk to you about."

"What about the rules?"

"I thought we could suspend them this one time . . ." She looked up from her unpacking and froze. "What's going on, Kevin?"

"Nothing."

"Something's going on."

He shook his head and buried his nose in his beer. Lisa stuffed the paperwork back in her case and zipped it shut. Then she sat back, hands folded, chin lifted, golden light streaming through the window and lighting up a sculpted set of cheekbones.

"How do you know?" he said.

"I love you, moron. I'm supposed to know. Now, what's going on?"

"Remember Rosie Tallent?"

An anxious moment flickered in her eyes and was gone. "Of course I do. Charges should have never been filed. And yours were the best stories the *Globe* ran all year."

"Yeah, well, something happened today."

"There's nothing coming out of our office."

"It's not about the case itself. Although I'd still love to find the real killer."

"So would I." Lisa coaxed a cigarette out of a pack of Marlboro Lights and lit up. Kevin breathed shallowly through his nose and stared at the Sevens's red painted walls.

"Kevin?"

She was still there, the familiar curves of her face conspiring to strip him of whatever it was that protected him against whatever it was he feared. He took a cleansing breath and edged out into the open, dropping his shield and baring his breast to the slings and arrows of his outrageous good fortune. Somewhere Shakespeare was having a good chuckle.

"It hasn't been announced yet, but I won the Pulitzer Prize today."

A couple of construction guys sat at the far end of the bar, eyes glued to the Sox pregame playing on a TV above the jukebox. In a booth along the wall, an artist type with a soft felt hat was drinking a dark beer and cleaning some brushes with a spotted rag. Across from the artist sat a college girl wearing chinos and a pink Izod who was dying to touch something special before she settled down in Wellesley and had her three kids. The artist didn't look particularly special, but he'd get better through the years as she retold the story to her friends over lunch. And then there was Lisa, eyebrows arched, perfectly manicured nails gripping the life out of her cigarette. Kevin didn't know whether the relationship would last, but she was the one he'd shared the news with. Regardless of what happened in the future, nothing and no one could ever take that away. And that had to mean something.

"Are you serious?" she said.

"Pretty serious, yeah."

"For Tallent?"

"Best investigative piece."

"Holy shit." She crushed out her cigarette and took his face in her strong, well-shaped hands, laughing as she kissed him and hugged him, pulling him close and laying her cheek next to his. Kevin felt the thick knot he hadn't realized was there loosen in his chest.

"You're impressed?"

"What do you think? Tell me about it." Her fingers brushed his cuff before cupping the inside of his wrist, and he suddenly worried she might start crying.

"There's not much to tell. Someone on the committee leaked it to my editor. I asked if he was sure and he said a hundred percent."

"Goddamn, Kevin. I'm so proud of you." And then she did cry. A single, lovely tear, wiped away with a single, lovely finger. And it meant everything.

"Thanks, Lis."

"I love you."

"Me, too. You want to celebrate?"

"Better believe it. Let's get some dinner, champagne."

"How about we just grab a couple of beers here instead?"

"That what you want?"

"I think so."

Lisa kissed him again. "You want to get drunk in the Sevens? Let's do it."

She motioned for the bartender. Kevin stopped her. "What did you want to talk about?"

Her eyes slid to her briefcase, packed with paperwork and still sitting on the bar. "It'll keep. Pulitzer Prize, Kev. Jesus." She threw down some cash. "Order us a round. And don't try to pay for it."

He watched her head off to the ladies' room, all legs and

heels and silk and smarts. A Picasso in motion. The two construction guys gave her a discreet look as she floated past, then back at Kevin. He tipped his nearly empty pint. They smiled and returned the favor. Kevin figured tonight would be as good as it got. So he'd enjoy it, before it all went to hell in the morning.

16

SHE BUMPED her hip against his as they picked their way along Charles Street, then began the narrow climb up Pinckney to where it wound back down into Joy. Lisa circled her arms around his waist as he fumbled for the key, running her lips across his neck, brushing up against the stubble on his cheek. They kissed in the darkened living room, with the anxious traffic below in the street and the front door still ajar. She kicked it closed as she led him to the couch. He started to take off his shirt. She tore it, buttons bouncing and rolling crazily everywhere. They started on the couch but wound up in front of a fireplace they'd used once, nearly burning down their apartment in the process. Kevin closed his eyes and lost himself. She watched him until the very end, then dropped her head back, bared her teeth, and let it wash over. When it was done, she lay curled on her side and stared at an inch-wide sliver of moonlight striped across his bare chest. She thought he might be sleeping and slipped from under his arm, padding into the bedroom to get a robe. By the time she returned, he'd put on a pair of blue boxers and found some cold chicken and half a bottle of wine in the fridge. They ate sprawled on the wooden floor, using pillows for cushions.

"My boyfriend, the Pulitzer Prize winner. I like it."

"You're drunk."

"Two pints."

"Imperial pints. That's twenty ounces. And you were drinking Guinness."

Lisa wasn't drunk but didn't mind that he thought so. She traced his flat stomach lazily with a finger. "You realize it's been almost a year."

"Be a year next month."

"Very good, Mr. Pearce. You remember how we met?"

"I know it was at a party."

"What party?"

Kevin picked at a piece of chicken. "Might have to take the Fifth on that one, Counselor."

"Idiot."

They'd met at a party thrown by one of her colleagues, a prosecutor named Ronnie Coleman. Ronnie loved to play match-maker and, for some reason, considered Lisa his greatest challenge. She told him she could get herself a date, or anything else she wanted, whenever she wanted. Still, Ronnie liked to dabble. So he'd introduced her to Kevin on a soft spring evening, with the windows open overlooking Marlborough Street and Alicia Keys playing somewhere in the background. Everything was perfect. Then Kevin opened his mouth. Most guys in Boston had one major problem. They couldn't get over themselves. Whether it was their career, their clothes, their imaginary prowess in bed, or just checking their hair in a mirror every five minutes, they were more boys than men. Kevin was all that for sure, but in an innocent, Hugh Grant sort of way, mumbling into his beer, barely making eye contact with her, and hustling back to his circle of pals first chance he got. He left the party a few minutes after they'd met without saying good-bye. At the door, however, his eyes sought her out and she raised her glass. He nodded and was gone.

It should have been nothing more than amusing, another child in a man's suit of clothes, but something lingered. She liked his disheveled smile, liked the way he walked, and especially liked that he wasn't a raging, fucking egomaniac. After he left, the party seemed washed out and boring. She found herself wishing he'd stayed. The next day she tracked down Ronnie, who provided her with the essentials. A reporter at the *Globe*. Never mentioned that. Covered crime. Never mentioned that. He must have known who she was. Never mentioned it. Lisa decided she wanted a second helping. Fortunately, Boston's a small town. She ran into him two weeks later at the Starbucks on the corner of Beacon and Charles. Away from the party, sipping his coffee, Kevin relaxed. And she found something there that comforted her, made her feel safe. Cared for. She remembered thinking that as he kissed her for the first time and she took him to her bed. The rest of it, of course, snuck up on her, belting her across the side of the head the way those things always did. She should have expected it, but who didn't say that? So she fell like everyone else who lived and breathed for a living fell. One minute he was a sweet guy she'd date for the summer. Then she caught herself looking at him as he walked into a restaurant and it all changed into something different, something thrilling, something electric. Something. She knew it would end. Everything ended one way or another. But she'd fallen, in that moment of time and space. Pretty fucking hard, too.

"Your pal, Robbie or something." She had to give him credit. Kevin was hanging in there, still trying to piece together their first meeting. "It was a party at his place."

"Ronnie Coleman."

"Ronnie Coleman. That's it. Lives on Comm Ave."

"Marlborough Street."

"Marlborough, right. Maybe I should give up while I'm ahead?"

"You're not ahead, but, yes, you should give up." Lisa pointed her toes and ran them along his shin. "By the way, are you ever gonna shave?"

He scratched at his stubble and pushed a hand through brown hair that fell halfway to his shoulders. "I'm going for Kurt Cobain, circa 1991."

"That's wonderful, Kevin, but this is the Pulitzer. Interviews, pictures, publicity."

"Am I running for office or something?"

"Just think about it, darling."

"You never call me 'darling.'"

"I never asked you to cut your hair, either. Tell me what you did today after you found out. Did you see your family?"

"I went back there, yeah."

"They must have been thrilled."

"They were excited. You want some more wine?"

She held out her glass and watched as he filled it. He never talked about Brighton. And never asked her about growing up in the 'Bury. It was part of their unspoken pact. Nothing about their pasts. Nothing about families, friends, old flames. First times, last times. Who they'd fucked. Who they'd fucked over. And nothing, especially nothing, about their childhoods. There'd only been the one exception. A gray Sunday morning when they'd just made love and were lying in the afterward, a bell from one of Boston's ancient churches tolling the hour then falling silent. Lisa recalled holding her breath and feeling the weight of everything that wasn't. No cars in the street, no rustle of breeze, no clap or shout. She'd wondered idly if they weren't the only people left in Beacon Hill, in all of Boston, in all the world, if perhaps she'd hear the clip of hooves striking off the cobbles below, the city's ever lurking past reborn as they'd slept. Then Kevin had touched the scar that ran along her scalp line, white against coffee cream skin, and asked where it came from. And she'd told him.

"Nigger, get back on that bus."

The cop glared at Lisa through the scratched Plexiglas shield covering his face and poked at her with the rounded end of his baton. Lisa's first instinct was to retreat back up the steps. Then she heard Mrs. Pendleton. The woman had a rawboned voice and smooth skin that shone in all its blackness. She dressed severely but professionally, face scrubbed of makeup and pretense. Fierce, intelligent, a leader. When she told her freshman class they'd "volunteered" to be the first bus into South Boston, they nodded as one and got on board. In the beginning it wasn't so bad—just a lot of hard, white faces, layered three and four deep on every block, staring at the caravan of yellow as it rolled past. Then they turned onto G Street and the first rock cracked a window. Mrs. Pendleton was standing in the aisle, explaining what to expect when it hit. She didn't miss a beat, smiling and thanking the locals for the warm welcome. The kids chuckled nervously. Then another rock hit, followed by a milk crate, a bottle, more rocks, and then too many objects to count. The school bus crawled to a stop in the middle of the street and began to sway on its springs as people hurled themselves at the windows.

Middle-aged men with faces carved out of roast beef, kids with zits and shaved heads carrying cut-down hockey sticks like war clubs, mothers with rollers in their hair and their children with signs that read WELCOME BONEHEADS and WHITES HAVE RIGHTS TOO! A thousand different flavors of ugly, coming at the windows in waves. Lisa kept her eye on Mrs. Pendleton, who only got calmer as the world got crazier. She strolled to the front, touching a child here and there as she passed before whispering to the driver. He shook his head at first, then edged the bus forward. The faces fell away as they picked up speed. Cops on motorcycles swung in on either side, escorting them the rest of the way down the block. The bus groaned to a stop and the crowd fell quiet. The driver looked back at Mrs. Pendleton, who walked down the aisle and crouched beside Lisa. Mrs. Pendleton had always made Lisa feel special, like she was destined for something "great." Maybe "great" started today. And maybe "great" wasn't really all that wonderful. Lisa wasn't sure, but when Mrs. Pendleton asked if she'd be willing to go first, Lisa found herself nodding. Then she was on her feet and walking to the front. The driver cranked open the door and there she was, with the cop and the Plexiglas shield, the black baton and the word nigger burning in her ears. And Mrs. Pendleton right behind her.

"What did he say to you, honey?"

"Nothing, ma'am."

"All right, then."

Mrs. Pendleton waited. They all waited. Everyone on the bus, the double line of cops in riot gear and more on horseback, the ranks of tight pale faces behind the cops who didn't want their children shipped off to a strange neighborhood halfway across the city, the million plus who'd sit safe and smug in their suburbs and watch on TV. All of them wondering if Lisa Mignot would make it to the front door of South Boston High School. Or if she'd be heading back to Roxbury in a pine box.

Lisa pushed the cop's baton away and stepped off the bus. Her eyes followed a pigeon, flapping its wings once and riding a gray wind across the façade of the school before perching on the corner of the building like a small, silent statue. Lisa took another step. There was a young white cop to her left. He slipped the visor up off his face and smiled. She smiled back. A green golf ball struck him just under the eye. He dropped to the ground and didn't move. The golf ball was followed by a baseball, slapping the pavement a foot or two in front of Lisa and sailing off into the crowd. Then it all came down. A fusillade of rocks and bricks, batteries and bottles, pinging off Plexiglas and popping all around her. Something told Lisa not to run. Running was fear. And fear was oxygen to the hatred burning all around her. So she ducked her head and just kept walking. Another cop went down to her right. Someone grabbed her under the arms and nearly lifted her off her feet, hustling her up the path toward the front door of the high school. She was twenty feet away when another golf ball snapped off the pavement. The carom caught Lisa near the temple. She went to a knee. There was a thread of blood on the curb and more on her hands. Above her a voice called her name. Then Mrs. Pendleton was there, wiping her face with a handkerchief.

"Can you go the rest of the way?"

"Yes, ma'am."

"Good, because if you can't make it, they don't stand a chance." Mrs. Pendleton pointed back toward the buses and a string of eyes staring out from the windows. Lisa nodded. The older woman took her hand.

"Head high, Lisa. Never be afraid."

And that was how they walked, hand in hand, the final five strides. And then, officially, South Boston High School was integrated.

Kevin wasn't a racist. Not a bit. Still, when she'd told him the story that Sunday morning, his face had clouded over. She was, for just a moment, one of "them"—the little black girl all of Boston had seen walking off the bus that day. She took a small sip of wine, rolled onto her back, and stared at a wooden picture rail that ran naked around their living room.

"What are you thinking about?" he said.

"Nothing. You. The Pulitzer." She lied because it was easy. Kind, even. Meanwhile, her mind turned to the part of herself she kept separate. Like a stone, it sat silent and cold and heavy in her stomach, absorbing neither heat nor light, reflecting only itself.

"Tell me something," she said, wary of the conversation now, leading things carefully away from where they couldn't go.

"Whatever you want."

She propped herself up on an elbow, the curve of her hip outlined in light from the street. "What does a Pulitzer mean for a journalist's career?"

He chuckled. "Good question. Probably nothing. If I wanted to leave Boston, maybe I could go to the *Times*."

"But you don't want to leave Boston." She knew he'd never leave. For Kevin, Boston was Boston. And everything else wasn't. Lisa didn't feel that way, but, again, why get into it? Especially now. Somewhere a cell phone rang, a soft purr coming from the general vicinity of the couch.

"I think that's mine." She dug around in the cushions until

she found her phone. "Gotta take this." She retreated down the apartment's short hallway, dropping her voice to a whisper. After another minute, she returned and started picking up clothes off the floor.

"What is it?" Kevin said, climbing to his feet and stretching.

"Remember I wanted to talk to you about something in the Sevens?"

"One of your cases."

"A girl was murdered last night. I can't go into all the details, but it's a big-time heater."

"And you need my help?"

She stopped collecting clothes and turned to face him. "What if I did?"

"Like I said, it's a violation of the rules."

"But you'd be willing to make an exception?"

"I'd be willing to make a trade."

She pulled him close, kissing him hungrily and running a rough nail across his cheek. Then she escaped into the bathroom, leaving him alone in the living room, half naked and bathed in a pale splinter of light.

———

Normally he'd have followed her right into the shower, but Kevin could tell she was wired for work. And, for the first time, she'd actually asked for his help. So he threw on a T-shirt and went into the kitchen to make coffee. They'd worked out the rules after three months together. She'd treat him like any other journalist in the city. No special access to anything coming out of the D.A.'s office. And it was a two-way street. If he dug up some dirt, she wouldn't expect to know until it hit the papers. Lisa had been the one who'd pushed for the Chinese wall. Now, for some reason, she wanted to tear the thing down.

"Hey." Her voice was muffled. Kevin walked back to the bathroom and cracked the door. The room was heating up and covered in a thin layer of mist.

"Yeah."

Lisa stuck her head out of the shower. "You making coffee?"

"Got a pot brewing. So what is it about your case that can't wait until morning?"

"They got some of the preliminary forensic work back."

"And it can't wait until morning?"

Lisa shrugged and slipped back behind the shower curtain. "It's DeMateo. He said he needed me so I go."

Frank DeMateo was the district attorney for Suffolk County and Lisa's boss.

"You want a ride?"

"I'll just jump in a cab, but you can do me one favor."

"What's that?"

"My briefcase is in the living room. There's a zippered pocket on the outside. Can you check and see if my ID's in there? If I left it at work, it's gonna be a pain in the ass getting into my building without it."

Kevin found her briefcase on the floor near the front door. He sat down on the couch and checked the pocket, but there was no ID. He opened the case, pulled out a couple of files, and dug around. Her ID was wedged at the very bottom, underneath a Snickers bar and a small makeup bag. Kevin stared at the picture of his girl, smart, smiling, beautiful, and about to burst with the fullness of it all. And this was her work ID. Kevin shook his head and swore to himself. His work ID looked like something out of the fucking Book of Revelation. And not the good Revelations, either. He started to shove files back into the briefcase. The last one was older, dog-eared, with a torn green cover and a typed label that read: HOMICIDE—1975. Underneath was the name of the victim: CURTIS JORDAN. Kevin felt his heart double pump in his chest and listened to the water from Lisa's shower, running like a dark, distant river. He followed the sound back to the bathroom and cracked the door again. The room was draped in steam now, her voice issuing from somewhere within its folds.

"Did you find it?"

"I did. How much longer you gonna be?"

"Five, ten minutes. Why?"

"Nothing. Coffee's ready."

"Thanks."

He started to leave.

"Kevin?"

"Yeah?"

A pause. "You all right?"

"Sure. Just sucks you gotta head out in the middle of the night."

"I'm sorry, babe. It's a messed-up case. I'll explain it all later."

Kevin closed the door and walked into the living room. They kept a small printer/copier on the floor by the desk. He powered it up and flipped through the first few pages of the old murder file. Phrases jumped out at him. "Deceased, twenty-six-year-old male, found on floor." "Cause of death: Thirty-eight-caliber gunshot wound to the chest." "Postmortem contact wound: Twenty-two caliber to the head." "Homicide: Unsolved."

Outside, the city was painted in shivering pinpricks of light. Inside, a radiator started to spit and the walls seemed to thump and swell. Poe's "Tell-Tale Heart" ran through his head like a cold dream and Kevin wondered if that wasn't his fate. He wiped his hands and laid the old file down on the desk. Lisa's laptop was open and running. A picture of the two of them at a Sox game served as her screensaver. He hit a button and the smiling faces dissolved into her e-mail browser. The latest message in her in-box was from her office and carried the subject heading: CURTIS JORDAN. Kevin opened it. The message was brief.

ATTACHED IS THE BALLISTICS REPORT WE TALKED ABOUT. CALL ME. F. DEMATEO

He opened up the report and hit print without reading it. Down the hall, the water was still running. After the report finished printing, he pulled out the file on Jordan. He'd copied maybe fifteen pages when the water stopped. Kevin turned off the printer and returned the file to Lisa's briefcase. She was toweling off when he walked back into the bedroom with coffee. He sat on the bed and watched as she got dressed—jeans and a loose-fitting Harvard sweatshirt.

"Coffee's good," Lisa said and lifted her mug.

"How long you think you'll be?"

"Dunno. Hopefully not all night." She straddled him on the bed and cradled his face in her hands. "I'm so proud of you, Kev."

"Thanks."

"I mean it. I feel like we're in this great place . . ."

"And?"

"And I don't want anything to screw it up."

"What could screw it up?"

"Nothing. I'm just saying." She leaned in to kiss him, the scent of lemon clinging to her hair and skin. "I gotta go."

"You gonna tell me about your case?"

"When I get back."

He walked her to the front door, then watched from the window as she climbed in a cab and disappeared down the hill. It was nearly midnight as he settled on the couch with his coffee and started to read—about a man he'd shot in the head twenty-six years earlier.

———

The phone jumped at a little after four in the morning. Kevin was lying on the couch, counting cracks in the ceiling. He let it ring twice, then picked up.

"Yeah?"

"Did I wake you?" Lisa's voice sounded hollow and echoed down the line.

"Not really." Kevin swung his feet to the floor. "How's it going?"

"These people are idiots."

"Who's that?"

"Take your pick. You know what, it doesn't matter. I need to ask a favor."

"What's that?"

"I need you to come down here. Tonight. Right now."

"To your office?"

"To Brighton, Kevin. You gotta come to Brighton and you can't tell a soul."

He knew he'd go. And knew he was going to lie to her. It wasn't something he wanted to do. And it wouldn't end well. But he'd lie anyway, as she'd lied to him. Sometimes it was just how things worked out. So he wrote down the address she gave him and hung up. Then he went into their bedroom and got dressed.

17

THE LETTERS were each a yard and a half high, alternating neons of orange and pink, blazing away in the predawn darkness at the corner of North Beacon and Market Streets. Had they all been working they would have spelled DUNKIN DONUTS. Even short two "D"s and an "N," the locals got the message. Kevin could see her as he pulled into the lot, set up at a table by the window. He ordered coffee and a honey-dipped doughnut from the sleepy-eyed woman behind the counter and made his way over. The reports he'd pilfered from Lisa's briefcase and computer were tucked inside his jacket pocket. He touched them with one hand as he slid in across from her.

"You all right?" she said, taking a sip from a cup kissed with lipstick.

"I haven't been working a murder all night."

"I get the feeling you don't like to come back here."

"Brighton used to be home to the city's slaughterhouses."

"Really?"

"Yep." Kevin gestured to the empty stretch of street running past their window. "Drove the cattle right down Market and butchered them along the river. Less than a half mile from where we're sitting."

"Yikes."

"The poet in me would say you can still smell the blood . . . especially if you grew up here."

"But?"

"Brighton's like anywhere else. Got its rough edges, got its skeletons. And like everyone else in this city, they think they're the shit and everyone else is from hunger." Kevin took a bite of the honey-dipped and dropped it back on its piece of wax paper. "Fucking heaven. You want a bite?"

Lisa shook her head.

"Suit yourself. You know this is the busiest Dunkin' Donuts in the country?"

"No kidding?"

"Assholes down in Weymouth say they're number one, but fuck them. It's Weymouth, for Chrissakes. Besides, this place is open twenty-four seven." Kevin took another bite and wiped his mouth with a napkin. "So you gonna tell me why we're here?"

Lisa turned the coffee cup in her hands and avoided his eyes as she spoke. "I'm gonna share something with you. Something no one but me, you, and maybe a dozen other people know. And it's not something you can report."

"If it's a story, I'd rather not know. That way if I get something on my own . . ."

"You can run with it and be a big hero. That's not what this is, Kevin. Not now."

The server glanced up from her work. Kevin waved her off and she went back to rearranging the jimmies on a tray of frosted doughnuts. Lisa massaged her temple with two fingers and dropped her voice. "Sorry, long night."

Everyone downtown knew she was a star. Fuck that, a mega-star. Lisa's problem was she viewed the world as a meritocracy. If you were smarter than her, then lead. If you weren't, then get out of the way. And no one in the D.A.'s office was as smart as Lisa. Needless to say, the white men she worked with trembled in her considerable wake. And fucked with her every chance they got.

"You need some rest," Kevin said.

"Yeah."

He touched the back of her hand. "Look, if you want this off the record, it's off."

"Thanks, babe."

"Not a problem. Now, tell me about your murder. I'm assuming it happened in Brighton?"

"A black woman was strangled and knifed in a house that was being built on Radnor Road. You know where that is?"

"Sure."

"We gave the story to the press late yesterday afternoon. Normally, it would be a one-day hit."

"But not this one?"

"We withheld the ID on the victim. And the exact location."

"Why?"

She shook her head. "I can't get into all that, but some people working the case wanted a little time with the evidence before we gave the name to the press."

"Who's handling the scene?"

"Good question. Boston P.D.'s on-site as the primary, along with the state police. It was your typical big-dick contest until the governor's office called."

"The governor?"

"They requested that the D.A.'s office pursue an independent line of investigation, at least for the time being."

"Who died, Lis?"

She nodded at what was left of the doughnut in front of Kevin. "You about done?"

He popped the last bite in his mouth and drained his coffee. She was already on her feet. "Let's take a drive."

———

They left the Dunkin' Donuts and headed up Market. The sky was just beginning to lighten and streetlights marked the way with soft splashes of light.

"Where are you going?" Lisa said.

"Thought I'd swing by Radnor. Just take a look."

"Not a great idea. They've got a couple of unmarked cars taking down the tag numbers of anyone who shows an interest."

"Scratch Radnor. Where would you like to go?"

"Just drive."

Kevin rumbled up Chestnut Hill Avenue, bumped over the streetcar tracks, and swung a left onto Commonwealth Avenue.

"Pull over," Lisa said.

Kevin parked on a hilly side street full of shitty apartments rented out to students and even shittier apartments reserved for Brighton's illegals. Lisa dug through a file and handed him a photo of a young black woman lying on her side in a cold puddle of blood.

"Her name was Sandra Patterson, twenty-seven years old. She was stabbed twice. Bled out on the floor."

"And what was Sandra doing on Radnor Road?"

"You ever heard of Habitat for Humanity?"

Kevin turned over the picture and looked out the window. Three Asian kids were coming down the block with book bags slung over their shoulders. Catching the early bus to school. Probably the charter to Latin School.

"Did you hear me, Kevin?"

"I heard you. That's who she was working for?"

"Habitat broke ground on the Radnor house ten weeks ago. Sandra was part of their construction team."

Kevin smiled blankly at the Asian kids. One of them waved as they walked past. Another gave him the finger. Somewhere a bird pecked at his soul and flew off with a piece. He passed the picture of the dead girl back to Lisa. "And the governor cares about all of this because . . ."

"Sandra Patterson was a state cop. She was working undercover as part of a drug op."

"In Brighton?"

"Your old neighborhood's been a player for years. Mostly local, cash-and-carry stuff out of the Faneuil projects and Fidelis Way. Some of the low-rise apartments along Western Avenue. Here and there in Allston."

"So why was Patterson in a house being built by Habitat for Humanity?"

"Two, three years back, we noticed some new patterns emerging. A lot more activity in the 'burbs. White kids selling bags of smack next to the Sunglass Hut in the Chestnut Hill Mall. Shit like that. They've also made a move on campus. BC, BU, Tufts, Harvard. The whole nine yards."

"And it's all running through Brighton?"

"Brighton's an edge neighborhood, bordered up against

Brookline, Newton, Cambridge. Plus it's got a lot of universities nearby."

"Who's the supplier?"

"Dunno. Whoever it is, they're not working out of any of the projects and, best we can tell, not hooked up with any gangs. They pick their spots, and they're damn good at covering their tracks. As you can imagine, there's been a lot of pressure to shut the thing down."

"They're moving dope in white neighborhoods."

"Rich neighborhoods, Kevin. Rich-ass suburbs."

"Why haven't I heard about any of this?"

"Because people like Sandra have been working undercover. She was enrolled part-time as a student at BC. A month ago, she told her boss she was gonna volunteer for the Habitat thing. She said Habitat itself wasn't the target, just cover for an angle she was looking at. Didn't seem like Sandra was close on anything so her boss didn't get a lot of specifics. We're not sure what happened after that, except it was a fuckup."

"Did you know her?"

"I met her. Sweet kid. Smart as hell, too."

"I'm sorry."

"Thanks. There's something else you need to see."

Kevin watched as Lisa dug into her file again. A folder fell off her lap, scattering Sandra Patterson's mortal remains across the floor of the car. Kevin reached down to pick up the photos. Lisa beat him to it and held up a head and shoulders shot of the victim. Patterson was lying flat on her back and might have been sleeping, save for the red button on her forehead and circle of thin steel wrapped around her neck.

"Sandra was strangled with what we believe to be a twelve-gauge piece of piano wire," Lisa said. "The gunshot was postmortem. Thirty-eight caliber."

Kevin studied the photo. Lisa kept talking.

"Forensics says whoever killed her tied off the wire enough to incapacitate, but not to kill. Then he used the knife."

"Did he take anything?"

"Took her driver's license, some money, and the sweatshirt she was wearing."

"Not your typical drug murder."

"It's Rosie Tallent, Kevin. Same M.O. Garrote and a knife. Single postmortem shot to the head. Black, female victim. And they both happened in Brighton."

Kevin handed back the photo. "Rosie was found in Allston. And it was five years ago."

"So you don't think the two are related?"

"Do you?"

"I think whatever this is, it's local."

"And you think I can take you inside?"

"You grew up here. And you wrote about Rosie's murder."

"I wrote about the man who was wrongfully convicted of Rosie's murder. And the legal process behind it. I never got into who actually committed the crime. The truth is I know as much about Brighton these days as you do about Roxbury."

"Exactly. And if Sandra Patterson was killed in a walk-up on Blue Hill Ave., I'd be calling in all my markers."

"Yeah, well, I don't have any."

"No one?"

"I've been gone a long time, Lis. You want a ride back to the apartment?"

"You're not going to help?"

"I didn't say that. You want a ride?"

Lisa stuffed all the paperwork back in her briefcase. Kevin turned over the engine and headed downtown, flashing through Kenmore Square and the Back Bay before hitting Beacon Hill.

"What are you going to do today?" she said.

"Drop you off. Then drive back to Brighton and bang my head against the wall."

"I love you, Kev."

"I want an exclusive if this ever sees the light of day, which, by the way, I highly fucking doubt."

He pulled up in front of their building and watched her disappear inside. Then he took out the business card Finn had given him. It read:

BOBBY SCALES
LEAD CARPENTER/ASST SITE SUPERVISOR
HABITAT FOR HUMANITY

Kevin clipped the card to the ballistics report he'd pilfered from Lisa's e-mail. It was short and sweet. An automated computer system had linked the thirty-eight used to kill Curtis Jordan in 1975 to postmortem gunshot wounds in both the Rosie Tallent and Patterson murders. A state firearms examiner subsequently confirmed the match as a thirty-eight caliber Smith & Wesson revolver. Kevin swore softly to himself. Then he put the car in gear and started rolling downhill. Thunder rumbled overhead and hard bullets of rain began to fall.

18

BOBBY SAT in his room and watched Barney Fife watch himself in a mirror. He was teaching Opie how to use a slingshot and wound up breaking a pane of glass in a bookcase for his trouble. Barney got all kinds of agitated until Andy stepped in and made it all better. Then Andy gave Opie a lecture on the dangers of the slingshot and sent the boy on his way. Bobby knew it was only a TV show, but Mayberry offered comfort. And there were many days, even more nights, when Bobby needed comfort. So he lost himself in the black-and-white images tumbling across the screen and barely stirred when the phone rang. Eventually, his eyes wandered to a clock he kept by the bed. Seven A.M. Damn, where did the time go? Bobby picked up the remote to turn off the set and paused. Opie had accidentally killed a bird with the slingshot and held the body in his hands. Six years old, trembling, crying, willing the bird to fly and tossing it up in the air, as if that could undo what had been done. No such luck, Op.

Bobby snapped off the set and lay back on his bed. He lived in a one-bedroom apartment above Joey's. The apartment was a dump, not to mention a firetrap, but it was convenient. And part of the routine that had become his prison. He got up and pulled a chair to the window for cigarettes. Bobby smoked and stared at an old Red Sox schedule he'd taped to the wall. Then he looked out the window. The shower had been cold and brief, washing the streets clean, leaving them slick and bright. The traffic up and down Market was light so it wasn't hard to miss the beat-up Volvo when it pulled in across the street. Bobby edged his chair back a foot or so and watched from the shadows as Kevin Pearce got out and took a look around. He was taller than Bobby pictured, a man now, but Bobby could still see the kid in him. The way he held his head as he glanced up and down the block, the hesitation in his step as he walked over to Johnny D's produce stand. The two of them stood in front of a display of bananas and talked. Bobby knew Johnny D was studying Kevin, the long hair and rumpled coat, probably trying to place him and figuring out how much to tell him. Finally, the produce man pointed back toward Joey's. Kevin shook his hand and headed that way. The first rays of sun slanted between the buildings and licked at his feet as he walked. Bobby flicked his cigarette out the window and took another ten seconds to study his childhood pal. He was like a letter that had been posted in the mail years ago and been circling through time ever since. The letter was gonna show up in Bobby's mailbox someday. And today was that day.

——

"Coffee?" Bobby pointed to a Mr. Coffee plugged into the wall. Kevin shook his head. He was standing in the doorway, unsure whether he was coming or going.

"Sit down." Bobby took a seat at the table and pushed forward a chair with his foot. Kevin sat down and looked around.

"I know. Forty-four years old and I live in a dump."

"I didn't say that."

"You didn't have to. It's cheap. And I don't need much. Just a place to shower, sleep, hang my clothes." Bobby was wearing black Nike sweatpants with white trim and a plain gray T-shirt. He nodded at the closet and a half-dozen collared shirts, neatly pressed and hanging in a row. "My life's simple. And quiet." .

"What do you do?"

"You know about the betting?"

Kevin nodded.

"Fingers died and there was no one else but me." Bobby spread his hands. "So I take the action and keep people happy."

"You like it?"

"It's not the kind of thing you walk away from."

"I saw Finn down at the park. He told me you also work construction."

"I hang Sheetrock six, eight hours a day. Then I come home, fix up some dinner, and go to bed. Twice a week, I have a couple of beers downstairs. And I go to mass most days."

"Mass?"

"I like Jesus. I like his life. So I go."

Kevin's eyes ranged across the room to a single shelf of books. "You read a lot?"

"Depends."

Kevin walked over and ran his fingers across a Bible stacked beside a Quran. Propped up at the end of the shelf was an old vinyl album from Johann Sebastian Bach. Kevin held it up.

"Where's the turntable?"

"That's Bach's mass in B-minor. Most perfect music ever composed."

Kevin put the album back and pulled out a paperback copy of *For Whom the Bell Tolls.*

"He's good," Bobby said. "But the macho stuff doesn't really work without the rest of it. Empathy, compassion, suffering. Your grandmother taught you that."

Kevin walked back to the table and sat down. "Are you pissed I came back?"

"I told you to stay away."

"And I did. For twenty-five years." He spoke with a quiet conviction, but Bobby saw through it.

"You've been in and out of Brighton."

"Only when I had to. And not for very long."

"A lot's changed. Everyone'll tell you that, first fucking thing."

"Sounds like you don't believe it."

"I do and I don't. The people I see, people who grew up here, people who stayed, they know what they know and can't imagine nothing different. Still walk around smug as shit, wanting to kick the piss out of anyone who tries to tell 'em otherwise. They'll hate you, by the way. Figure you came back just to rub their faces in it. You sure you don't want coffee?"

"No, thanks."

Bobby poured himself a cup, fixed it up with milk and sugar, and brought it back to the table.

"What about the rest of them?" Kevin said. "The ones who didn't grow up here?"

"What about 'em?"

"What are they like?"

"Who gives a fuck? You keep in touch with your sisters?"

"Colleen, here and there. Bridget, not so much."

"Haven't been back to Champney?"

"You know I haven't."

Bobby took a precious sip from his coffee and rubbed his lips together. "Finn told me about the Pulitzer. Un-fucking-believable. Congratulations."

"Thanks. Actually, it was a story about a Brighton guy. James Harper. He was convicted of killing a woman named Rosie Tallent."

Bobby got up again and pulled out a trunk from under the bed. He dug around until he found a manila envelope and tossed it on the table. It was stuffed with clippings from the *Globe*.

"Second time in as many days that I've seen a collection of my stuff," Kevin said.

"I read everything you ever wrote on Tallent. I'm proud of you, Kev. Your grandmother would be busting . . . when she wasn't telling everyone 'I told you so.' Doesn't mean you should have come back, though. You shouldn't have."

"Why?"

"Same reason you stayed away in the first place. Out there you've got your future. Something special."

"And back here I've got a past?"

"Eat you whole, brother. Bones and all."

Bobby laid down the thirty-eight with the gray tape on the grip. The silver twenty-two sat beside it. Kevin took a seat on the bed and stared at the guns as Bobby filled up a trash bag with clothes. They were in his room above the cab office. Less than a mile away, Curtis Jordan's body was cooling on the floor of his apartment. Bobby threw a pair of torn-up jeans in the bag. The smell of cut grass and turned earth blew through an open window.

"I can get my own clothes," Kevin said.

Bobby shook his head. "Just wear mine. Most of this stuff is too small for me anyway. You got any blood on your shoes?"

Kevin stuck up his feet, shod in a pair of black Cons.

"Take 'em off." Bobby found a pair of no-name, beat-up sneaks in a closet and tossed them at Kevin. Outside, a car engine coughed, then settled into a throaty rumble.

"Where am I going?" Kevin said.

"New York. You're gonna stay with your aunt for a while."

"How am I gonna get there?"

"Shuks is downstairs. He's gonna drive you."

"Why?"

"Cuz that's how it is. You gotta go. And you gotta go now."

"What about the wake?"

Bobby sat down on the bed. Kevin's pupils were blown wide open. Quiet fear vibrated between them like a tuning fork. "Not gonna happen, buddy. I'm sorry."

"At least I got to see her in the basement."

"You never should have been involved, Kev."

"I had a gun, too."

"You weren't gonna pull the trigger."

"You don't know that."

"But you do. And that's important. Did anyone see you in the building?"

"No."

"You're sure?"

Kevin nodded.

"Let me take a look at that shirt."

Kevin pulled off his shirt. Bobby checked it for blood and threw it in the closet.

"Put on one of mine."

Kevin shrugged on a long-sleeve polo and rolled up the sleeves so it fit. Bobby picked up the thirty-eight in one hand and the twenty-two in the other. He stashed the guns in a dresser drawer, then tied up the bag of clothes in a knot.

"When will I be back?" Kevin said.

"Two weeks. A month, tops."

The kid was never coming back. And would never leave if he caught even a whiff of that simple fact. Bobby shoved the bag of clothes in his chest. "Come on. Shuks is waiting."

"I'm gonna miss you, Bobby."

"It's just for a month. Cool?"

"Cool."

"Good. Now, let's get moving."

"I ran like a coward." Kevin flicked at the news clippings with a finger.

"You were a kid."

"I ran like a coward. And I let you take the weight."

"That's your ego talking."

"I know how I feel."

"So what's next? You gonna walk over to Station Fourteen and give them a statement?"

Kevin shook his head.

"Then what?"

"I guess I just needed to come back. To see you. Say what I said."

"Consider it done. Now go."

They sat in silence. Bobby sipped at his coffee and stared at a watery patch of sunlight on the wall.

"I was thinking about stopping by Champney," Kevin said.

"Did Colleen tell you Bridget and I had a thing?"

"I heard it wasn't a big deal."

"It wasn't. Bridget helps with Fingers's operation. Handles all the bookkeeping."

"That's how she pays the bills?"

"She earns it, Kevin. Girl's organized as shit. And she likes money." Bobby took the clippings back to the trunk and packed them away.

"Can I ask you something?" Kevin said.

"Go ahead."

"I've written hundreds of pieces for the *Globe*. Why pick out Tallent to save?"

"How do you know I didn't save everything you've written?"

"Did you?"

"No. Tallent was your best stuff. And she was from Brighton. Hell, it won the Pulitzer so I must know something." Bobby pushed the trunk back under the bed and sat down at the table, leaning forward with his shoulders and chest, fingertips touching, voice hushed as if the entire world and everything in it depended on whatever came next. "It's never gonna be like you want. Never in a million fucking years. You try to fix things from back then, you try to meddle, even a little bit, and poof." Bobby exploded the world with his hands. "It all comes apart. People start getting hurt. You know what I'm saying?"

"I think so."

"It was good to see you, Kev. Proud as hell. Don't ever forget that."

"I won't."

"Good. Now go, enjoy your life. And stay the fuck out of Brighton."

Bobby showed him to the door and watched from the high window as he crossed the street. The kid was a grown man now, with grown-man habits, like lying through his teeth. But that was all right. He'd returned as Bobby knew he would. Knew he must. What would come to pass Bobby didn't know, just that it had always been and would happen now and there was nothing either of them could have done that would have changed a word of it. And that gave Bobby some peace. He freshened his coffee and sat at a small desk he'd set up in a corner of the room. From a side drawer he took out a photo, curled at the corners and faded with age. Sixteen kids standing in front of a school bus, a wooden roller coaster behind them, dropping from the sky like an enormous bird of prey. PARAGON PARK, LABOR DAY, 1972 was scrawled in pen on the back. Bobby was fourteen, third from the left in the front row. He sipped at his coffee and rubbed the photo with his thumb before putting it back in the drawer and rinsing out his cup in the sink. Then he turned on the shower and knocked out two-hundred push-ups while the water got hot.

19

LISA MIGNOT hit the pause button and waited for her boss to speak.

"They're talking about Curtis Jordan," Frank DeMateo said.

"We don't know that."

"Play it again."

Lisa hit rewind. She was sitting in a delivery van a block from Bobby Scales's apartment. Her boss was buried in the basement of the Suffolk County D.A.'s office. They'd gotten the order for the wiretap yesterday afternoon, just before Lisa met Kevin for drinks. The judge had bitched and moaned about the proposed scope of the tap. Then they told him the dead girl was a cop and he signed whatever the fuck they wanted. One of the black bag guys, a kid named Danny Mendez, planted the bug in Scales's apartment while he was at mass yesterday afternoon. Now Danny sat in the driver's seat and monitored the wire while Lisa and Frank ran through the conversation between Scales and Kevin for a second time. The recording had barely finished before Lisa jumped in.

"The court order's specific. We're listening for anything that might pertain to Sandra Patterson's death."

"And if we happen upon anything else, we're free to go after it. In this case, it might very well lead us back to Patterson. In fact, that's the whole point."

There was a pause on the line. Lisa needed a cigarette. And some space. Frank DeMateo was giving her neither.

"Kevin's not a criminal, Frank. And he sure as hell isn't a killer."

"I think you're right."

"But we need to look at it?"

"We need to look at Scales. And Kevin's our way in. You knew this was a possibility."

"Fuck."

"You want out?"

"I want you to trust me."

"What does that mean?"

"If Scales is our guy, he goes down."

"And your boyfriend?"

"He just won the Pulitzer Prize. On the Rosie Tallent murder."

"He was involved in the Jordan thing, Lisa. Maybe nothing criminal, but he was involved."

The possibility had always been there. She'd ignored it best she could even as she agreed to use Kevin as a stalking horse. But it had always been there. He could lead her to Scales, yes, but Kevin could also wind up being implicated. And there was very little she could do to protect him. "Let me see it through."

The district attorney for Suffolk County grunted. Lisa couldn't tell if it was a good grunt or a bad grunt. She decided to assume the former. "When do you tell everyone Sandra was a cop?"

"Press conference, probably later on today. Tomorrow at the latest. I'd love to announce an arrest at the same time."

"Be nice if it was the right guy, Frank. What about the staties?"

"What do you think? Crawling the fucking walls."

"Do they know about the wire?"

"I told them timing was critical, and we already had the people in place. They're working forensics with the city's homicide guys."

"Does anyone know who we're looking at?"

"Not yet, but we're gonna meet after the presser. At that point, all bets are off."

"What does that mean?"

"Just get me something on Scales. I'll handle the rest."

DeMateo cut the line. Lisa flipped her phone shut. Danny pulled off his headphones and slid closer.

"He hasn't said a word. I'm guessing he's still in the shower."

"Once he leaves, I'm gonna head out. You sit on the wire in case he comes home during the day. I'll be back around four. Then you can take off."

"What did the boss say?"

"Usual bullshit. Sounds like we might get big footed once they go public."

"Can they do that?"

"Typically, no. But this isn't typical, so maybe. It's nothing you have to worry about. We have the wire today and tonight for sure. Let's see what we get."

"You think Scales is the guy?"

"He worked with Patterson at Habitat. And he keeps clippings from Rosie Tallent's murder under his bed."

"Is that it?"

"You sound like the judge. That's all I'm gonna talk about."

"Can I ask you a question?"

"One more."

"This other guy on the tape, Kevin. Is he your boyfriend?"

"Who told you that?"

"Forget it. It's none of my business, anyway."

"We live together."

Danny lifted an eyebrow. "Does he know he's being listened to?"

Lisa nodded at the phones in his lap. "Get back on the wire."

Danny slipped on his headphones. Lisa knew what he was thinking. She'd pinned a bull's-eye on her boyfriend. Now, they'd all see where it led.

20

KEVIN MET Mo Stanley at the Mirror Café in Brighton Center. Three old-timers stared at her as she got a cruller and coffee, whispering furiously among themselves when she decided to join him at a table in the back.

"You couldn't give me a call?" she said, slipping off a backpack and tucking it under the table by her feet.

"Sorry."

"For Chrissakes, I've been leaving you messages . . ."

"I'm sorry."

"It's fine."

"Doesn't sound fine."

"The Pulitzer Prize, Kev?"

"I know."

"Seriously, the Pulitzer fucking Prize? I'm numb. I mean I was numb, like, yesterday."

"Jimmy told everyone?"

"He told me, then I told him to keep his trap shut. You'd let everyone know when you were ready, which, by the way, should be soon."

"I owe you one."

"Bet your ass you owe me. What's with the freak show up front?"

"Brighton's finest. You know how it is. Beautiful woman walks in they've never seen before . . ."

"Save it for someone who gives a shit. You want a piece of my cruller or what?"

Kevin smiled and was rewarded with a smile bouncing back across the table. Mo was a Quincy girl, earned her stripes for the *Globe* covering crime in Dorchester and Roxbury. As she liked to say, the real fucking deal. She could have been a knockout if she'd wanted to. Instead, it was short hair and no makeup. She never wore a dress unless she had to and didn't let too many people know too much about her. Add all that up and the newsroom concluded lesbian. Kevin knew that was wrong. First, because she'd told him. Second, because they'd rolled around in the front seat of his car after a night of drinking at Mister Dooley's on Broad Street. They'd talked about it the next morning and decided it was best to leave the whole thing alone—which never really worked, but that was what they'd decided to do anyway. The truth was he cherished her friendship. Really, he cherished everything about Mo. Of course he never said a word to her about any of it.

"So, what's it like?" she said, tearing open a package of Splenda and stirring some into her coffee before setting the cup to one side.

"You'll have one of your own soon enough."

"Yeah, well, until the Pulitzer committee gets around to my clip file, allow me to live vicariously."

"It's no different than before."

"Like hell it isn't."

"How do you figure?"

"For one thing you don't seem to have to show up for work anymore. They just gonna send you a check every other week and trot you out for the Christmas party?"

"I'm working."

"I know, Patterson."

He'd called her before he went to see Bobby. He figured she'd be in early and knew she'd be working the Patterson homicide. And even if she wasn't, she'd know more about it than anyone in the newsroom. That was just Mo. So he'd told her in a general sort of way about the connection between Patterson and Rosie Tallent. She'd immediately jumped to the possibility of a serial killer. Kevin had let the idea ride.

"You get a chance to take a look at anything?"

She reached down and pulled a legal pad from her backpack. Mo had strong, square hands and flipped through her notes quickly, mumbling as she went.

"Mo?"

The reporter stopped flipping and looked up, hints of pique in both cheeks. "What am I going to get out of this, Kevin?"

"I told you. There's a link between Tallent and Patterson."

"What kind of link?"

"A forensic link."

"You're getting this from someone inside the investigation?"

"I can't tell you that."

"Your girlfriend, maybe?"

He'd been careful to keep Lisa out of the conversation. Mo, however, was too damn smart. And Kevin should have known better.

"You don't want the story, Mo, just say the word."

"I want it."

"You sure?"

"Yes, but I can only sit on the Tallent connection for a day or two, tops."

"That's all I need. After that, I give you everything, including all my sources."

"We'll do a joint byline."

Kevin shook his head. "It's all yours. Fair enough?"

"Yeah."

"Good. Now, we need to find out if there are other cases out there."

Mo broke out her Mo grin, which typically translated to *I'm the best reporter in the city so fuck you and the horse you rode in on.*

"You already got one," Kevin said.

"How'd you know?"

"Cuz you got that look on your face."

"What look?"

"Never mind. What did you find?"

"It's my guy in the cold squad."

"How much detail did you have to give him?"

"Relax, the guy's a year from retirement and thinks of me as the granddaughter he never had. He'll keep his mouth shut. In fact, he'll be more than happy to lie, cheat, and steal for me if that's what we want."

"Tell me about the case."

Mo crowded closer. Kevin could feel the heat coming off her skin, the hot thrill of a journalist sinking her teeth into a story. Fucking narcotic. He took a sip of his coffee and waited.

"Her name's Christine Flannery."

"Never heard of her."

"Why would you? She's a white Rosie Tallent, lived in Southie. I know, it's not Brighton, but hear me out. They found her body two years ago, dumped in a stairwell a block from Government Center. Stabbed twice in the chest." Mo reached into her backpack and pulled out a file.

"What's that?"

"A summary of the autopsy report and a set of crime scene photos. I told you, anything I want." Mo pushed across the report and finally took a sip of her coffee. "God, that's good. M.E. says they found ligature marks on her neck. Page 3." She directed Kevin's attention to the bottom of the page and read the highlighted passage aloud for him. " 'Strangulation used as a means to *control and incapacitate* the victim rather than *kill* . . .' "

Kevin scanned the summary. "Says the ligature marks showed signs of slippage, indicating she was probably strangled with a nylon or a sock." He flipped the report shut and pushed it across the table. "I'm looking for a piano wire, Mo. And a postmortem gunshot wound to the head."

"I know what you're looking for, but these things don't always match up perfectly. This woman was dumped in a stairwell downtown. Killed right there or very close by. My guy says whoever did it probably didn't have a lot of time."

"So he couldn't go through his ritual?"

"Maybe there is no ritual. Maybe it's just convenient to strangle them, then use the knife."

"But the gunshot. There's nothing convenient about that."

"So without the gunshot, you can't see a link?"

"Didn't say that."

Mo dropped her voice to a fierce whisper. "Then what the fuck are you saying?"

"I don't know."

"This isn't about a serial killer, is it, Kevin?"

"I don't think so."

"And the ritual crap isn't all that important?"

"It's important, but not critical."

" 'Important, but not critical.' You know what, fuck you." She stood up and began to repack her notes.

"I know as much as you do, Mo."

She stopped packing. "You've never lied to me before, Kev. Why start now?"

He touched her sleeve. "Sit down."

She shook him off, but took a seat. "Patterson was working undercover on a drug sting when she was killed."

"I already told you that."

"Yeah, but you never told me how it all ties together. And you never told me how your girlfriend fits into all of it."

Lisa again. Mo was circling. And Kevin needed space.

"Let me take a look at the photos." He pulled across a stack, flipping through a handful of morgue shots before stopping on a run of pictures from the dump site and the tangle of body parts that made up Christine Flannery, layered across three steps leading down into what looked like a basement. Kevin was guessing she was close to six feet, cocaine thin, with her skirt hiked up and a tattoo of a turtle crawling up a pale left thigh. She had her mouth open—front teeth little more than black nubs—and doll eyes half shut with that glassy look that told you the body was a shell and its owner had moved on to greener pastures.

"How old was she?" Kevin said.

"Thirty-six. Long string of arrests. Possession, hooking. All street-level stuff. You know the drill."

"And she lived in Southie?"

"Old Colony. Had three kids. No husband."

"Kids?"

"I assume they're in the system somewhere. Foster homes, adoption."

Kevin flipped through a few more photos, stopping on a close-up, snapped from a high angle peering down and across the body. "What's that?"

Mo leaned in for a look. "What?"

Kevin studied the image and waggled his fingers impatiently. "You got any more of these? Tight shots, head and shoulders."

Mo dug through the pile and found a few more pictures. Kevin nodded to himself as he cycled through them.

"What is it?" Mo said, frantically scanning his discard pile, wondering what she'd missed.

Kevin pulled the photos into a neat stack and pushed them across the table. "Where did you park?"

"Around the corner."

"Pull your car up to the light. I'll be waiting."

"Where are we going?"

"Just follow me."

———

A dozen or so kids formed a human chain, tethered to a wall and swinging back and forth across the schoolyard. A solitary dark-haired boy, maybe ten or eleven, lurked at the far end of the yard with another dozen classmates between him and the end of the chain. The boy jogged back and forth, looking for an opening. Three kids tried to trap him in a gully, but the boy squirted free and began his run, twisting and turning, dodging and cutting, getting ever nearer to the end of the chain of students stretching out to meet him. The other team closed ranks, one of the kids clipping the boy on the shoulder but not holding him long enough. He circled again, slower now, his pursuers sensing weakness and moving in. The boy feinted another run, then found a gap and broke through, a final desperate dash, riding a wave of speed as his pursuers collapsed on either side, touching hands with a girl on the end of the chain and freeing the members of his team who scattered to the four corners of the yard. The boy drifted in the flotsam and jetsam of his run, cruising the perimeter again, taking congratulations in stride even as the game of Relievio wound up for another round.

"Memories, Kev?" Mo was squinting and holding her hand up to the morning sun slanting across the back lot of Saint Andrew's Elementary. "Let me guess, you went to school here?"

He'd been that kid, sprinting from the beginning of recess until the end, before school, after school, during school. Always running, never getting caught. He recalled one fall afternoon and a single game that became a death march and his signature Relievio moment. The other team consisted of six kids, all fast, all tough, all smart. They hunted him across the blacktop for two hours. He ran that day in a pair of cheap leather shoes, nails gone through both soles, feet a bloody fucking mess. By the end, his own team was telling him to quit, right up until the moment he made his run and freed them.

"I went here through sixth grade," Kevin said.

"Had enough, huh?"

"It wasn't so bad. How about you?"

"Sacred Heart in Quincy. Eight years of nuns. Another four in high school." Mo nodded at the school's redbrick façade. "How does any of this tie in to Christine Flannery?"

"They used to have an all-girls high school here. Saint Andrew's Academy. Closed down a few years back. When I was a kid, I remember they gave out this thing called a Miraculous Medal at graduation. Silver medallion of Mary hung on a blue string." Kevin pulled out one of the crime scene photos from the dump site. "This woman's wearing one. At least I think she is. Come on."

They cut across the yard and ducked inside the big front door. Chalk dust and erasers, floor polish and Windex, streaked windows and hazy sunshine. The sights and smells flooded his bloodstream, bubbling up to fill his eyes, ears, nose, and throat.

"Look the same?" Mo said.

"Smaller."

The school probably should have had some sort of security at the front door, but there was nothing, so they wandered down one hallway, then a second. Some of the classrooms were full and they could hear a nun blowing on a pitch pipe, then leading her class as they ascended, then descended the scale of notes.

"What's with the A's and B's?" Mo pointed at the figures "2A" and "2B" stenciled in white over a pair of adjacent doors.

"That's how they split up the classes. In the first grade you were designated an A or a B. Then you stayed with that class all the way through eighth grade."

"How did they decide who went where?"

Kevin shrugged. "It's the nuns so who knows. I was a B. Come on."

They ducked into a classroom, empty except for an old nun set like a chunk of granite behind a desk at the front of the room. "Can I help you?" She spoke without taking her eyes off her work.

"We're looking for some information," Kevin said, aware of his voice in the close quarters of the classroom.

"Perhaps you'd like to know how we separate our A's from our B's?" The nun pulled off her glasses and looked up. She had a long face, with eyes so pale as to be nearly transparent and cheeks that were heavily scarred.

"You heard us?" Kevin said.

"I did indeed."

"This is Mo Stanley. I'm Kevin Pearce."

"You write for the *Globe*."

"I do."

"And you went to school here."

"I did."

"I went to Catholic school as well," Mo said.

"But not at Saint Andrew's?"

"No." Mo fell back to lick her wounds.

"You've never been back, Mr. Pearce?"

"Not until today, no."

"We're very proud of the success our students have had. We like people to know it's because of the training they got here."

Kevin would have laid a bit more of the credit for whatever he'd done at the doorstep of Boston Latin School, but the nun was tough, the nun was ornery, and the nun was well within striking distance.

"Yes, ma'am. I tell people about Saint A's all the time."

"I'm sure you do." She came out from behind her desk and extended a hand full of long fingers and surprising grip. "I'm

Sister Lorraine." Kevin had vague images of a younger version of the nun, standing by the door to the boys' room, watching over them as they tried to take a piss.

"I always taught on the A side of things," she said, "so I never had you in class."

"That's too bad," Mo said, fully recovered now and tickled as all hell to get back in on the fun.

"Yes, he was boisterous enough as I recall, but I'm guessing that's not why you're here."

"It's about a former student," Kevin said.

Sister Lorraine pulled a couple of chairs off the wall and gestured for them to sit. Then she closed the door to the classroom and took her place again behind the desk, clenching her hands in front of her and dropping her chin like a hammer the way only a nun can. "As I recall, Mr. Pearce, you usually write about death, so excuse me for not being more excited at your request for information."

"I understand, Sister."

"I assume something's happened to one of ours."

"Yes, ma'am." He could smell the soap on the nun's skin and suddenly wished he was anywhere but here.

"What's his name?"

"Actually it's a she," Mo said.

"I don't know if she went here," Kevin said, "but I'm pretty sure she went to the Academy."

"Chrissy . . ." The name crumbled off the nun's lips.

"How did you know that?" Mo said.

"Chrissy McNabb."

"The last name we have is Flannery."

Sister Lorraine shook her head. "That was her married name.

There were three of them, all girls. Went to grammar school and the Academy. Lived with their aunt on Bigelow Street." She lifted an accusing finger and pointed it at Kevin. "I think Chrissy was the same year as one of your sisters."

The dam broke and it all came pouring in, torrents of blind memory bathed in streaks of sunlight—a young girl, younger than Kevin, running across the tarred playground with trailing white ribbons in her hair, chasing after Bridget, smiling and giggling, holding in a five-year-old's secret with her hand over her mouth as she went. Kevin pulled out the crime scene photo and placed it facedown on the desk.

"That's her?" The nun jutted her chin toward the photo while keeping her eyes fixed on him.

"Be good if you can confirm it."

She pulled the picture across and lifted it, taking a look, then pushing it back. Outside kids were still playing in the yard. Light from the window cut fresh wounds across the nun's pockmarked face. "I kept in touch with her."

Kevin started to say something, but Mo touched his sleeve and the response died in his throat.

"She had a lot of problems. A lot of girls do. I guess there's always one that just strikes a nerve." The nun skinned back her lips. "Fat lot of good it did."

"I'm sure you did all you could," Mo said, brushing her hand before pulling back again.

"She'd show up at all sorts of strange times. I'd give her a little money, some clothes, a coat and boots for the winter. The last time I saw her, I tried to get her to see her aunt—she still lives in the house on Bigelow—but she wouldn't. Anyway . . ."

A bell rang somewhere and the hallway filled with kids, running up and down, laughing, yelling, heading to and from class.

"You know they're going to close this place down?"

"I didn't," Kevin said.

"This year or next, no one's sure, but it's already been decided. There was a rumor they were going to turn it into a day-care center. A friend told me she saw plans for a recycling plant. Rich, huh? Hang on a minute."

Sister Lorraine got up slowly, the crush of so much life bending her frame inexorably to its will. She returned a few minutes later with a long cardboard box, opening it at her desk and running her spider fingers along a series of index cards until she found what she wanted. It was a registration form from 1969. Chrissy McNabb's kindergarten picture was attached.

"Is there anyone else in Brighton she kept in touch with?" Kevin said, taking a quick look at the card then putting it on the desk next to the crime scene photo. "Anyone else she talked about?"

The nun shook her head. "All she talked about was the drugs. Where she was gonna get the money for whatever she needed, how it was gonna be the last time. Always the last time."

"Did she mention a dealer?" Mo said. "Anyone who might have helped her get drugs or money?"

"I gave her money. If you're looking for someone to blame, blame me."

"That's not what we meant."

"I know what you meant. She never gave me any names. Well, she gave me one. Fidelis Way. That's where she did her 'shopping.' Her words, not mine."

"I'm sorry we had to bring this to you," Kevin said.

"I'd rather know."

Kevin got up to leave. Mo got up with him, pressing close against his back. Sister Lorraine rubbed the kindergarten photo with a thumb as she spoke.

"Do you know where they buried her?"

"I can find out," Kevin said. "But it'd be better if you left us out of it."

She shrugged because that didn't matter—a petty concern from an alien world. So they left her in the sun-streaked room, with the windows open and dark green shades banging in the breeze. Alone with her stack of registration cards and muted memories of the girl with white ribbons, playing on a playground so long ago.

21

BOBBY WALKED down the loading dock and smelled the smells—the tang of diesel overlaid with the waft from fat bags of onions and garlic, pallets of soft strawberries and heaps of overripe bananas. He stopped in front of a display for TaVilla Tomatoes and soaked in the sights—big men, skinny men, dark men, hairy men, men with bellies and ground-up cigars stuck in their mouths scribbling furiously into order books, men who never said a word, men who couldn't keep their yaps shut, men whispering fervent whispers and screaming in shorthand produce gibberish about oranges out of California and a load of lettuce that somehow disappeared in fucking New Jersey. It was the New England produce market at a little after ten in the morning, and another day of bartering, bickering, conniving, and thieving was coming to a glorious close. Most of the buyers were headed to the bar, the off-track, or a strip club—hopefully all three if the money held out. Bobby sifted through the crowd and found his way to a building at the far end of the dock. A dozen illegals, quick hands and quiet eyes, worked in a drafty, dimly lit warehouse, stuffing celery hearts into plastic bags and packing them into boxes on pallets. A large Italian with snow-white hair, beetle-black eyebrows, and a nose that resembled an egg-plant watched Bobby as he crossed the room. Bobby nodded. The Italian's name was Sal Riga. He explored the cavernous reaches of one of his nostrils with a thumb that seemed made for the job, looked at whatever it was he'd excavated, and wiped it on his blue polo shirt. A Vietnamese roughly the size of Sal's latest bowel movement ran up to the man and began gesticulating wildly. Sal followed the Vietnamese through a doorway covered over by hanging plastic strips.

Bobby slipped out of the packing room and walked past a run of empty truck bays. A Chelsea rat named Obie Liston stuck his nose out from behind a pile of packing crates and sniffed at Bobby as he went. Obie was a scrawny little fuck with a red wiffle cut and a couple of green and yellow shamrocks intertwined in a tattoo across the back of his neck. He ran book for most of the market when he wasn't boosting cars and running a chop shop out of his mother's garage. Chances were Obie didn't like Bobby on his turf. Fuck him. Bobby took a left at the end of the last bay and slipped into a small connecting room. Through the door-way, he could see another expanse of empty warehouse. In the very center of the room, a waterfall of cabbage—chopped-up bits of red, white, and green—fell gently through a hole in the roof and disappeared down a dark blue chute. Somewhere above him, heavy machinery thumped and throbbed.

"You like coleslaw?"

Bobby jumped. For a big man, Sal Riga moved like a fucking cat.

"Should I?"

"Every morning we sweep up all the shit off the floor and run it through the chopper upstairs." Sal nodded at the cabbage waterfall. "Drops down the chute, gets processed, and bagged in the basement."

"So I should pass on the slaw?"

"Probably no worse than the fucking hot dogs and sausage they feed us. But, yeah, I don't eat the shit." Sal slammed the metal door shut. The only remaining light came from a single bulb encased in a metal cage over the door. "I told you to come in the other way."

"Sorry, I got turned around. Does it matter?"

The Italian shrugged massive, meaty shoulders.

"What's this about, Sal? You paid up last week."

They'd met five years ago in a BU bar called T's Pub. They were both drinking Bushmills and got to talking about sports, then betting. Bobby had the Pats that weekend getting a point and a half at Miami. Normally, a guy like Sal would make his bets with someone like Obie, but the line that week was two. Sal put down five hundred with Bobby and cashed, winning on the hook. The following week he called in another bet and won again. Pretty soon Sal was one of Bobby's biggest players, plus he brought in other guys from the market. And they all had money. Bobby shaved a little off the lines and still made out pretty well just because of the cash they laid out. A typical Sal bet was five to ten large. Some of his pals bet more.

"What's the line on the C's tomorrow night?"

"I think it's six."

Sal nodded. "Probably gonna want to make a wager."

"Just let me know." Bobby waited. The machines had gone quiet for the moment, and Sal still hadn't answered his question. Why had he wanted Bobby to come in to the market? And why were they standing in this tiny, shitty fucking room, belly to belly, talking about a bet that could have been handled with a phone call?

"Something came up." Sal started slowly, like he had all the time in the world. "Something I wanted to talk to you about face-to-face." The Italian shifted his weight in his shoes. He wore loafers with argyle socks. The sides were all broken down to shit and one of them was missing its tassel. "I got a business proposition for you."

"Yeah?"

"The guys who own this company"—Sal ran his eyes around the room—"guys who pretty much own the whole fucking market. They want to buy in. Be your partner."

"No thanks, Sal."

"You haven't heard what I got to say."

Bobby didn't have to hear. Sal worked for Frank "Cakes" Grisanti out of Providence. The Grisanti family ran most of the big books in New England, as well as prostitution, loan sharking, racketeering, and anything else they thought they could make a buck in.

"Your boss shakes more off his dick than I make in a year on my book."

"Who said anything about your book?" Sal's eyes had narrowed to black slits. He was close enough now that Bobby could see the patch of fur growing along the bridge of his nose, right up into his eyebrows. One step from the fucking Franklin Park Zoo. Bobby knew he needed to tread carefully.

"Guess I'm confused then."

"Don't play fuck-fuck with me, Bobby."

"I'm not . . ."

"The shit. Dope, weed, blow. Whatever the fuck else you got

going on. We know you're pushing it into the suburbs. Newton, Brookline, Wellesley, for Chrissakes. We know you're on the
campuses. Listen, Cakes is old school. Hates niggers and won't
do business with them. So we let them run their shit in the city
and fucking kill each other. But this is different. You're different. We're thinking we help you expand, first to the South Shore
and then all the way down to the Cape. We put up the money.
Provide the manpower. You share in the profits." Sal plugged a
toothpick in his mouth, rolling it with his fingers between slick,
banana lips. "I'm even gonna give you a bonus. Just cuz I like you
and want us to get off on the right foot."

"Yeah?"

"You're wondering how we know about your operation?"

"Wondering about a lot of things, Sal."

"You heard of a place in Brighton called the Corrib?"

"Pours a nice pint of Guinness."

"There's a mick who drinks in there that's running his mouth.
Says he's either gonna get paid or put you out of business. You
know the mick I'm talking about?"

"I got an idea."

"There you go. So we got a deal?"

"I don't do partners, Sal. If I did, you and your boss would be
at the top of the list. But I just don't."

Sal pulled out the toothpick and pointed it at Bobby. "You
sure?"

Bobby shrugged. "Pretty sure."

Sal nodded. That's when the coleslaw bag went over Bobby's head. He could still see Sal through the lettering on the bag,
staring dully at him as the plastic sealed tight to his nose and
sucked his lungs dry. Bobby thrashed with his arms, probably

the stupidest thing you could do, but he'd never been suffocated with a coleslaw bag before so what the fuck did he know? The guy behind him doing the suffocating, on the other hand, he had experience. Deftly he stepped to one side and cinched the bag like a fucking vise grip. Bobby couldn't hear a thing. Was he screaming, scuffling, putting up any kind of a fight? His eyes found Sal again, little more than a shadow now in a shrinking circle of light—soon to be followed by eternity at the bottom of a landfill in Revere. Bobby fought down the gorge of panic rising in his throat and threw cold water on his brain. If he had thirty seconds to live, he'd use them wisely. First, he stopped trying to breathe. What was the point? He relaxed his neck and shoulders, letting himself drop to his knees, arms and wrists limp, fingers scratching his epitaph in the empty air. Whoever was behind him leaned close, giving the plastic a final, vicious twist, eager to finish the job and get to the bar for a drink. Bobby bowed forward until his forehead almost touched the floor, then snapped his head back, a final burst, a wild, lucky shot that caught his assailant on the tip of the nose, stunning him and sending him reeling into the shadows. The bag slipped off and Bobby charged forward, filling his lungs with sweet oxygen and ramming a shoulder into Sal's soft belly. Sal vomited sausage and peppers all over his loafers. Bobby reached for a knife strapped to his ankle and slit his best customer from navel to breastbone. Sal took one look at his intestines, steaming coils trailing out onto the concrete, and howled, trying blindly to stuff organs back where they belonged before curling up on the floor like an infant and mumbling to himself. The man who'd tried to strangle Bobby was crumpled against a wall. He was just coming around when Bobby took him by a handful of hair. The man's eyes widened, dark brows arched in dual question marks. Bobby cut his throat with a single swipe. Then he walked back to Sal, who was somehow still alive and actually trying to bargain for his life. Bobby cut his throat as well and wiped his knife clean on the polo.

He slipped through the coleslaw plant and found his car where he'd parked it. A mile from his apartment, he pulled into a long lot by the river and pushed open the door just in time to get sick. A car blew past, some guy leaning out the back window yelling "COOOOKIES." Bobby flipped him off, then got out and walked down to the water. The morning air felt cold and clean and cleared his head. He'd like to think he got sick because he'd just gutted two men. But the truth was he felt nothing for Sal or his pal. They'd tried to kill him. And they'd stacked the deck. So fuck them. He got sick cuz he got sick. Nothing more. And what did it matter anyway? He had a day, maybe less, before Cakes sent someone up to find out what happened to Sal. And then Bobby Scales was a dead man.

22

THE DEVELOPERS had come in. The developers had left. They'd
pulled down most of the frame housing on the adjacent blocks,
transforming monthly rentals into what passed these days for
the American dream—townhomes and condos, one redbrick
building after another, stacked with row after row of tinted windows looking back coolly at the street. Inside, the march of the
mundane rolled on: granite countertops, stainless steel fixtures,
a small, phony fireplace, and, if you really made it big, a master
bath with the spa package. Kevin stared at the patch of weeds
growing in the middle of this suburban wet dream. Fidelis Way.
In the 1970s, there'd been no mistaking it. Loud and black and
poor and sweaty. Drug-ridden and desperate. Do-rags and homies
hanging on the corner, selling blow for a dime a bag; teenage
moms sitting on the stoop in the early evening, watching their
kids and waiting for the bullets to fall; old black men playing
speed chess and slugging malt liquor out of paper bags; brothers
driving ten miles an hour down the street in pimped-out rides,
hands on the wheel in their best gangsta lean. That was Fidelis.
The life. A siren's song, luring young men with a little cash they
thought was a lot and depositing them in an early grave for their

trouble. In the '80s, the city threw a bunch of money at the problem, giving Fidelis a new name and transforming it, along with Columbia Point in Dorchester and the D Street projects in Southie, into "mixed income" housing. Underneath the skin of fresh paint, however, Fidelis remained Fidelis. Young professionals who paid a half-million dollars to live a block away drove past with their windows up and doors locked. That was as close as any of them wanted to get to anything real, unless, of course, it was Friday night and they were looking to score an eight ball or a bag of weed. Kevin held a different view. He was fifteen the last time he'd visited Fidelis. And the peeled eyes of a dead man followed him everywhere he went.

Mo had left him the file on Chrissy McNabb. He flipped through it one more time, then packed it away beside the materials he'd taken off Lisa's computer. As usual, Mo was right. McNabb looked like she might be part of the pattern, killed by the same person who did Sandra Patterson and Rosie Tallent. McNabb also had a connection to Fidelis Way, which brought Kevin full circle to Curtis Jordan. And Bobby. He could have just straight out asked Bobby about the thirty-eight. Where was it? Who had it now? How was it mixed up in all this? Maybe he should have, but Kevin was still hoping for another way out. So he'd settled on Fidelis. He was about to get out of the car when his phone buzzed and his youngest sister's name flashed up on the screen.

"Colleen."

"Is it true?"

"What's that?"

"The Pulitzer."

Kevin leaned back against the headrest. "How'd you hear about that?"

"Never mind. Is it true?"

"Yeah."

"Amazing. Will you meet anyone famous?"

"I don't know, Coll."

"Everything you touch turns to gold. That's what I tell everyone. Everything you touch turns to gold." His sister's voice ran circles around him, gaining speed with each revolution.

"Let's just keep it between us for now."

"Oh, okay."

"I just want to low-key it, you know?"

"I understand." The merry-go-round sagged, slowed, then wheezed to a halt.

"Thanks, Coll."

"No problem. You know me. Get excited at the drop of a hat."

"Nothing wrong with that."

"We're all proud of you, Kev. Mom and Dad would be, too."

His parents had passed the year before Shuks—his father first from a massive heart attack, his mother six months later when her car skipped off the Jamaicaway and hit a tree. Kevin's was the wooden face at the back of the church as they sprinkled holy water over his father's coffin and Colleen walked up to the pulpit and looked at him in the narthex and smiled but did the favor of not mentioning him in her eulogy. For his mother, it was back to the basement at McNamara's and fifteen minutes alone with her before they closed the lid. He remembered sitting at her feet and staring up the length of her broken body, thinking about her washed-out eyes twenty years earlier and the blood on his hands, then mother and son walking up the stairs to his grandmother's apartment. He knew he should have been touching her cheek, kissing her fingers, trying to crawl in the coffin with her, but all he could think of was the opening line of Camus's *The Stranger*.

Aujourd'hui, maman est morte.

"Where are you now?" Colleen's voice cut through the tissue of memory.

"Actually, I'm sitting in front of Fidelis Way."

"What are you doing over there?"

Kevin glanced across the street at the squat outline of the projects. "Nothing, really, just working a story. Was thinking I might stop by Champney later."

"Seriously?"

"Thinking about it."

"It'd be great if you went back, Kev."

He had no idea why it would be "great," and no idea why he was even thinking about it. But he was. "I assume Bridget's still living there."

"She is, but I'm not sure she's home right now."

"Is the key in the same spot?"

"Yes. Can you believe it?"

"I can believe it."

"Bridget's doing so well, Kev. She really is."

"How about you?"

"What about me?"

"How's life treating you?"

Colleen was married to a guy named Scott Carson. They had one kid, a thirteen-year-old named Conor, and lived in Newton. He'd met Conor once and never been to their house.

"I'm fine," she said.

"Scott and Conor?"

"Everyone's great. Just great."

Kevin could hear the shift, her voice squeezing and tightening, hardening to a fine sheen.

"I gotta get going," she said.

"Maybe I'll swing by your place after Champney. Say hello."

"Probably not the best day for that. Listen, I'm in line at the bank and this teller is staring at me . . ."

"No problem."

"I'll call you next week. We can grab lunch downtown."

"Sounds good."

"Perfect. Congrats again, Kev. I'm really happy for you. And be careful. It's still the projects, you know."

She hung up and he thought about the baby sister he'd never been able to do enough for. And the tickle at the back of his brain that told him it was too late in the game to make up the difference. Kevin shoved the phone in his pocket and got out of the car, walking up the grade toward Fidelis. He brushed past the fresh-looking community center the city had built and cut between two buildings into the core of the projects. Hidden from the street, this was the old Fidelis, the Fidelis of the '70s, what the locals called the "FWP." Two young girls, probably sisters, were framed in a window to his left. Kevin made eye contact and they ducked out of sight. A kid with a Yankees hat on sideways stepped out of a doorway.

"Five-O?"

Kevin shook his head.

"You buying?"

"No." As a journalist, Kevin's job was to visit the nastier parts of the city, places people discussed from a distance but actually knew very little about. For the most part, he'd always felt safe. Reporters had no skin in the game and weren't considered targets by gangs. This time, however, might be different. He wasn't there for a story, no matter what he said. And bangers had a way of seeing right through that shit.

"If you ain't buying, then why you here?" The kid with the Yankees hat was maybe thirteen and weighed less than a hundred pounds. His movements were quick twitch. All Kevin could think of was a young Mickey Rivers.

"I just want some information."

"Fuck information."

"You don't even know what I want," Kevin said, which had to be true because Kevin didn't know what he wanted. Mick the Quick lifted a corner of his shirt. He had a heavy pistol stuck in his belt.

"You gonna shoot me?"

Mick seemed surprised. Most white people probably saw the piece and ran.

"I'll pay you," Kevin said. "Just let me talk to someone."

Mick glanced behind him. Kevin could see more heads periscoping up in windows. Liquid shadows collected in breezeways.

"Be careful what you wish for, Casper. Come on."

He led Kevin down a turning path to the building Curtis Jordan had died in. By the time they got to the door, the shadows had soaked back into the flat brick walls. Mick stepped inside. Kevin followed. An older kid with skin like cocoa and shoulder-length dreads laid a gun up against Kevin's cheek. Behind it, he spoke with a thin Jamaican accent.

"You looking to get clipped, brother?"

Kevin licked his lips. "I'm just looking for information."

"Fuck him." That was Mick. He had his gun out as well and seemed to like waving it around.

"Shut up." The Jamaican crowded Kevin up against a row of mailboxes. Slashes of graffiti scored the walls here and there. A set of eyes burned from beneath a stairwell, then blinked out. "What sort of information?"

There was intelligence in the Jamaican's voice. Kevin took out a picture of Chrissy McNabb on the slab.

"She don't look too healthy."

"She was one of your customers. They found her body downtown."

The Jamaican shrugged. Kevin pocketed the photo. "How about a guy named Curtis Jordan? He was shot in this building."

"Lots of people got shot in this building."

"I'm a reporter for the *Boston Globe*. Maybe I can help find out who killed him."

"Why you care who killed Curtis?"

Bingo. A gangbanger who wasn't even twenty knew about a nothing murder twenty-six years cold. That meant something. Had to. "It's what I do," Kevin said. "It's a story."

"Let me pop this motherfucker," Mick said, hot to get in on the fun. The Jamaican motioned for quiet with two fingers, then raised his gun, butt first, cracking it like a whip across the side of Kevin's skull. He dropped to a knee, the scuffle and squeak of sneakered feet all around him. It was young Mick, rounding first and digging hard for that extra base. A second blow drove Kevin to the lobby floor.

"Look at me."

Kevin looked up at a forest of waving dreadlocks, a diamond-encrusted grill gleaming in the very middle.

"What's your name?"

"Kevin."

"I think you want to hurt someone, Kevin. Kill someone, maybe."

"I'm just looking for a story."

"Your eyes say something else. You been here before?"

"No."

The Jamaican's face narrowed at the lie. He rifled Kevin's pockets, taking the morgue shot of McNabb, then disappeared up the stairs, young Mick nipping hard at his heels. Kevin struggled to his feet, a lump already starting to swell at the back of his head. His phone buzzed once in his pocket. He flipped it open and read the text that was waiting there.

GO C BRIDGET. SHE'S DOING GREAT . . . AND GET
OUT OF THE PROJECTS!! LOVE, COLLEEN

This time Kevin took his little sister's advice to heart, snapping the phone shut and hauling ass out of Fidelis as fast as he could.

———

The Jamaican's name was Deron. He walked up two flights to an apartment at the end of the hall. A woman stood there, staring out a window as the white boy left.

"What did he want?" She spoke without turning. Deron

thought a lot about shooting her, but only late at night and only when he was by himself.

"He's a reporter. Asked me about a girl." Deron pulled out the morgue shot. The woman took a look.

"We know her?" she said.

"Junkie. No one's seen her in a long time."

"Guess we know why. Anything else?"

"He asked about Curtis. Said he wanted to do a story."

"He's lying."

"He knew this place."

"Everyone knows Fidelis."

"He knew this building. I think he knew Curtis."

"What's the problem, Deron?"

"You know the problem. Cops tweakin'. My crew tweakin'."

"Your job is to handle the street. If you can't do your job, I've got plenty of pups down there that wanna eat."

Deron could feel the heat rising in his chest, but kept his face still. Now was not the time and this was not the place. He ducked his eyes and headed for the door.

"Deron."

He turned. She had a small gun in her right hand and he realized his hesitation had cost him. The truth was bosses didn't hesitate. And Deron was a born lieutenant. He knew that now. And that was a good way to die. The Jamaican's teeth sparkled as he took two neat slugs in the chest. He was dead before he hit the ground. The woman bent over the corpse, prying its lips open and plucking out the diamond grill with two fingers. Then she left.

23

IT WAS quarter past two and Bridget Pearce was looking to tear someone a new one. She banged her shopping cart through the swinging doors at Horrigan's and bumped across the rutted lot. A grocery clerk offered to help with the bags, but she waved him off, stopping at Friendly's to get a vanilla Fribble before lugging everything out to her car. The witches behind the deli counter hadn't helped matters. That was for damn sure. She'd felt her face flush when they asked about her brother's Pulitzer. She'd played it off as shock, surprise, joy, but inside her stomach was churning, and she wondered what they saw in her, how much they knew, and why she cared at all. But she did. Always had. She couldn't get her key out of her purse so she put one of the bags on the hood of the car and the other at her feet. Then she popped the locks and loaded up the backseat. She'd just slid behind the wheel when the passenger's door snicked open and Obie Liston slipped in beside her.

"Hey, Bridge."

She hadn't seen the bookie from Chelsea in at least five years. Back in the day, Obie liked to drink Kahlua and cream at the

Fish House in Lynn. One night he'd grabbed Bridget's ass in the bar there and she'd bounced his balls up into his tonsils with a wicked knee. She leaned down to help him up off the ridiculous disco dance floor they had in the place and told him next time she'd cut off whatever he had hanging between his legs (if he had anything left hanging between his legs) and use them as fuzzy dice for her rearview mirror. Then, for no goddamn reason at all, she went outside and cried in an alley, with the music playing and laughter from the club floating all around her. But that was a long time ago. Didn't mean she still didn't hate the little prick. Just that it was a long time ago.

"What the fuck do you want?"

Obie pulled out a half pound of sliced cheese wrapped in deli paper and opened it on his lap. "Land O'Lakes white, the good stuff. You want some?"

"I'll pass, thanks. Now, tell me what you want or get the fuck out of my car."

Obie folded up a slice and popped it in his yap. "Funny thing. I'm driving around town, thinking about a meatball sub for lunch, when I get this call. Rhode Island number. It's a guy I know who's hooked up with Cakes Grisanti. You know Cakes?"

"Not personally, no."

"So this guy tells me one of Cakes's boys is on his way up here. Gonna pay a visit to your boss."

"I don't have a boss, Obie."

"You know who I'm talking about."

"Why would Cakes Grisanti care about Bobby?"

Obie grinned.

"Damn, what's wrong with your teeth?"

"What?" He pulled over the rearview mirror and took a look.

"Fuck. My gums bleed when I get nervous. You got a tissue or something?"

Bridget shook her head. Obie the asshole tore off a piece of deli paper and did the best he could. When he was satisfied, he turned back to Bridget and smiled.

"How they look now?"

"Like they're rotting out of your head. Christ, your breath is awful."

"But the blood's gone?"

"Yeah, it's gone. Get back over to your side of the car. And open the window."

She cracked the driver's-side window. Obie picked up the thread of his story.

"So my buddy asks if I could find Bobby Scales. Like right now."

"Why?"

"Why? What do you think, why? So the guy coming up from Providence could pay him a visit." Obie made his finger into a pistol and dropped his thumb like a hammer.

"You've been watching too much *Sopranos*. What's Providence care about Bobby for?"

"This is what the guy told me. Said something happened this morning." Obie tilted his head and studied Bridget in a way that gave her a chill. When you came right down to it, he was cunning in his own piece-of-shit way. Nasty, too.

"You think I know something about that, Obie?"

"You tell me."

"What do you want?"

"Holy shit, I haven't seen one of those since I was a kid." Obie pointed out the window at a mechanical horse tucked between a rack of Horrigan's shopping carts and an ice machine. "The Smiling Mustang" was painted in big blue letters across the side. "We had one called Trigger. Gray with a red mane. Ten cents a ride. Damn, I loved that thing." Obie gobbled up a couple more slices of Land O'Lakes and began to bounce in his seat.

"Sorry, Obie, I don't have any change."

He stopped bouncing. "I wasn't gonna ride the thing. I'm just saying, takes me back. You know what? Fucking forget it." Obie's gums were bleeding again, filming his teeth and leaving a glisten of red along the edge of a half-eaten piece of cheese he held in his hand.

"Let's get back to Bobby," Bridget said. "You want my help, tell me what happened."

"I told you, I dunno."

"Then get out of the car."

"Fine. I heard they found two of Cakes's guys dead this morning down at the produce market."

"The produce market?" Bridget knew Bobby had clients down there. Still, it didn't make sense.

"Someone cut their throats."

"And you think that someone's Bobby?"

"I don't think nuthin'. Providence thinks it's Bobby."

"How did you find me?"

"Luck. I figured I'd cruise Brighton, swing by Bobby's place maybe. But first, I needed something to eat so I came down here for the cheese. And there you were."

She didn't believe him, but what did it matter? He wanted Bobby. And was willing to make a deal.

"How much do you know about Providence, Obie?"

"It's the mob. Prostitution, loan sharking. These days they launder a lot of cash through legit businesses. Drugs."

"Bobby doesn't deal in girls and he doesn't push dope. That's Fidelis."

"Around here, sure. But Providence handles all of New England and down the East Coast. Big coin."

"And what's that got to do with Bobby?"

"I'm just saying, that's what they do."

"What time will they be here?"

"Who knows? Maybe tonight. Maybe tomorrow. Maybe they're already here."

"And you want me to rat him out?"

"Don't get so fucking dramatic. Just tell me where he is. Maybe all they want to do is talk."

Bridget stared out the window at "The Smiling Mustang," white metal teeth curled in a goofy grin, paint peeling in a half-dozen spots, and the springs all shot to hell. Bridget bet the thing didn't even work. "What's in it for me?"

"If I handle this right, Providence is gonna give me Bobby's book. Set me up with some money, really expand."

"You live in Chelsea."

"That's where you come in. Day-to-day management of everything in Brighton and Allston. You get a cut up front, make double, triple anything Bobby ever made." Obie rolled a couple more slices of cheese into a tight torpedo and popped them in his mouth.

"And if I say no?"

He shrugged. "I find him anyway. And you're out of a job."

"How about I warn Bobby, he bugs out, and Providence thinks you tipped him."

Obie shook his head. "That ain't you, Bridget. First of all, you're greedy as fuck. Plus you're ambitious and smarter than even Bobby. Why do you think I picked you?"

"So you did follow me here?"

"Followed you around that fucking supermarket for a half hour."

"I bet you're the one who called Providence. Probably saw Bobby in the market this morning and figured why not."

"They called me."

"Why the fuck would Providence call you?"

"Does it really matter? Either you step up or you don't. That's how these guys work. So what's it gonna be?"

"Get out."

"You serious?"

"You're right, I won't say a word to Bobby. If he got himself in deep with those guys, he'll have to get himself out. But you're wrong about the rest. Yeah, I like money, but I'm not a fucking rat. You know why? Cuz rats wind up working with scum like you and then one day you're having a conversation in a car about me and I wind up on the wrong end of a visit from some guido. So get out of my car and take your fucking cheese and shitty-ass fucking breath with you."

Obie gave her the finger and climbed out. Bridget rolled down her window the rest of the way.

"And Obie . . ."

He stopped and turned.

"If you think those guineas won't make a meal out of someone like you, you're even stupider than I thought. Do yourself a favor. Tell them you couldn't find Bobby and go home. Lock the door, turn out the lights, and be happy you did something half-way smart for once."

Bridget watched Obie make his way to his car, then pulled up Bobby's number on her cell. Her finger played across the SEND button but didn't push it. She put the phone away and started to back out of her space. Asshole Obie nearly sideswiped her, laying on the horn and laughing like a maniac as he peeled out of the lot. Bridget hit the brakes, causing one of the shopping bags to topple and the top of her Fribble to pop off. The milkshake spilled all over the floor where it mixed with the unspooled yolks of four or five broken eggs until you couldn't tell one from the other in a sprawling, sticky mess.

"Fuck." Bridget leaned her forehead against the steering wheel and felt trembly, like she was gonna start crying for no reason at all. Fucking Fish House all over again. A young couple who looked like they were from Cambridge or Wellesley or Connecticut or some goddamn place stopped in the parking lot to stare at her.

"Mind your own fucking business," Bridget screamed through the open window and watched the young couple stuff themselves into their Subaru and peel out into traffic without even looking. That made her feel a little better. Bridget pulled some paper towels from one of the bags and cleaned up the backseat. Then she ran into Friendly's and bought another shake. It was 3:15 by the time she got back in her car. Depending on traffic, the drive across town was a half hour. And she was running late.

24

AGGIE LIVED on the first floor of an aging brownstone in Jamaica Plain. She was eighty-eight and had suffered at least two major strokes. Maybe more, according to her doctors. They'd wanted her in a rehab facility with hot and cold running nurses, but her great-niece wouldn't hear of it. And Bridget Pearce was the money. So Bridget made the decisions.

She'd found Emmanuelle working in Watertown at a produce store called Russo's. Emmanuelle was an illegal who split her time stocking bananas out front and hosing down pallets of cherry tomatoes in the back. Bridget offered the soft-eyed Guatemalan twice what she made at Russo's to take care of Aggie—twenty-four seven. Emmanuelle jumped at the chance. That was four years ago.

Bridget walked up the sagging steps to the apartment and banged on the front door. Emmanuelle was there in a flash, sugar on her lips, inviting her boss inside. Bridget sat on a small, neat couch while Emmanuelle bustled around in the kitchen. Cut flowers scented the room, and the furniture gleamed under a fresh coat of polish. A bamboo fan beat gently overhead and classical music played in the background, the two combining to cover up the hiss and thump of an industrial-strength respirator wheezing away in a bedroom down the hall. Emmanuelle came in with tea and a plate of gingersnaps. Bridget smiled and did the honors, pouring cups for both of them.

"She's doing wonderfully," Emmanuelle said. Bridget nodded at the comfortable lie. In four years, Aggie had made no discernible neurological progress. She ate when fed, moved her bowels when prompted, and three times a week got into a wheelchair so Emmanuelle could push her around the block. She couldn't speak but seemed to know where she was and followed any visitor around the room with a slack jaw and rinsed-out eyes. Not that Aggie got a lot of visitors. Early on Colleen had wanted to visit, but Bridget poured cold water on the idea until her sister gave up. Now, besides Emmanuelle and the doctors, it was just Bridget, twice a week like clockwork. She broke off a piece of cookie, soaking it in her tea before nibbling off an edge.

"How are you doing?" she said, gesturing for Emmanuelle to sit closer. The girl slid maybe an inch across the sofa.

"I'm fine, ma'am. Just fine. You want to see her?"

"In a minute. Tell me about your family."

"It's all good. My niece, Jacinta, she started middle school."

"She's that old?"

"Sí, sí. Thirteen."

This was their routine. Tea. A couple minutes of small talk. Then Bridget would go in. But first, the money. She pulled out a roll of bills and began to peel off twenties. "Here's your cash for the week. And a little extra for your niece."

Emmanuelle tried to give back the extra, like she always did. And Bridget refused, like she always did. The girl supported an extended family of at least twelve that Bridget knew of, so the cash came in handy. And it kept her on a short leash. With the money taken care of, Emmanuelle quickly slipped on her coat. Bridget saw her out and watched from the front windows as she walked neatly down the street. She'd be gone for two hours. More than sufficient. Bridget headed back to the bedroom and opened the door.

The ghost of her grandmother sat at the foot of the bed, unfiltered cigarette in one hand, lips peeled back in a deathless grin. Her great-uncle, Shuks, floated near the ceiling, diving at Bridget as she approached the bed before disappearing in a long, winding sigh. Bridget gave as good as she got, shooting a withered smile back at Gram, then pulling a chair within whispering distance of her patient.

"They're not gonna help you."

Aggie responded by rubbing together a toothless set of gums. The closer Bridget's great-aunt got to death, the more she looked like she was just being born. Her body was barely a bump under the covers, shrinking under the assault of chemicals, disease, and the inevitable wasting of old age. She'd lost all but a strand or two of hair, her skull covered with deep wrinkles that looked like ancient runes you might see carved on a cave wall somewhere. Bridget got a sudden urge to run her hands over them and discern what sort of message they held. Instead, she stood up and circled the bed, inspecting the machinery that kept her great-aunt alive—machinery she paid the tab for. Bridget tweaked a tube dripping clear fluids and tugged at some wires that ran along the floor and disappeared under cool sheets. When she returned to the chair, she held up the white Friendly's bag. It was Aggie's weekly treat, fed to her through a straw. Emmanuelle had cried and kissed the back of Bridget's hand the first time she'd asked to feed the shake to Aggie. Since then it had become part of their routine. Bridget pulled out the Fribble and poked a straw through the hole on top. Aggie watched closely, rubbing a furred tongue across lips cracked and blistered with fever. Bridget found some ointment Emmanuelle kept nearby on a tray and rubbed it on the sores. Her great-aunt purred low in her throat like an old tabby and began to shift her legs under the sheets. Bridget made a quieting motion with one hand and picked up the Fribble, fitting the straw to Aggie's lips. Her eyes grew wide while yellowed cheeks worked overtime drawing up the vanilla goodness. Bridget let her get a good taste, then plucked the straw from her mouth, watching her lips dry suck like a fish out of water. Bridget pulled off the cover and took a sip herself, allowing a mustache of thick cream to form before licking it off.

"That's enough for today," she said and tossed the cup in the trash. Aggie moaned and popped her lips.

"Now, stop that." Bridget cleaned her great-aunt's face and hands with a warm washcloth and plumped her pillows. By the time she kissed her forehead, the old woman was back to looking at Bridget like she was a god. She left the room, closing the bedroom door softly behind her, and headed down the hallway toward the kitchen.

A rear door opened to a set of stairs leading down to the building's basement. Bridget had rented out the lower levels when she took the first-floor apartment, agreeing to pay extra provided she, and she alone, had access. The scumbag landlord had jumped at the cash. Bridget told him she'd change the locks and cut the keys herself. She tugged open a second door in the basement and pulled out a flashlight as she navigated another set of steps. The subbasement smelled of rats, dead and decaying in the walls. Bridget could hear the live ones, urgent nails chattering against the concrete as they scurried in advance of her approach. She hit the bottom of the stairs, her light finding the first storage bin. Bridget checked her watch. If everything went well, she'd be done in an hour. She punched in an alarm code, opened the bin, and grabbed a canvas bag. Sitting on the cold floor, Bridget pulled out bundles of cash and piled them around her. She'd just begun to count when her cell phone buzzed. Bridget looked at the number on caller ID and picked up.

"What's up, Finn?"

Finn McDermott breathed through his nose and didn't say a word.

"Finn? You there?"

"I can hardly hear you."

"What do you want?"

"You seen your brother?"

"Not yet. Why?"

"I seen him down at Tar Park yesterday. He was asking 'bout Bobby."

"So what?"

"I don't like him sniffing around."

"He's not sniffing anything."

She'd started skimming off Bobby's book years ago. He had more than he needed and she had squat, so fuck him. Finn didn't care as much about the cash as he did banging her and he was cheap insurance. If Finn wanted to think they were partners, that was all right, too.

"I paid our money a visit today," she said, picking up a stack of twenties and counting silently.

"Where are you keeping it?"

"None of your business."

"It might be good if I knew."

"It might be good if you go fuck yourself. What did we agree on?"

"Just be careful. Bobby's not a dummy, you know."

"We're fine. You still wanna meet tonight?"

"I should be done by eight, eight thirty."

"I can't get there till ten."

"What's going on?"

"Nothing. You want to meet or not?"

"Bridge . . ."

"I'll see you at the Cask. If I'm not there by ten thirty, I'm not coming."

She hung up and finished counting the stack of twenties. Somewhere above her, there was a groan in the pipes. Bridget pulled out a ledger book filled with her best friends—black columns of figures, etched in small, precise script and marching down the page in picture-perfect order.

25

KEVIN GOT out of his car and made the slow walk up Champney Street. Leaves in the trees rubbed together in the breeze, scouting up whispers all around him. He lingered on the sidewalk, staring at windows curtained against the day. There was no grace left in the old homestead, no sense of nostalgia, or even foreboding. Just a lawn mower resting in pieces on the porch, along with a stripped-down bike frame and rusted hunk of chain. A black sedan rolled down the block and knifed to the curb.

"Kevin Pearce?"

The voice pulled Kevin from his slow-churning fog. Father Lenihan had been the priest at Saint A's for three decades. As far as Kevin knew, he was the only one left in a parish with more tumbleweeds than parishioners rolling down the aisle every Sunday.

"Father, how are you doing?"

"Doing well, thanks."

Kevin moved closer but didn't offer his hand. The priest leaned across so the late-afternoon sun blanched his face, lighting up the veins in his eyes and cobwebbing in cheeks and nose.

"You look good, Kevin."

"I'm kind of surprised you recognized me."

"You're the spit of your mother. What brings you back?"

"No reason. Just thought I'd see the old neighborhood."

They both turned their gaze down the block. A pair of sneakers was slung over a telephone wire and cars swirled around Oak Square, their shapes cutting fast and dark in the murk. The priest spoke first.

"It's not like it was."

"That's what everyone says, but I'm not sure if they mean it's better or worse."

Lenihan nodded as a chunky white kid stepped from the alleyway of a two-family across the street. He stopped next to a statute of Mary on the Half Shell stuck in the front yard. The kid gave Kevin and the idling car a Boston once-over then disappeared back from where he came, leaving the Virgin to fend for herself.

"I heard you work for the *Globe?*" the priest said.

"I'm a reporter."

"Good for you."

Kevin's newspaper had been the one to expose the cancer feeding on the archdiocese of Boston. Kevin knew the reporters from the Spotlight team working the story. He'd checked early on to see if Lenihan's name, or any of the other priests from his childhood, had made their lists. Lenihan hadn't. A couple of others from Brighton had. Kevin would like to say he'd felt some foreboding of evil, some skin crawl at the back of his neck when he was a kid and they were leaning over him, touching his shoulder, tousling his hair, correcting, disciplining, teaching him right from wrong, but he hadn't felt a thing. Saint A's had never been a home for him growing up—not like some kids—but when he was there, he'd always felt safe. Now he just felt sick and wanted to get away from the whole thing as fast as he could. The old priest didn't have that option.

"Have you seen anyone yet?"

"I saw Bobby Scales this morning."

"Bobby. You know he comes to church just about every day? Sits in the back when I light the candles for mass. He thinks I don't know he's back there, but I do." Lenihan sparked up an old-school Irish smile that had Kevin leaning against the side of the car.

"Should I tell him you're onto him?"

"Let's keep it our secret."

"No problem."

"Lord knows we can't be driving away the ones that do show up." The priest peered up at Kevin like a beggar at Christmas looking for the tickle of a coin in his cup.

"I'm sorry, Father."

"It is what it is, but you probably know that better than most." He lifted his chin toward 8 Champney. "Does she look any different?"

"Yes and no."

"Like everything else?"

"Exactly."

"Welcome home, Kevin. Say hello to everyone for me."

"I will, Father."

Lenihan offered a half wave that might have been a blessing and eased his car away from the curb. Then Kevin was alone again. Just him and the house. The house he'd grown up in. The house where she'd died. The house he'd run from. He walked across the slabbed sidewalk and felt the soles of his shoes scratch as he climbed the steps. The screen door he'd cycled through a million times as a kid was still on the job, except now it was torn in more spots than not and hung by a single screw screwed into a single hinge. He opened it with two fingers and reached for the key under a piece of fitted wood that made up part of the doorstep.

The door swung wide, a rectangle of sun on the floor of the hallway and the smell of old paint and dust in his nose. Kevin rocked on the threshold, tracing the outline of his parents still scratched in the cushions of living-room couch and chair. His old man's voice snapped on a string tied to the back of his neck and he remembered the warm feeling of imaginary piss running down the leg of a nine-year-old and the thrill, the pure fucking thrill, of uncut fear the way only a child can experience it. And keep it. And nurture it for a lifetime. He saw his mother, anchored in the corner, eyes hollowed and drawn at the mouth, the husk of her life peeling away in thin layers of regret. He thought all of that was done—the thump of dirt on wooden coffins announcing an end to a part of his life that had ended long before. Maybe not. He swallowed against the dry spot in his throat and stepped into the room. On a table near the front windows were a collection of things he'd missed. A blurry picture of Colleen in her cap and gown, high school diploma in hand, smiling and giving the camera a thumbs-up. Nearby were a couple more high school shots of Colleen and one of Bridget, holding her elbow while she stood on the back porch of the house and smoked a cigarette, narrowing her eyes and staring at something irritating in the distance. He sat down in one of the old chairs, green stripes with pink flowers, and touched a tender spot the boys from Fidelis had raised near his temple. Then he got up and walked into the kitchen.

It was like the living room, except everything was even older and grayer. He saw the same cups he drank milk out of as a kid. The same bowls he'd used for cereal. Same knives, plates, forks. He walked over to the pantry that had once served as his bedroom. Scratched into the door frame was a ladder of pencil marks where they used to measure their heights. He noticed an old phone jack in the adjacent hallway, a tangle of wires spilling out across the floor. Kevin recalled the heavy black phone that used to sit on a table with a single chair beside it. His father, tumbling down the hall at night, pissed on whiskey and beer. The pull and recoil of the rotary dial and his voice like maple syrup, talking sweet to his women, telling them he was going to leave his family, begging them to wait, describing what he'd do to their bodies when he saw them. Then he'd hang up and crawl into bed with Kevin's mom. The memory turned his saliva into sawdust, and a hot pulse quickened in the hollow of his throat.

He moved deeper into the pantry. The room's only window was painted shut. Kevin crouched down to examine a section of wall underneath it. In 1967, the Red Sox were worse than bums. They were irrelevant. At the start of the season the oddsmakers pegged them at 100–1 for the pennant. Kevin didn't much give a damn about oddsmakers back then. He jumped the bus to Fenway on Opening Day and sat in the bleachers with Shuks and eight thousand other diehards as Lonborg beat Eddie Stanky and the White Sox, 5–4. He listened that season on a transistor, sound down low at night, and scratched final scores into the wall beside his bed. At first, it was a game here or there. As the Impossible Dream unfolded, his entries on the wall became more frequent and the '67 team became his family, the soothing voices of Ken Coleman and Ned Martin welcoming him in every night, providing a place where he could feel safe and warm and even loved in a crazy sort of way only he could understand. Kevin rubbed off a thick layer of dust with his thumb and turned up a couple of scores etched in black ballpoint.

APRIL 14
Sox 3
Yanks 0
Billy Rohr one-hitter!!

JULY 27
Sox 6
Angels 5
Ten innings

He scrubbed a little more and found an entire string, scribbled in the wandering script of a sleepy third-grader.

AUGUST 24
Sox 7
Senators 5

AUGUST 28
Sox 3
Yanks 0

SEPT 5

Sox 8

Senators 2

At the very bottom of the wall, he unearthed a final, faded entry.

OCTOBER 1

Sox 5

Twins 3

Final Standings

Red Sox 92-70

Twins 91-71

Tigers 91-71

AL Champs . . . World Series!!!

IMPOSSIBLE DREAM

He'd gone to that last game, a bunch of them had, storming the right-field gates twenty at a time. Some of them got caught, but Kevin was far too quick. He sat on the concrete steps of the bleachers, a few feet from the bullpen, and watched Lonborg finish it off. Then he ran onto the field and rolled around in the green grass and red clay and lived a moment that only comes once in a young boy's life and only if he's terribly, terribly lucky.

Kevin clapped the dust off his hands and got to his feet. At the other end of the hallway his parents' old bedroom was closed off. He touched the smooth doorknob but didn't turn it, threading his way back through the kitchen and out onto the porch. The wooden posts groaned as he leaned on the crooked railing

and looked over the backyard of his youth. Old Towne Taxi had
closed up years ago, but the office was still there, windows dark
and the dirt parking lot overgrown with hip-high weeds. Kevin
picked his way across the yard and climbed the short run of steps.
The front door was locked. Now that he was closer, he could see
the door itself was heavy and new, as was the shiny deadbolt lock.
He walked around to the side of the building and tried a window.
Locked as well. Inside, a red alarm light blinked patiently on the
sill. Beyond that, the main room looked empty except for the
outline of a desk pushed up against a wall. Kevin wondered if it
was his grandmother's desk, who used it, and why was the place
alarmed anyway? He followed a faint path toward the back of
the building. The trees had grown thick here, forming a canopy
with the roof and creating a deep tunnel of shadow. As he turned
the corner, something came whistling out of the darkness. He
ducked and heard the woody thump of a baseball bat off the side
of the building. It was a wild swing and Kevin thought whoever it
was either had piss-poor aim or only intended to scare him. He
stepped in, catching a thin wrist with one hand and twisting the
arm of his attacker at the elbow. A boot lashed at his knees, clipping him on the shins. He swore and pivoted, increasing pressure until he heard the bat drop. A hand grabbed at his hair and
pulled him to the ground. They rolled into the weeds and then
out of the shadows. Kevin wound up on top, kneeling astride his
attacker.

"Fucking Bridget."

"Brother Kevin." His sister was wearing jeans and a loose-
fitting white shirt. She flared her nostrils, the old man's crazy
circling in her eyes and stirring the blood they shared. Some
Thanksgiving Day tables were populated by doctors or lawyers ar-

guing the finer points of their respective professions. Others had relatives stabbing each other with silverware and chewing on the drapes for dessert. Bridget blinked and the eyes went sleepy—dark and impenetrable. Kevin got to his feet and helped her up.

"Did I hurt you?"

"Hell, no." She rubbed her elbow and picked up the bat. "What are you doing sneaking around back here?"

"What are you doing coming at me with a Louisville Slugger?"

"Still got a lotta fucking rats in this neighborhood. Tried to break in three different times in the last year."

"Is that why you got the alarms?"

"Sure." She walked back toward the front of the cab office. Kevin followed.

"I didn't see any alarms in the house."

"They don't try to get in up there."

"What's back here?"

"Nothing, but the rats don't know that. Fucking pack of morons." She'd parked her car at the edge of the dirt lot. A couple of shopping bags sat in the backseat. "We can leave the car here. Just grab a bag."

They started to walk across the yard, Bridget slightly ahead of him. He'd only seen her a handful of times over the years, never more than a minute or two of mumbled small talk. Now he studied her profile, bathed in the pinks and purples of early evening. At thirty-eight, his nasty kid sister had grown into a cruelly efficient woman, with a wiry body and mean line to her upper lip that was the genetic birthright of Boston women who traced their roots back to the working kitchens of Ireland and England. A tweak here and there and Bridget might have been beautiful. Instead, she'd had to settle for common.

"You been inside the house?" she said.

"Just for a minute. You should find a new hiding place for the key."

"You gonna tell me how to run this place?"

"I'm just sayin' . . ."

"I told you. No one wants to get in except me. Come on."

———

Kevin sat at the kitchen table and watched her unpack groceries. She shoved a stack of French bread pizzas and some fish sticks in the freezer and slammed the fridge shut. Then she took a seat across from him, settling in the chair with a heaviness that belied her spare frame.

"So, Pulitzer Prize. Mr. Big Shot."

"How did you find out?"

"People down at Horrigan's were talking about it. You know how that goes."

"It's not a big deal."

"Course it is." She rubbed her forefinger with her thumb and turned over a spoon on the table. "If I'd known you were coming, we would have had a party."

He pictured her raising her head and cackling, like a hyena over a fresh kill, jaws run red with blood. But she just sat there, frowning like he was a puzzle with a few pieces missing.

"You look old," she finally said.

"Thanks, Bridge."

"Everyone's gotten old. Or dead. You hear about Shuks?"

Kevin nodded.

"Went right after mom and dad. All the brothers are dead.

One after another." Bridget popped each of their dead great-uncles in a row with her finger. "You know about Aggie?"

"I heard she's in a nursing home."

"That's what they wanted, but I said fuck that. Got her an apartment in J.P. with a live-in caretaker. Who told you about her?"

"Colleen."

Something smug flickered in Bridget's face, and Kevin felt like he'd just picked sides.

"So you keep in touch with little sis?" she said.

"You know I do."

She gave a colorless shrug as if the subject was hardly worth the breath she'd spent bringing it up. "She lives in Newton now." Bridget hit the name of the town like it wasn't a big deal even though Colleen thought it was.

"I know."

"With the scumbag husband and loser kid."

"Jesus."

"You don't think Scott's a scumbag?"

"What's going on with Colleen?" His voice sounded reedy, quickening in spots like his mother's.

"Nothing. Everything's just fine and dandy."

Bridget got up and began to put away the rest of her groceries. Kevin walked back out to the porch. After a couple of minutes, she came out.

"You haven't shown your face here in twenty-five years. What did you expect?"

He opened his mouth to respond, but again found he had nothing to say. And so they stood there, Bridget studying him in a manner that was uniquely hers.

"You saw I took out the phone in the hallway?"

He flushed up into his scalp. "So what?"

She blinked and he knew she knew about all of that so long ago and who really gave a good fuck anyway. Kevin pointed to the dark staircase.

"Who's upstairs?"

"Top floor's empty. I got a young couple on the second. Paying eight bills a month."

Kevin started walking up the first flight. She trailed close behind.

"You remember Chrissy McNabb?" he said.

"You mean the junkie?"

"You knew about that?"

"Everyone knew about Chrissy. Her aunt still lives on Bigelow. Why?"

"You guys were in grade school together."

"Hated that fucking place. Why you asking about her?"

"No reason." They climbed another flight. "How's your life going, Bridge?"

"I sleep in the same bed I did as a kid. How do you think it's going?"

"I'm sorry."

"Don't be. I made my choices and I'm good with it."

But he was sorry. She was his kid sister and he couldn't help it. "How long you think you're gonna stay in the house?"

"Is that why you're here? Let me guess, you and the little princess wanna sell the place?"

Kevin stopped on the landing. "I just want to make sure you're gonna be all right . . ."

"I pay the taxes, heat, electric. Put in a new water heater last year."

"I'm just saying, if you're ever short . . ."

"If I'm short, there's always Bobby." A lash of a smile.

"I heard you two dated."

"We're on a break."

"Fine. You're on a break." Kevin circled the final flight and took a seat on the top step, a few feet from the door to his grand-mother's old apartment. Bridget settled just below, sitting at an angle, nostrils slitted, eyes running. Feral now. Hunting.

"What is it?" he said.

"Nothing."

"I'm not one of your toys, Bridget. You got something to say, just say it."

"You ever hear of the Royal Hotel?"

"The flophouse on Boylston?"

"Colleen's husband's shacking up down there. Every Tuesday like clockwork. Sometimes, Wednesdays."

Colleen's marriage flashed past like a car wreck on the side of the road.

"Have you talked to her?" Kevin said.

"It's none of my business."

"Then why do you seem to be enjoying it so much?"

"Actually, I think it's sad. What's even sadder is that little sis-ter knows about it and doesn't do a damn thing. I guess she loves that house in Newton too much." Bridget inched closer. "Now, tell me about *your* girlfriend."

"What about her?"

"I heard she's a half-breed."

"Fuck off."

Bridget undid a button, then two, allowing her blouse to slip. From his perch, Kevin could just glimpse the purple twists of scarred flesh, bunched up at one shoulder and running in long, liquid strokes across her back. Then she turned to face him. She wasn't wearing a bra and her right breast rested in a cup of pinkish light. Ducking just beneath it was another scar, this one thin and precise. Bridget ran a finger along it. "A nigger gave me this, brother. Just about where we're sitting. Or maybe you forgot?"

"I didn't forget. For Chrissakes, cover yourself up."

She pulled her blouse closed and held it with two fingers. "Why are you really here?"

"I don't know." Kevin nodded at the door sitting just over his shoulder. "Maybe I just wanted to see it one more time."

"I got a key if you want to go inside."

"This is close enough."

Bridget smiled softly. "The old man always said you were a coward."

He left her sitting on the steps, smoking a cigarette, one long leg crossed over the other, blouse still partially undone. As he hit the bottom of the hill, Kevin snuck a final look back at number eight. Night was coming quickly and the building's edges were blurry against the blue-black sky. A silhouette appeared in the bay window he'd always thought of as his father's, staring out at him before disappearing in a shifting of curtain and sash. Kevin was tempted to retrace his steps up the hill. In the end, he thought better of it and left.

———

Bridget pulled back from the window and wondered about her brother. She understood greed. Understood lust. Understood revenge. The more subtle range of human emotion, however, had always been beyond her knowing. And that worried her. She turned down the lights in the living room so there was just a glow from the street and left by the back porch, picking her way through weeds and shadow to the front door of the old cab office. The lock turned easily and the door swung silently on its hinges. She punched in the alarm code and settled behind her grandmother's desk, pouring herself a drink from a bottle of Stoli and lighting a cigarette. There was a sound outside. Bridget reached for a side drawer but wasn't quick enough. Colleen's husband stood in the doorway.

"I told you not to come around today."

Scott Carson took a step inside. "Who was that leaving the house?"

"Your brother-in-law. He didn't ask for you."

Scott's eyes skittered toward the bottle. She put a hand on it and topped off her glass. He took another step.

"You're embarrassing my sister, Scott."

"I'm not . . ."

"You're laying pipe across half the fucking city and she knows it."

"Colleen doesn't know nothing."

Bridget pulled an envelope from the side drawer, counting out two hundred in twenties and pushing across the stack. "Go home and make nice to her. And act like you mean it."

Scott grabbed at the money. "Can I get a drink?"

She poured him a short glass. He drank it in one go and looked for another.

"You remember a girl named Chrissy McNabb?" Bridget said, refilling his glass and watching as he put it away.

"McNabb?"

"Used to live on Bigelow. Crackhead, street whore, blow-job-for-a-pipe kind of girl. Hasn't been around in a couple of years."

"Doesn't ring a bell. Why?"

"Never mind."

Scott held up the fold of money. "Will Bobby know about this?"

"Bobby doesn't give a fuck."

"Where is he?"

"None of your goddamn business."

Scott licked his lips and blinked his eyes, fighting with whatever it was he had to say.

"What is it?" she said.

"I heard some things 'bout him."

"About who?"

"Bobby."

"Fuck what you heard. Now get out of here."

She knew he wanted to take a run at her. Shoot her, kill her, fuck her. All three if he could fit them in. She could smell it on him, hoped and prayed the prick would try his luck. But he tucked tail and ran. She crushed out her cigarette, finished her drink, and pulled out a compact. Her lips looked pinched in the small circle of glass. She touched them up with some gloss and wondered again what her brother was up to. Then she thought about Bobby. She had a pretty good idea about the kinds of things Scott Carson was hearing on the street. And none of them were good. Fucking Bobby.

26

THE MONEY was stuffed in a coffee can on a shelf in the closet. Bobby counted it at the kitchen table—just shy of twenty-two K. He could get his hands on more, but it would do for now. Bobby took out a couple hundred, wrapped the rest in newspaper, and packed it in a suitcase along with three days' worth of clothes. He hadn't figured on disappearing until tomorrow. Still, there was a lot to do before he left. And maybe, if things broke right, he wouldn't have to leave at all. Under some loose floorboards he found a nickel-plated nine-millimeter with a black grip. He checked the clip and set the pistol on the table. Outside cars were lined up at the light, everyone doing the long shuffle up Market Street, heading home from work. Bobby took out the old picture of Paragon Park and laid it down beside the gun. The last thing was the knife. He'd wiped it clean with bleach and was about to strap it to his ankle when he heard a sound on the stairs. Bobby slid the suitcase into the closet and crept to the door for a look through the peephole. Seamus Slattery was on the other side, good eye flicking back and forth. It was the nervous patter of a man who'd pushed in his chips and called for the dice. A man who was already dead but just didn't know it. Bobby felt the knife handle, hard and dry in the hollow of his palm. The Irishman raised his knuckles and hesitated, then rapped on the door.

27

IT WAS nearly eleven and Joey's was wall-to-wall with drinkers. Kevin sat in his car and watched the windows—rusted red with barroom light and alive with a floor show of men and women, drinking and smoking, cussing and conspiring, flirting, fighting, and one couple, Kevin was quite certain, fucking in a shadowed corner by the ladies' room. Laughter bellied out into the night as the door opened and four women in tight dresses, high heels, and higher hair wobbled out of the place. They gave Kevin's car a passing glance as they helped one another across Market Street. After a stop at the ATM, they made their way into an Irish joint called Porter Belly's. As the door swung open, Kevin caught a glimpse of a coarse, immigrant face muddied with heat and alcohol. He was standing on a stage with a mike in his hand, crooning to Marvin Gaye's "Sexual Healing" for all he was worth. At his feet were a tight coterie of big-hipped women, swaying in perfect tempo with the singer's beer belly, freed from its flannel shirt and having a hell of a good time hanging out half a foot over his belt. Kevin caught it all in the space of a door opening, perfectly framed and mercifully covered up again as said door swung closed. He dropped his head against the driver's-side window and thought about his visit home. The memory left him cold and sick and hollow inside, Bridget's words tumbling through his head like a can being kicked down an empty street.

The radio was tuned to an all-news station, every hour on the eights. The weather sucked. Boston drivers, even worse. He turned up the volume as they got to the news. Sandra Patterson was the lead. Late that afternoon the Suffolk County D.A. had gone public with an ID. DeMateo hadn't given many details, except to say that Patterson was a state cop, she'd been murdered somewhere in the Allston-Brighton area, and a task force would be formed to handle the investigation. Kevin switched off the radio and checked his phone. No message from Lisa. He wondered if she'd attended the presser. DeMateo tried to get her on TV every chance he got. Never allowed her to speak, but always gave her a prominent spot just behind him. The D.A. was nobody's fool. Lisa was black—but not too much so—and looked fucking amazing. On screen or off. Kevin cut his eyes across the street. A man walked past Joey's in a buttoned-up peacoat and sheltered in the lee of the building. His face was a smudge, but Kevin thought he recognized something in the bow of his legs and the way he shifted his weight on his feet. The man reached into his pocket for a can of Copenhagen and Kevin was sure of it. He was looking at Billy Sweeney—yet another stillborn legend conceived in a place that was full of them.

Late afternoon. The world quiet and empty save for the chatter of hockey sticks, one against the other, and plumes of breath like cold, white smoke, billowing bright against an achingly blue sky. Kevin and a pack just like him were hard at work, chasing Billy Sweeney's flickering form across Chandler's Pond. While everyone else strained and struggled, chopping up the rough ice with their skates and hacking at each other's shins, Billy floated through, around and above it all, turning this way and that, puck tethered to his stick on an invisible string, blades flashing and hissing as they cut smooth, fast curves across the pond. Three years older than Kevin, Billy had scored a scholarship to Catholic Memorial and centered their first line as a freshman. In his sophomore year CM won the state title and Billy was named the Globe's player of the year. By the time he was a junior, BC and BU were drooling over him even though he barely weighed a buck-twenty. There were a dozen Sweeneys in all and no money except the change their mother found in the cushions of the couch every morning, but it didn't matter. For Billy, everything was gonna be comped. Boy fucking wonder. Kevin was fourteen and Billy a senior at CM when he pulled up one summer night in a fire red Monte Carlo with a white kid from the Faneuil projects everyone called Shifter. They asked if Kevin wanted to go for a ride. It was hot and still and Kevin was bored as hell so he climbed in the back. Shifter was driving. He was an albino with hairless brows and lids and eyes that glowed like the sun. They had a cooler filled with ice and a dozen Rolling Rocks in the front seat. He wasn't gonna ask, but Billy offered so Kevin popped a beer and sank into the padded seating, feeling the AC on his feet and watching the tops of the houses float past. They'd gone almost a mile before Kevin noticed the screwdriver stuck in the ignition. Billy told him it was a hotbox, but not to worry. They'd taken it from the lot of a car dealership in Allston and the owner wouldn't report it until morning. Kevin was planning to jump out at the next light when police flashers lit up the back window of the Monte. Shifter would have run, but they were stuck in a line of traffic. When a second cruiser pulled alongside, Shifter nudged the car to the curb. Billy swore once and Shifter's red eyes flicked to the glove compartment. Kevin felt like one of those Roman galley slaves lashed to his oar as the captain rammed into some other fucking boat and all the losers below drowned like rats. The cop ran a quick light across the interior and ordered everyone to the curb. The glovie contained a bag of weed, a gram and a half of coke, and some pills. Kevin was supposed to be headed to college someday. Billy Sweeney, the NH fucking L. But now something else was going on. They were cuffed and taken in the back of a wagon to Station Fourteen. Kevin had been in his cell less than an hour when Bobby came down the hall. Somewhere behind him, there was a whirr of gears and a short, sharp buzzing, then the door to Kevin's cell popped open.

"Let's get you the fuck out of here."

There was no paperwork to fill out, no statement to sign, no court date. Just him and Bobby walking out the front door of the cop shop, Bobby's arm slung protectively across his shoulders. At that age, Kevin didn't know what love was, but he sure as shit knew loyalty. And he knew he could count on Bobby to have his back. A lot of guys in the neighborhood talked that kind of game, but damn few backed it up. Bobby always did.

Shifter and Billy Sweeney walked that night as well. Just because Billy Sweeney was Billy Sweeney. And Shifter was with him. Not that any great lesson was learned. Two weeks later, Billy climbed out of another hotbox in Somerville and started running toward the bright lights of the Mystic projects. A cop yelled at him to stop and fired a warning shot. The bullet came up off the pavement and caught Billy in the hip. He managed to get away, but his lottery ticket to BU, the NHL, wherever, got ripped up and tossed in the trash. From then on, he was just like the rest of them, nothing but a wannabe pond player.

Kevin watched from the front seat of his car as Billy crossed Market Street, head down, chin tucked into his chest, moving like an old man before his time with the *Herald* stuck in his pocket and a pronounced limp. He disappeared around a corner and Kevin got out. More forms, huddled in a pack and covered up in thick jackets, stumbled out of Joey's as he approached. A guy in a long gray coat knocked into him, staggered against his buddies, and kept going, leaving behind nothing save a perfunctory "asshole" for Kevin to ponder. A bouncer in a black T-shirt stood at the front door of the bar, arms crossed, impervious to the cold. He shook his head, shaved and oiled to a high sheen and gleaming under light from the street. "Fucking booze, right?"

Kevin waved it off and walked around the corner to the entrance for Bobby's apartment. He hiked up the stairs and rapped on the door.

"It's open." Bobby was sitting in a chair, remote in his lap, TV tuned to some cop movie in black and white. A suitcase sat on the bed. "There's beer in the fridge." Bobby pointed without taking his eyes off the tube.

"No, thanks."

"Sit down, then."

Kevin took a seat on the edge of the bed.

"You ever watch Andy Griffith?"

"Not in a while."

"Ever tell you Opie reminds me of you?" Bobby finally looked over. Kevin shook his head.

"There's one episode where he kills a bird and you can see the whole world in his face. Great acting."

"Ronnie Howard played Opie."

Bobby clicked off the set and dropped the remote to the floor.

He had a thick bandage wrapped around his left hand. "I thought I told you not to come back."

"There's something I didn't tell you this morning. Something you need to see." Kevin pulled out the pages he'd copied from the original murder file on Curtis Jordan. Bobby gave them a quick read.

"Curtis Jordan got what he deserved."

"I know that."

"But it still eats at you."

"I went into Fidelis today. Asked around about Jordan."

"And?"

Kevin touched the bruising near his temple. "The locals weren't too happy."

"Fucking Opie." Bobby gave Kevin a hard-skinned smile and went back to reading. "Where did you get all this?"

"My girlfriend's a prosecutor with the D.A.'s office. I lifted it out of her bag."

"That's gotta be good for the relationship."

"They're shaking the tree, Bobby."

"No one gave a shit back then. Why would they care now?"

"There's more." Kevin took out Bobby's business card. "You hear about that dead cop? Woman by the name of Sandra Patterson?"

"Just saw her picture on the news."

"She worked at Habitat for Humanity. In fact, they found her dead inside one of your houses. Radnor Road."

Bobby hooded his eyes, plucking the card from Kevin and flashing it between the tips of two fingers. "You talk to anyone else about this?"

"What do you think?"

Bobby pointed his chin at the door Kevin had just walked through. "Go downstairs and grab a beer. I'll be down in five."

———

Kevin found a corner walled off from the main crush. Just him, a bumper pool table, and three Irishmen sitting at the other end of the bar and inventing new ways to use the words *fuck* and *cunt*. A fourth old-timer wearing a beat-up Red Sox hat joined them and ordered a round of drinks. Then Bobby came in. He was wearing a long black overcoat that nearly touched the floor. Kevin watched his progress in a Powers Whiskey mirror. So did the rest of the room. The bartender threw down a coaster as Bobby pulled out a stool.

"Bud?"

"Thanks, Ray."

The bartender returned with a longneck bottle. Bobby took a healthy pull before swinging his face closer in the smoke and light.

"Grew up here," Kevin said. "Don't know a soul."

Bobby laughed.

"What's so funny?"

"Tommy." The beat-up Sox hat surfaced from the end of the bar like a cartoon prairie dog popping out of its hole.

"Come here." Bobby pushed out a stool with his boot. The old-timer took a seat. Up close his skin looked sallow and was covered with rough splotches of brown, two or three of which were growing hair. One eye wandered, with a black pupil that was as big and round as a nickel. The other shivered in its socket, bouncing from Bobby to Kevin, wondering what they wanted and why.

"Tommy, you recognize my friend?"

The eye stopped bouncing and tightened in on Kevin.

"This is your old shortstop, Kevin Pearce. Kevin, your second baseman, Tommy Doucette."

Doucette's face split into a grin, revealing tiny teeth peppered with bubbles of brown saliva in the cracks and crevices. "Kevin fucking Pearce. I thought you were dead."

Bobby tapped Doucette lightly on the arm. "He writes for the *Globe* now."

"Sports?"

"I'm an investigative reporter."

"No kidding." Doucette circled his finger once in the air. "Ray, give us a round."

"My treat, Tommy." Bobby nodded for the bartender to set up Doucette's buddies. Ray obliged, pouring a fresh rum and Coke for Doucette and placing three overturned shot glasses in front of his companions. They lifted their drinks Bobby's way and went back to cursing.

"Kevin, what happened to you?" Doucette said, as if his own life was anything but a walking, talking, fucking train wreck.

"Family stuff," Kevin said.

"You just disappeared."

"I know."

"We would have won the city that year. I swear it . . . ." Doucette's voice trailed off, his good eye contemplating the past floating belly-up in his glass.

"I'm sorry, Tommy. It was just a thing."

Doucette waved him off. "Fuck it. We were kids."

"Kevin just won a Pulitzer," Bobby said, measuring the old teammates, one against the other.

"Oh, yeah?" Whatever joy there might have been in Tommy Doucette had been drawn out long ago, leaving behind nothing but a rattling, rasping emptiness. "Congratulations." He toasted Kevin and polished off his drink in two swallows. "I better get back. Bobby?"

"Next Tuesday, Tommy."

Doucette scrambled to his feet. Bobby gripped his arm and put him back on the stool. "What you owe plus another point."

Doucette nodded. Bobby let him go and watched as he scurried back to his pals. "The old double-play combination."

"What happened to him?" Kevin said.

"Guy's a fucking wreck. Did five years in Walpole for boosting cars. Word is they passed him around pretty good."

Kevin recalled a blazingly hot July afternoon—Tommy Doucette getting beat like a bitch by some kid from Rogers Park. The other kid was bigger, sure, but Tommy didn't even try to fight. Just covered up on the melting blacktop and let the kid put it on blast until he'd punched himself out. Doucette was thirteen at the time and there was nothing he could have done, short of killing someone, to get back what he'd given away that day. So he became what he'd become—fresh meat in someone else's food chain.

"How much does he owe you?" Kevin said.

Bobby shook his head. "Doesn't matter. Tommy ain't going nowhere."

Kevin felt the sleeping dogs of childhood, awake again and growling in his gut. "I saw Billy Sweeney tonight."

"Oh, yeah. You say hello?"

"He probably wouldn't even know who I was."

Bobby didn't respond.

"What's he doing now?"

"Used to work for the T. Now he collects disability and drinks down the Stockyard. Gets pissed on drafties and starts telling everyone how fucking great he could have been. Why?"

"No reason. Who else is around?"

"Most of 'em are gone. Your first baseman . . ."

"Brian Tarpey?"

"Polished off the better part of a quart of vodka driving home from New York. Killed himself and a couple of high school kids on the Pike." Bobby began to count off the dead on his fingers. "Joey Nagle, found in his car behind the Corrib. Blew his heart out with a speedball. Sully died of fucking hepatitis, if you can believe that."

"Jimmy Fitz?"

"Liver went three years ago. They waked him in the Grill. Laid the body out on the bar and everything. Cops said it violated the health laws or something, but they wound up letting it go."

"How about the Coreys?"

"Paulie's a punk. David ate a bullet in the bathroom of a YMCA in Mattapan. You met Finn at the park."

"Yeah, I met Finn. Told me he sells T-shirts for a living."

"His best seller last year had STEINBRENNER SUCKS on the front and JETER SWALLOWS on the back."

"I saw that one outside the Cask."

"Probably Finn. You ever get down to Champney?"

"Bridget scares me."

"She should. Your sister likes to collect information. Then she collects people. Keeps them on a little string in her pocket. It's all petty stuff, but she's mean as hell about it."

"Have you seen Colleen?"

"Not lately, why?"

"Nothing."

"Hey, look at me." Bobby's presence muscled its way into the conversation, his voice low and punishing. "It's that fucking husband, isn't it?"

"How did you know?"

"Shitbag drinks in here every now and then. Tries to bang anything that moves. I wanted to tell Coll, but you know . . ." Bobby shrugged off the thought of getting involved. Someone shoved quarters into the bumper pool table. The balls rolled smoothly under the table along wooden rails and clicked against each other as they came to a halt. Bobby ordered a couple shots of Jack. Strains of Van Morrison's "Wonderful Remark" lifted and floated in from the other room.

"Great fucking song," Bobby said.

"Yeah."

"Any idea what it means?"

Kevin shook his head.

"I bet Van just made it up as he went along. Said 'fuck it,' let everyone figure it out for themselves."

The bartender came down with the bottle of Jack and poured their shots. Kevin swallowed the whiskey and wiped his mouth with the back of his hand. "The girlfriend I was telling you about . . ." He was trying hard, and failing mightily, to keep the edge out of his voice.

"The prosecutor?"

"She's working the Sandra Patterson case. Asked if I'd poke around here for a day or two. See what I could turn up."

Bobby took his time, peeling the label off his beer bottle with his thumb. "So she thinks her cop killer's from Brighton?"

"She had the Jordan file in her bag like I told you . . ."

"Yeah, I've been thinking about that. Doesn't it seem a little convenient?"

"What do you mean?"

"Maybe she wanted you to find the file. Figured you'd take one look and come running to me."

An image popped into Kevin's head—Lisa shedding water as she leaned out of the shower, smiling in the steam and heat, asking Kevin to dig through her bag. "That's not Lisa."

"I'm supposed to take your word on that?"

"I came here to tell you what was going on, Bobby. Nothing more, nothing less."

"And I can trust your girlfriend?"

"You can trust me."

The label came off in one curled piece. Bobby laid it flat on the bar. "I knew Sandra Patterson. She had a different name at Habitat, but I knew her."

"How well?"

"Talked to her once or twice on the job. Sure as shit didn't know she was a cop."

Doucette and his Irish buddies had cleared out. The kids shooting bumper pool were in their own world, laughing and preening, studying their shots and looking at themselves in the whiskey mirrors every chance they got. Kevin pulled out the ballistics report.

"More presents from your girl?" Bobby said.

"It's a ballistics report dated the day before yesterday. Links the gun that killed Curtis Jordan to Patterson's murder. Also links it to Rosie Tallent."

Kevin watched Bobby's eyes as he read. When he was done, Bobby shoved the paperwork back across the bar. "This gonna fuck you over for the Pulitzer?"

"What? No. If anything it helps prove James Harper was innocent. But that's not the point."

"What is the point?"

"If they think you did Jordan, they're gonna come after you for the others."

"Know what I think?"

"What?"

"Someone's playing games with you."

"Everyone knows you were a suspect in the Jordan thing. With this connection . . ."

Bobby held up a finger. "Stop talking."

Kevin went quiet.

"Wait here a second." Bobby walked behind the bar, whispered something to the bartender, then disappeared through a door. He was back in a moment. "Let's go."

The temperature had dropped and small bits of moisture blew off the rooftops, sparkling in the cut of the streetlights before being swept into the night. Bobby's coat billowed with the wind as they crossed Market and Kevin thought he caught a hint of metal underneath as Bobby levered himself into the car. Then Kevin slipped behind the wheel and they drove off.

28

THE CHESTNUT Hill Reservoir sits on the eastern edge of Boston College's main campus, a stone's throw from the football stadium and Kelley Rink. During the day, it's filled with joggers circling the mile-and-a-half loop. At night, it's pretty lonesome. Kevin pulled into a small parking lot beside the Resie and killed the engine.

"What are we doing out here?" he said.

Bobby just sat, listening.

"Bobby . . ."

"How often you think about dead people?"

"Cut the shit."

"I'm serious. How often?"

Shuks's face dropped down onto the hood in front of Kevin, pulling at a Lucky and streaming smoke across the windshield before dissolving back into the night. "No idea."

"You don't think about 'em hardly at all. Nobody does. Why the fuck would we? Truth is once you're under the ground, you're gone. I loved your grandmother, but who's gonna know she even existed in fifty years? Hell, who's gonna know we existed?"

"We'll know."

"We'll both be dead."

"Yeah, but we'll know. And that's gotta count for something."

"Everything from this world goes into the dirt with you, Kev. Just how it is."

"You are one cheerful motherfucker."

"You still got your soul. Wanna hear about that?"

"Not really."

Bobby chuckled, banging his wrapped hand lightly against the window. "It's the whiskey. Gets me talking ragtime."

"What happened there?"

He held up the bandage and unzipped a seamless grin. "You worried?"

Kevin kept his face still. "Didn't say that."

"I cut it with a Skilsaw at work. No big deal." Bobby dropped the hand into his lap. "The report you showed me on the ballistics. It said the bullets they took out of Sandra Patterson and Rosie Tallent matched the thirty-eight that killed Jordan. Right?"

"Yeah."

"And you're wondering where that gun is?"

"Something like that."

"Come on." Bobby climbed out of the car, long coat pulled tight around his body. They slipped through a hole in the fence and wound their way down a black path skirted on either side by twisted stands of trees and overgrown bushes. Bobby took out a silver flashlight and clicked it on. A crust of frost ran along the edge of the bank; a thickening mist swirled and scurried across the water. It smelled like rain.

"Just follow the waterline." Bobby pointed with his flash and began to walk. Kevin followed, moonlight dodging his footsteps between cracks in the trees.

"I tell you I'm gonna be heading out of town for a bit?" Bobby's voice was rough with the cold.

"You didn't."

"Got some business to take care of. Be leaving tomorrow. This way."

They walked the curve of the bank for another hundred yards, then moved up into the tree line. Bobby stopped at a small clearing and propped the flashlight against a rock. His face was soaked in yellow, and his shadow sprang to life on the screen of foliage behind him.

"Right here." He toed the ground with his boot.

"Right where? What are you talking about?"

Bobby pulled a small shovel from under his coat, unfolded it, and began to dig. "I marked this place out years ago. I knew the land was protected because of the Resie. No one was gonna build condos here or any of that shit. As for this particular spot, you didn't see the signs but it's loaded with poison ivy."

Kevin jumped back. "Fuck."

"Small price to pay." It was awkward to shovel with the bandage, but Bobby managed. Kevin didn't offer to help. After about ten minutes, Bobby dropped to his knees. He'd broken through the hard cover and the soil underneath was soft and yielding. When he spoke again, his breath came in small bursts of cold. "Know what I've got down here?"

"Why don't you tell us, Mr. Scales?" A second light clicked on, harsh and white in their faces. "Get up on your feet, slowly. Keep your hands where I can see them and stand by Kevin."

Bobby did as he was told. Lisa Mignot stepped forward. She was wearing jeans and a short leather jacket with a silk scarf that bled red wound around her neck. She wore black leather gloves and had a gun in her right hand.

"Now, who wants to tell me the story?"

———

Neither Kevin nor Bobby said a word. Lisa dug a toe into the hole Bobby had started and nodded at him. "Finish."

He threw the shovel at her feet. "Do it yourself."

"Bobby, this is my girlfriend, Lisa Mignot. She's a prosecutor for the Suffolk County D.A. and, apparently, licensed to carry a gun."

"Looks like I was right," Bobby said. "She's been using you, Kev. Planted those files where you'd find them, then followed us out here."

The truth of Bobby's words flashed across Lisa's face, all the worse because of her beauty. Then, it was back to business.

"I could have come out with a car full of cops," she said, "but I didn't. I'm alone and no one knows I'm here. I wouldn't have done that if I didn't want to help you. Both of you. And, believe me, you need it."

"Dig the hole, Bobby."

"Fuck her."

"Dig the hole. Whatever it is, she's gonna find it anyway."

Bobby picked up the shovel and began to dig. Four shovelfuls later, the edge of his spade hit something metal. Bobby wedged a cream-colored box out of the black earth.

"Leave it, Mr. Scales." Lisa hadn't holstered her gun. She pointed with it toward the base of a tree. Bobby did as she asked.

"What's in here?" Lisa said.

Bobby didn't respond. Lisa looked at Kevin.

"No idea."

She crouched down, fumbled with the catch for a moment, then pried the box open. "It's empty."

"Guess you can put the gun away," Bobby said.

"You want to tell me why you buried an empty box in the middle of nowhere?"

"I'm fucked in the head. Ask Kevin."

Lisa holstered her weapon. "Come here." She crooked her finger and walked down the bank to the water. Kevin followed.

"What's supposed to be in there?"

"I told you. I have no idea."

"We've got a wire in his apartment."

"So he's a suspect?"

"He's up to his eyeballs in this, Kevin. And if you're not careful, you will be, too."

"Was he right about the file on Jordan? Did you leave that out for me?"

"I didn't think it would turn out like this."

"Fuck, Lisa. Fuck."

She wet her lips and peeled her eyes back toward Bobby, who was sitting with his spine up against a tree and his bandaged hand resting on a knee. "I was telling you the truth. I'm the only one who heard the wire tonight. And no one else knows I'm here."

"You offering a deal?"

"I keep this quiet. He tells me what was supposed to be in the box."

"Curtis Jordan killed my grandmother."

"I read the file and I'm sorry. But Bobby Scales was the investigation's number one suspect."

"He was never arrested."

"It was 1975, Kevin. The cops in Brighton probably threw a fucking party when they heard another project nigger bought it. Thing is, the gun's back in circulation. And two days ago it was used to shoot an undercover cop."

"If someone killed Jordan and kept the gun, why pull it out and use it years later? Makes no sense."

"You're right, but these things don't always make sense. And you know that as well. Either way, your friend's involved." She shifted her weight, gun creaking in the leather holster clipped to her belt. "You know it's possible he's playing you."

"How?"

"He takes you out to where the gun is supposed to be buried and, surprise, surprise, it's gone."

"You're telling me this was a show?"

"He lets you see the empty hole, gets you to believe someone else dug up the thirty-eight and is killing the women. I was a complication he didn't count on, but so what? It's still just an empty hole."

"You believe that?"

"I met the guy five minutes ago."

"Maybe I killed Jordan."

"I *don't* believe that."

"Part of you does. Part of you is thinking that might be exactly what happened."

"To be honest, I had you pegged for the twenty-two. Post-mortem contact wound to Curtis Jordan's head. At fifteen, that's plenty of weight to carry around."

Kevin started to turn away. She touched his shoulder. "No one's interested in who pulled the string on Jordan. Least of all, me. We just want the gun."

"Postmortem wounds were part of the M.O. on Tallent and Patterson."

"You didn't have anything to do with killing those women, Kevin. I know that."

"How can you be so sure?"

"Easy. I love you. I understand you. And I fucking live with you."

"Not anymore."

"Really?"

"Pack up your shit and leave the key."

She stared at him like someone she might have known once, then blinked her eyes frozen and didn't seem to see him at all. On her way up the bank, she kicked at a root before crouching so she was level with Bobby. "I'm gonna sit on this for another day or two. Talk it over with Kevin, then call me. Otherwise, we come get you. And if I were you, both of you, I'd think about getting a lawyer." Lisa tucked a card into Bobby's hand and left. She never looked back at Kevin. And she took the box with her.

29

"YEAH."

"Frank. It's Lisa."

"Something pop on the wire?"

"It's not gonna work."

Frank DeMateo moved the phone from one furry ear to the other. He should have been home in bed with his wife. Instead, he was standing in a pitch-black lot behind the Winship Elementary School in Brighton. "Scales has got the gun. Or he knows where it is."

"Maybe he got rid of it."

"And someone found it and just started offing people? I don't believe it. Has he said anything?"

"He's been in his apartment all night. No visitors. No calls."

"Fuck." The district attorney for Suffolk County dropped his head back and stared at a couple of muddy stars, nearly lost in an inkblot sky. He had a bad feeling and wasn't sure if it was about Scales or his colleague. Maybe both.

"What do you want to do?" Her voice ran smooth and still.

"Shut it down."

"You sure?"

"The task force is gonna come in and push everyone around anyway. Let them set up their own fucking wire."

"Where are you?"

"I'll tell you about it tomorrow."

"Am I gonna be off the case?"

"That's up to the task force."

"Which means I'm off."

"Shut down the wire, Lisa. We'll talk tomorrow."

"Good night, Frank."

DeMateo stuffed the phone in his pocket and began to walk. He was half sorry. And that was only if he tried real hard. Lisa Mignot was too smart for his own good. On top of that, she was black. As the only elected Republican in Suffolk County, DeMateo sat in slot number one on the Dems' hit list. And Mignot was their wet dream. If she'd gotten lucky with the wire and broken open the Patterson thing, he'd have been as good as fucked in the next election cycle. Now, however, he had a shot. All he had to do was make a case against Scales, which was why he was out in the damp and the fucking cold, chasing ghosts in Brighton.

The Winship lot was split into two levels with a set of concrete stairs connecting them. DeMateo strolled down the steps, jingling loose change in his pocket like he had all the time in the world. A uniform was waiting on the lower level.

"What's your name?" DeMateo said.

The cop rubbed his hands together and stamped his feet. He had clean, white teeth that flashed in the night when he spoke. "Officer Clavell, sir. Jose Clavell."

"You found the body?"

"Yes, sir. It was rolled up in a tarp."

"Show me."

Clavell chased the path with his flashlight, leading DeMateo to a pickup pulled next to a Dumpster and the wall of the school. Clavell turned his light on the backseat as the D.A. stuck his head in. The tarp was peeled open like an overripe banana, revealing a head of black hair with a pale streak running parallel to the part.

"This is how you found him?"

"Yes, sir."

"What's with the eye patch?"

"EMT said he lost an eye."

"No kidding. Nothing wrapped around his neck?"

"Neck? No sir."

"Cause of death?"

"EMT said it was multiple stab wounds to the chest."

"And the tarp was just like this?"

"It was taped up at both ends with electrical tape. I cut it open. That's how I made the ID."

"But the body's the same? Head back. Mouth open. All that shit's the same?"

"Yes, sir."

DeMateo knew what Clavell was thinking. What was the Suffolk County D.A. doing out here in the middle of the night on a nothing murder? DeMateo had already gone ten rounds with the detectives working the scene. Then, their boss. He had every right to be here, but there was a protocol involved. Fuck protocol.

"Name's Seamus Slattery?"

"Yes, sir. He lives the next street over on Mount Vernon." Clavell pointed vaguely toward an iron fence.

"The pickup is his?"

"Yes, sir."

"Priors?"

"Busted for possession twice. Cocaine and weed. Both times dismissed. Couple drunk and disorderlies. A DUI last year. He was an Irish citizen."

"Erin Go Fucking Bragh. What about a green card?"

"Ten years ago."

DeMateo took the light from Clavell and probed the back-seat. "Tell me what you see there."

"That's his right hand, sir."

"I know that." DeMateo held the light steady on the corpse's palm, flung awkwardly toward the two men as if inviting them inside.

"It's bandaged, sir."

"You got a knife?"

Clavell produced a small pocketknife. DeMateo reached in and cut away the white gauze pad wrapped around the corpse's hand. "What do you see now, Officer?"

"It looks like a puncture wound."

"Maybe two, even?"

"Yes, sir."

DeMateo pushed the light up to the dead man's face. "Looks like he might have gotten bashed in the head as well." He snapped off the light. Thirty yards away, two detectives were huddled by a crime services truck, drinking coffee and chatting with one of the techs.

"The woman who called this in, she saw this guy getting beat up yesterday?"

"Yes, sir. Said she saw it out of her window."

"She say anything about him getting a nail put through his hand?"

"I didn't ask her."

"Why the fuck would you?"

"Sir?"

"The puncture wounds were covered up by the bandage. Besides, if she'd seen something like that, she probably would have mentioned it."

"Yes, sir. I think the detectives are planning to interview her."

"Where does she live?"

Clavell again pointed toward the fence line.

"Show me." DeMateo started to walk across the lot as fat drops of rain began to fall. Clavell fell in step. It was five minutes before anyone realized they were gone.

30

THE SKIES opened just as he ducked inside. Bobby let the door swing softly behind him and started up the darkened staircase that led to his apartment. From somewhere above came the scuff of leather on wood. Bobby took out the nickel-plated nine he had stuck in his belt. It didn't figure that Cakes had moved that quickly, but who else would be paying him a visit at three in the morning? Halfway up the first flight, he heard a second sound, this time a sniff, followed by a wet sigh. A woman's sigh. Bobby thumbed on the safety, slipped the gun inside his coat, and climbed the rest of the way. Her face was cut in half by light filtered from the street. Rain drummed on a skylight overhead, a muffled sound making Bobby feel like they were the only two people in the world.

"Did you get wet?" she said.

"What are you doing here?"

"I need to talk to you."

He opened the door to his apartment and Colleen Carson followed him in. She perched on the edge of a chair, clutching a large black bag in her lap and taking a slow look around. "This is nice."

"Spare me."

They'd never talked much after she got married. Then he'd started dating Bridget, and they'd never talked at all. Bobby cracked a window and felt the wind and rain sucking at his fingers through the gap. He could smell her scent mingled with the storm and thought about fifteen years ago and an Irish bar on Harvard Avenue called Toner's.

Happy hour. Some guy with a nicked-up guitar playing Neil Diamond on a small wooden stage as if his life depended on it, which it probably did. Everyone was stiff as fucking doorknobs, hooked arms and red, sweaty faces, singing and dancing and drinking fifty-cent drafts, doing all the Boston shit everyone thinks is so great, but only up close or from a great distance. Colleen Pearce sat at a table with a handful of beer mugs, two cigarettes boiling in ashtrays, and a girlfriend keeping a close eye on who was where, what, and when. The last time Bobby had seen Colleen she'd been maybe fifteen. Not anymore. Guys came up to the table. Guys left. Finally, her friend went to the ladies' room and Bobby slipped into the empty chair. He asked if she was a Pearce even though he knew damn well she was. Colleen smirked and wondered aloud if it always took him that long to make a move. They talked—easy, fun, stupid talk. Thrilling talk. Young talk. She smoked and he watched her smoke, committing every gesture to memory, stringing them together like pearls. They had a couple more drafts, just enough so it was good. At some point the friend returned and disappeared again. They swayed and sang along with everyone else to Billy Joel's "Piano Man." She covered his hand with hers like they were an old married couple and it was the most natural thing in the world. When they left, the city seemed mellow and scratchy after the smoke and noise of the bar. They got a pizza at Pino's in Cleveland Circle and watched the Green Line rumble past and talked about the stuff they'd been waiting to talk about their whole lives, but never found the exact right person who'd know when to talk and when to listen. It could have gone anywhere from there, but Bobby knew better. He'd already dug his trenches and built his walls, strung long, looping runs of razor wire around his heart. So he dropped her off at Champney around two in the morning and watched her go into the house. She called a couple of times after that, but he ignored them. Two nights before Christmas, he saw her through a window downtown. She was with a college- looking guy, sitting at a table in a restaurant. Colleen was laughing with her chin up and covering the man's hand with hers. Just like an old, married couple. Bobby felt a pull inside that surprised him. A year later, she married Scott Carson. And life moved along.

"You know I wouldn't come unless it was important," she said, something anxious eating at the edges of her eyes.

"What do you want?"

"I'm not exactly sure."

That was a lie. She knew what she wanted. If you weren't making a bet, it was the only reason to pay Bobby a visit. He was the guy everyone grinned at uncomfortably in the street and avoided until that moment when they needed someone to take out the trash cluttering up their lives. It was his thing, why he walked like he did.

"Where's your husband, Coll?"

"He's got guns."

"Where is he?"

"I don't know. Gone. He keeps a shotgun in the house and some sort of machine pistol."

Scott Carson was a smug, arrogant prick who treated Colleen like a piece of townie ass. That was Bobby's take, not that anyone ever asked him. And that wasn't Scott's only problem.

"Tell me about the drugs."

"I don't know anything about that."

Bobby got up and opened the door. "If you're gonna lie to me, there's not much I can do."

"Bobby." She had so little and thought it mattered so much. And she'd use whoever was around to keep it safe. He could blame her, but why bother.

"Tell me what you know, Coll. It goes no further."

"Fine." Her voice had turned quick, defiant, skipping over words like a stone across a shallow, green pond. "I know he's been dealing."

Bobby closed the door and leaned up against it. "How long?"

"I've known for six months."

"Did he tell you where he was getting his product?"

She shook her head. "We needed the money. Fucking bills in Newton, Conor's school. But the guns and the rest of it. Christ, I'm afraid he's gonna come in one night and kill us."

Bobby walked to the window and shut it. Then he pulled up the shade so he could get a better look at her in the patches of light. Her sweater was thin cashmere, and her collarbones stuck out like fish ribs. Bobby noticed swelling along one heavily powdered cheekbone. His eye tracked down to a faint necklace of fingerprint bruises around her throat. He moved closer and touched them with his finger.

"He's got girlfriends, Bobby. Little girls he fucks in a hotel downtown. Last week I sat in the lobby and watched him walk in with one of them. Then I went into the ladies and got sick."

A single, tardy tear slipped from the corner of her eye, trickled down a sticky cheek and into the side of her mouth. "What happened there?" She pointed to the bandage on his hand.

"Nothing. Where's his stash, Coll?"

"Stash?"

"The drugs. Money."

"Scott doesn't let me see that stuff."

Bobby sat down again and leaned forward, hands clasped loosely between his knees. He was in no hurry and they both knew it. She pulled a small cigar box from her bag and pushed it onto the table. The inside was stacked with cash, twenties, fifties, hundreds, sorted into neat bundles, each bundle wrapped in a piece of paper covered with figures and names. Underneath the cash was a Ziploc bag containing twenty or thirty lottery tickets, folded in half and paper clipped. In the crease of each ticket was powdered cocaine—looked like teeners and eights. Bobby took a quick peek at the names on the money wrappers. Then he put the cash and drugs back in the box and closed it.

"There's a little more than four thousand," Colleen said. "I don't know what the drugs are worth."

Bobby tapped his fingers on the table. Outside the wind and the rain took turns banging drunkenly against the side of the building. "Pick up your son tonight. Get all your shit together and get out of the house."

"But . . ."

"No 'buts.' Pick up Conor and leave." He scratched out a name on a piece of paper. "This is a long-term hotel in New Hampshire. Get yourself a room and lie low until you hear from me."

"You just took all my money."

He walked over to his suitcase and returned with a thousand in twenties and hundreds. "This'll keep you for a while."

She grabbed at the money and stuffed it in her bag. "What if he tries to find us?"

"Scott won't be bothering you anymore."

"Really?" There was a crack in her voice, a glimmer underneath of something shiny and hard and mean.

"You should get moving, Coll."

"He'll be at the Royal Hotel this morning. I mean, I think he'll be there. He usually gets a room."

Bobby didn't respond. She stood up to leave, pulling on her coat, suddenly anxious to be as far from whatever she'd set in motion as possible.

"One more thing," he said. "Don't tell your sister about any of this."

"I can tell her I'm leaving for a while . . ."

"No."

"Why not?"

"Cuz she likes to talk. Cuz she doesn't like you. And cuz she can be pretty fucking nasty when she wants to be."

Colleen eased back into her seat. "There's something else we should probably talk about."

The sudden shift should have bothered him. But it was Colleen, and he'd always been intrigued most by whatever came next.

"What is it?"

Her eyes moved to her bag. Thunder grumbled and a long fork of lightning lit up her face. Bobby saw Sal Riga there as well as the other dead man from the produce market, the one with dark eyebrows raised in double question marks. Then Colleen Carson reached into her bag and pulled out a gun.

31

LISA BLINKED her eyes open. The clock sunk into the dashboard read 6:00 A.M. She'd planned on getting a hotel room but wound up parked in front of their apartment, wrapped in the bigness of the storm as it rolled in off the ocean, staring up at the sleeping windows until she herself dropped off. More rain blew up Pinckney Street, pinging off the roof of the car and cascading across her windshield. A man stood in the doorway of a hat shop, smoking a cigarette and staring at the cold water as it collected in the gutters and washed back down the hill. Blurry lights came on in a café. A woman stuck her head out and pulled in a stack of soggy newspapers left by the front door. Lisa was her first customer, sitting in the front window with hot coffee as the rain tapered to a mist, then stopped altogether. The sun made a tentative appearance just as Kevin stepped out of their building—now his. He kept his eyes glued to the pavement and headed straight for his car, bumping down the hill with a look neither left nor right. Lisa waited ten minutes, then crossed over and walked up four flights. She could have put off things for a day or two, but something told her this needed to be done quickly. She let herself into the apartment and looked around. A still life of her time with Kevin looked back. On the mantel stood a reproduction of a New England whaling schooner etched in scrimshaw on a pale piece of bone. A cheap watercolor they'd bought in P-Town hung off the wall. Opposite it were framed pictures of them on the ferry to Nantucket and another watercolor, this one marginally better, of the Chatham lighthouse. She walked into the kitchen. Stuck to the fridge were ticket stubs from a Pats game and a single photo from last Christmas Eve. The snow had started falling in earnest around five. They'd filled a thermos with cocoa and walked through the city, sidewalks empty, bare black branches patterned against the low New England sky. As night fell, fresh light blazed from the windows of the Brahmin brownstones, illuminating stone steps and carved archways dressed in thin coats of white. They got a drink at the bar in the Ritz and listened to the carolers in the cold outside Arlington Street Church. Their night ended on a bench in the Public Garden. The snow had thickened, falling in sheets across the moonlight. An old woman took the photo, smiling at them as they smiled back and she remembered something lovely from her past. Lisa plucked the snapshot off the fridge and stuffed it in her pocket. She'd allow herself one.

In the bedroom, on the top shelf of the closet, were her suitcases. She pulled down the two rollers and filled them with clothes. Fifteen minutes later, she had her Civic loaded with everything she owned. And then it was time to leave. She leaned against the car and took a last look up and down the block. People were going about their business, doing what they did yesterday, would do tomorrow and the day after. She was the interloper, always had been, her life an exercise in make-believe, right down to the apartment in Beacon Hill and lily-white boyfriend. That was unfair to her, to Kevin, to their time together, but she felt it all the same and knew she always would. It was her greatest strength and biggest weakness—a solitude she wore like a second skin. And the unblinking mind that went with it. Lisa pulled out her car keys and bent to unlock the door. A woman wearing Wayfarer sunglasses brushed past, knocking her into the side of the Civic. Lisa whipped around, swinging a fierce elbow but missing as the woman walked off. Lisa took a deep breath and let herself settle. Then she was back in the car, possessions packed tightly around her, rolling out of Beacon Hill, rolling with regret, rolling with anger, but rolling just the same. A cell phone buzzed from somewhere deep inside her bag. It was Frank DeMateo. He wanted her to meet him at the morgue. Fuck him, too.

———

Bridget Pearce slipped the Wayfarers onto her forehead and watched the Civic until it took the corner at the bottom of the hill. Then she walked slowly up the block, past Kevin's building, to her rental. Bridget wasn't sure what she'd hoped to find at her brother's place, but the girlfriend was nothing if not interesting. Maybe even useful. Bridget cruised back down Joy Street, flipping off a couple of tourists who'd wandered off the sidewalk to take a picture. Then she turned onto Cambridge and disappeared into the choke of traffic headed downtown.

32

SCOTT CARSON climbed the back stairs of the shit bag Royal Hotel one lousy fucking step at a time. Nick had given him a room on the fourth floor looking out over an alley. Prick was actually pleasant, smiling and calling him Mr. C. as he handed over the keys, telling him he could have the room for the rest of the day even though Scott had only paid for the morning. Ass wipe. Scott stopped once on the climb up, sitting in a stairwell and smoking a cigarette as the blood thundered in his ears and a cockroach the size of small beagle crawled past him on the wall. He pushed into his room at a few minutes before seven, immediately cracking open both windows in a futile effort to remove the stink of whoever had been in there before. In the bathroom he wiped the sweat off his face and touched at the puffiness in his cheeks and eyelids. He was overdue for a vacation. Maybe Vegas. Suck up some sun, pool time, a little gambling. Fuck knows he deserved it. But first, there was the matter of his wife. He'd figured it was gonna be difficult to get rid of her. Then he got the call. And just like that Colleen wasn't a problem anymore. It bothered him if he thought about it too much so Scott decided not to. He found a water glass on a shelf over the toilet and pulled a flat bottle of scotch from a paper bag. The girl he'd hired for the morning was listed as eighteen, but the guy at the service assured him she was fourteen. Tight. That was what the guy had said. And insatiable. Nice word, *insatiable*. Scott poured himself some whiskey and bolted down a handful of Vicodin. Then he took a blue pill. Followed by a second. What the fuck, why risk it when you can be thick as a barn post all morning? There was a small knock on the door. Scott drained what was left in the glass and checked himself again in the mirror, pushing at the loose folds of skin under his chin and carefully rearranging random strands of hair on his head. Another knock. Scott felt himself getting hard even as he walked across the room and gave himself a quick adjustment so she wouldn't see the boner first thing.

"You're early . . ." His mouth opened and closed once, dick shriveling, balls sucking up into his stomach. His guest took a step into the room and closed the door. Scott's face crumbled into soft pieces. "What are you doing here?"

The first shot felt like a bee sting. Scott looked down at the hole in his shirt and thought it should hurt more than it did. He coughed and saw the hole bubble with a froth of blood. Another pop and a second hole joined the first. Scott had somehow found his way to the floor, looking up at stains on the ceiling and wondering if they were some sort of Olympic-sized cum shots. He could hear his heart now, rasping in his chest. There was something liquid between his lips. He wiped them and his sleeve came away red. The toe of a shoe brushed his nose as someone stepped over his body. Rough hands on his clothes and in his pockets. He turned his head and watched a dark figure climb out of the window and onto a fire escape that ran down the side of the building. Then Scott was alone. He tried to yell but only managed the bones of a dead man's whisper. Nick was probably outside in the hall, listening at the door and having a good laugh. Let him laugh, the fucking loser. Scott coughed again, the blood like thick syrup in his throat, filling his lungs, drowning, choking. Word around Brighton had always been not to fuck with the Pearce girls. Scott smiled a sticky grin. He'd never paid the talk any mind. Lesson fucking learned. He coughed a final time, blowing what was left of his life in bright blood all over himself. It was barely seven when he turned his head toward the morning sun and died.

33

BOBBY ROLLED into the abandoned lot at exactly 7:40, listening to the engine tick in the morning quiet before getting out. He worked quickly and calmly, stripping the grimy plates off his Jeep with a flat-head screwdriver and tossing them into the backseat of a blue Toyota. The cars were parked side by side next to a field ugly with hunks of grass and rock. Bobby's suitcase followed the plates, along with a small black gym bag. The Toyota turned over on the first try, its engine settling into a soft, efficient hum. Bobby pulled out of the lot and drove a mile and a half, parking on a side street a block from Saint Andrew's. He walked back to the church with his head down and the gun in his pocket. Best he could tell, no one had followed him. And no one had seen him.

He sat in the last pew for eight A.M. mass and didn't take Communion. Afterward, he waited for the church to empty before walking over to the confessional. The green light was lit, indicating a priest was inside waiting for his next sinner. Bobby knelt in the swirling dust and darkness. The wooden partition slid across with an oiled rasp. Seams of light bled through the wire mesh, stitching a ragged pattern across his face. Bobby squinted and struggled to see his confessor but could only make out a black shape cloaked in some sort of sacramental glow. He blessed himself, mumbled some words, and listened to some mumbled back. A pause ensued—a holy space waiting to be filled with the litany of his sins.

"I haven't come to confess."

A dry rustle as Father Lenihan shifted in his vestments. "I'm sorry?"

Bobby shoved the picture from Paragon Park through the hole in the screen. "Saint Regis Home in Cambridge. Nineteen seventy-two."

The rustling stopped. A pair of veined hands held the photo under a wavering circle of light. "Can I ask your name?"

"You wouldn't know it, but I come to mass here almost every day."

"I'm sure I'd know your face."

Bobby felt himself shrink into the back of the confessional box as shame did its work, hollowing from the inside out. He licked his lips and rallied.

"I was never abused. At least not by any priest. But I saw stuff. And I saw you."

"Son, let's go into the sacristy and talk . . ."

"I always got the feeling you wanted to help, wanted to stop it. But you were young and couldn't protect shit."

The silhouette dipped, forehead pressing against the metal facing of the screen, breath whistling softly between his teeth.

"I didn't come here to lecture you, Father. Not gonna piss and moan about my life, either."

"We can get you help. I can make sure . . ."

"Don't need it. Don't want it." Somewhere at the back of the church, a door opened and slammed shut. Then, a bell began to toll. Bobby took out a small volume and read.

At the center of our being is a point of nothingness which
is untouched by sin and by illusion, a point of pure truth,
a point or spark which belongs entirely to God, which
is never at our disposal, from which God disposes of our
lives . . .

"Thomas Merton."
"Very good, Father."
The priest's hand snaked through the hole, raking Bobby's arm and clamping on to his wrist. His voice, when he spoke, was strained to a whisper. "You must understand I did what I could."
Bobby's fingers touched the grip of the gun in his pocket. "I'm sure you did. Thing is, Father, sometimes even good men just need to die."

———

The heater in his car sounded like a five-pack-a-day smoker, wheezing and hacking, lukewarm air coughing out of the car's floor vents in fits and starts. Kevin hit some buttons and pounded on the dashboard, hoping to intimidate the thing into kicking on. Heaters just didn't work that way. He punched the off switch and sat in silence, staring at the heavy red door of Saint Andrew's Church. Bobby hadn't offered two words on the ride back from the Resie. As he got out of the car, he said he'd be at eight A.M. mass. Kevin had briefly considered talking things out right there, but figured it'd keep. Besides, he'd had Lisa filling his head. Part of him thought she'd be waiting at the apartment when he got back from the Resie, and fought the urge to call when she wasn't. The rest of him laughed at how willingly he'd sold his soul for a handful of trinkets. He pulled out one of her old winter hats he'd found in the backseat and held it to his nose, breathing in her scent still clinging to the knitted wool. He remembered the first time he'd kissed her. He couldn't believe it was really happening, a woman like that, lips running across his like a sizzle, turning his knees to water and his dreams into flesh and blood, thrilling and scaring the hell out of him all at the same time. People like him, people who'd never really had it, didn't understand love, wound up giving it too much weight, seeing it, touching it, imagining it everywhere. She'd understood that from the start. And so she'd played him for a fool. And he'd lapped it up with a fucking spoon. Sad thing was, given the chance, he'd do it all over again. Kevin threw her hat in the glove compartment and slammed the fucking thing shut.

Folks had begun to trickle out of mass in ones and twos, mostly old people, mostly women. He considered walking inside, but something malignant blinked in his belly and he stayed where he was, stretching his fingers and rubbing the early morning cold out of his knuckles. He wondered where Bobby was and whether he'd show up at all. And if he didn't, where did that leave things? Kevin turned on his cell and punched in the number for his boss.

"Are you our writer-in-residence now?"

"Hey, Jimmy."

"Hang on." Jimmy Edwards shuffled the phone from one ear to the other. Kevin figured he was getting up to close the door to his office.

"We could use you in the newsroom, Kev."

"I might be onto something."

"Yeah?"

"The cop murder."

"Patterson?" Jimmy's voice tightened and Kevin knew he had him hooked.

"Mo and I have been working it."

"Why's this the first I'm hearing about it?"

"My fault. I told Mo to keep it quiet."

"So talk to me."

"Not yet."

"Fuck you, not yet. The cops won't give us shit. The governor's sniffing around." A pause. "Is your girlfriend handling it?"

"Let me talk to Mo."

Jimmy took that as a yes. "How long you gonna need?"

"Mo."

"Tomorrow. Your ass, my office. By the way, you didn't hear it from me, but Stanley's got a job offer."

"In town?"

"*Chicago Tribune.* Heard it was for good money, too."

"No shit."

"Hang on. I'll get her."

His boss was gone before Kevin could ask another question. Then Mo came on the line.

"What did you do to him?" she said.

"Jimmy? Nothing."

"He's antsy about Patterson, right?"

"I told him we were working it together. He's fine."

"Yeah?"

"Sure. You get anything more on McNabb?"

"Not much. Her murder wasn't exactly a high priority. I did get a look at the rest of the autopsy report."

"And?"

"The knife was similar to the attacks on Sandra Patterson and Tallent."

"How close?"

"I'm not a fucking M.E., Kevin. The measurements on the wound looked to be about the same. Blade was a half-inch wide. Four to six inches in length. Probably one of a million sold in Boston every year."

"A million?"

"I'm just saying, it's a common size knife."

"But you think McNabb's connected?"

"I thought that from the beginning."

"Me, too."

"So what's next?"

"I need another day. Then I give you everything."

"They really want me to file something."

"One more day." Kevin paused. The red door of Saint Andrew's Church swung open and a couple of blue-haired old ladies tottered out, gesticulating madly as they negotiated the church's front steps. From somewhere above, a bell hammered out nine strokes and fell silent.

"Where are you?" Mo said.

"Never mind. Jimmy told me you're looking at a job in Chicago."

"I told him that in confidence."

"So you gonna take it?"

"Maybe. The *Chicago Tribune*'s starting a new I-unit. Money's good. People seem nice. Who knows, right?"

She was leaving. He heard it in her voice and felt it in the way his stomach dropped.

"I'm happy for you, Mo."

"Don't be too happy. I'm not gone yet. Have you checked your messages?"

"I had my cell turned off."

"Smart, Kevin. I left you a message about an hour ago. They found another body in Brighton last night. Guy named Seamus Slattery."

"Never heard of him."

"Yeah, well, he was stabbed twice in the chest. No ligature. At least nothing I know about."

"Can you get a look at the file?"

"I don't think so. My guy tells me your girlfriend's flagged it."

"No kidding."

"So this is news to you?"

"News to me."

Saint Andrew's red door swung open again and Bobby Scales walked out.

"Sorry, Mo, I gotta go."

"Where are you?"

"Another day. Then we sit down and talk."

"How good is this, Kevin?"

"Good."

"Political?"

"What isn't?

"Dirty?"

"As hell." He paused. "A day, Mo. Day and a half, tops. Then it's me and you. We get some beers, we talk about Patterson. And all the rest."

She started to speak, but Kevin cut the line. Bobby climbed in without a word. He was wearing a leather bomber jacket that was cracking at the seams and worn at the elbows.

"Where you been?" Kevin said.

"Mass, then confession."

"Haven't been to confession in years."

Bobby shrugged. "It's not for everyone."

———

They chugged up Washington Street and crossed over into Newton. The promised land. When they were kids, Kevin and his buddies would cruise the neighborhood on bikes looking for dinner. They'd find a backyard with an unattended grill and swoop in with pocketknives, spearing as many fat steaks as they could before riding into the wind. They'd eat somewhere in the dark, licking the juice off their fingers when they were done, thrilled they'd gotten a free meal from the "rich Newton fucks." That was then—when they were kids with nothing to lose, a whole world to fuck with, and all that mattered was "right now." Kevin pressed down on the accelerator, feeling the car surge and tires sing as he swung a left onto a long, rambling stretch of road. Bobby sat beside him like a tombstone on a hill, staring blankly out the window. A park floated past, soft fields slumbering under a melting blanket of spring frost. An older man, professorial type with glasses and a green wax jacket, walked out of the park with a golden on a leash. The dog walker waved at the car. Everyone in Newton waved. It was like a village law or something. They went for another mile or so, past sweeping driveways and deep carpets of lawn rolling up to the front steps of one massive manse after another. Bobby finally stirred to life, directing Kevin to circle back into the city. Like everything else, even Newton got tedious after a while.

"I figure we should talk to a lawyer," Kevin said as they coasted to a stop at a red light.

"You mean you want to take your girlfriend's advice?"

"She's moving out."

"She was doing her job, Kev." Bobby was wearing a smaller bandage on his left hand and picked at the tape wound across his knuckles. Kevin noticed red marks streaked across his wrist.

"What's that?"

"What's what?"

"Looks like you got clawed or something."

Bobby examined the marks for a moment, then dismissed them with a shrug. The light changed and Kevin eased through the intersection.

"I tell you I saw Father Lenihan the other day?"

"Small world."

"You know the *Globe*'s doing all those stories on the church and stuff?"

"I read 'em, yeah."

"I know the reporters working that. Checked all the lists they got for pervert priests. Lenihan's not on any of them."

"Why you telling me?"

"You go to church there. Thought maybe you'd like to know."

They crossed back out of Newton and banged through a run of axle-scraping potholes.

"When you gonna ask about the Resie?" Bobby said after the road had smoothed out.

"I'm not."

"Good."

"Whatever you had buried there . . ."

"You know what it is."

"Whatever it is, you should tell the lawyer."

"How well you know lawyers?"

"Apparently not as well as I thought."

Bobby chuckled and gestured for Kevin to turn onto Tremont Street. They bumped along some old streetcar tracks, a picket line of two-families and three-deckers, all crooked and humpbacked, rough nails and wood, running up and down the side streets. Bobby gestured again, the smallest of motions with his good hand. Kevin rolled into an empty lot and stopped. They each looked up at what everyone in Brighton called "the Steps."

34

THEY NUMBERED eighty-nine in all, smooth stone slabs marching through a thicket of terraced woods to the back door of Saint Andrew's Church. The steps were put in for all the God-fearing folks who lived in the low-lying neighborhoods up and down Tremont Street. For six decades they'd climbed their way to absolution on Sunday morning and hustled back down after mass for another fun-filled week of cursing, fighting, and all-purpose sinning. Bobby led the way up, never explaining why they'd stopped or where they were headed. About halfway to the top, he gestured to a break in the trees and walked into a clearing populated by the crumbling remains of what had once been a small building. Bobby kicked at a cluster of beer cans and settled on the damp turf, his back against the building's only remaining wall. Kevin stopped ten feet away.

"Not gonna find any lawyers here, Bobby."

"Know who used to live here?"

Kevin shook his head.

"All the Irish nuns. They'd walk up the steps every day to wait hand and foot on the priests. Sit down. You're making me nervous."

"The gun's making me nervous."

Bobby zipped open his jacket and pulled out a thirty-eight-caliber revolver. Its grip was wrapped in gray tape. "Recognize it?" He laid the gun on the ground by his boot. Kevin squatted on his heels. The trees were still heavy with rain. They crowded close, shutting off the rest of the world, creating a leafy amphitheater for just the two of them.

"So you did pull it out of the hole."

"It's your grandmother's. She kept it in a strongbox along with her cash."

"She never told me."

"Why would she? I went up there the morning after she died. Figured the cops or someone would have grabbed it, but there it was. Stuck up on a shelf in the china cabinet."

"And you took it?"

"I used it to kill the prick that butchered her." Bobby picked up the weapon and offered it, grip first, then put it back down. "Your girlfriend squeezed you last night with the file on Jordan."

"And you think you're vulnerable?"

"You tell me."

A breeze swept across the hill, shaking rain from the tops of the trees. Kevin felt Bobby studying him in the drifting light.

"I've always been good with killing, Kev. If anyone knows that, it's you."

"You saying you killed those women?"

"If it's me or them, it's gonna be them. You should have seen that. You should have seen that first fucking thing."

Bobby climbed to his feet, gliding across the clearing to sneak a look down the steps. He held the gun in his right hand, down low by his side. They were maybe fifteen feet apart when he turned and pointed. A simple, clean gesture. Kevin put up his hands as if they could stop a thirty-eight-caliber slug from doing what God and man intended. Bobby touched a silent finger to his lips. He'd use the same gun he used to kill the man who'd murdered Kevin's grandmother. And no one would hear a thing. By nightfall Kevin would be in the ground, buried in the soggy woods behind the nuns' house, just down the hill from where he'd taken his First Communion. All this and more raced through his brain at warp speed as Kevin mimicked Bobby, slipping his own finger to his lips and not making a sound. Such a willing victim in the end. Maybe he thought he'd get points for that. Bobby gestured for Kevin to go to his knees and zeroed the gun on his forehead. The two men stayed that way, grim, gray statues among the trees. Then Bobby lifted his chin, raising the gun a fraction so it was aimed just off Kevin's shoulder. From his left, Kevin heard the chatter of leaves. A raccoon waddled out of the crackling brush and stared down the slope at both of them. He had curved, black claws and razored teeth drawn up in a vicious smile. A second raccoon peeked his head out from under a bush and hissed. Then the pair slithered back into the scrub, disappearing in a whip of black-and-white fur.

"Fucking hey." Bobby lowered the gun. The killing moment, if that's what it was, had passed. "You all right?"

"Just a little jumpy."

Bobby reached down and helped Kevin to his feet, gripping his triceps and pulling him within a whisper. "You really think I'd hurt you?"

Kevin shook himself free, hot fear draining out of his belly and down into the black earth. Bobby slipped the thirty-eight back under his jacket. "I'm gonna need you to stay here and chill for a bit."

"Where you going?"

"Not sure. Maybe me and Finn will head down to Florida like he's been yapping about all these years."

"You didn't kill those women."

"You saw the piece."

"Let's go in and talk to them. Try to cut a deal."

Bobby bared his teeth in a smile their raccoon friends would have been proud of. "How old are you now?"

"Forty-two."

"And how many holes you dug?"

Kevin didn't respond.

"Killing someone changes you, bro."

"I was there, too."

"Being there isn't pulling the trigger." Bobby produced a small object from his pocket. "You left this behind the day you went to New York. Never thought I'd be able to get it back to you."

Mother of pearl. Smooth and hard and pale. Kevin took his grandmother's pendant in his hands as the world dropped away. He turned the pendant over, feeling its curve and shape. The last time he'd held it, it had been decorated in blood.

"Everything changed when she died," Bobby said.

"I divide my life into before and after. Even now."

"Then don't make it all for nothing. You really wanna help, buy me a day with your girlfriend. Then tell 'em what you know. I did Curtis Jordan. You tried to stop me."

Another gust of wind kicked up the hill, calling an end to their meeting. Bobby ran silently to the top of the steps and vanished without looking back. Kevin sat in the grass, rubbing the pendant under his thumb, recalling the drift of smoke from her cigarettes and the soft whistle of the kettle in the morning as it came to a boil, wondering what it might have been like if she'd lived and knowing he'd never, ever fucking heal. That was the price he paid for the time he'd had with his grandmother, the bullet wound in his hip and limp he'd carry with him until the end of his days. Gladly. He took his time walking back down the steps, scraping his heels against the chipped stone as he went. He'd just gotten behind the wheel when two squad cars pulled into the lot, flashers rolling. One cop got out with his service revolver drawn. A second approached and asked Kevin to step out of the car.

35

SEAMUS SLATTERY gazed at the ceiling like a one-eyed jack while a morgue attendant ran baseball stitches across his chest. The air was alive with the muddy scent of viscera, mingled with the acidic smell of bile and piss. The afterbirth of an autopsy. Ten feet away, Frank DeMateo took a bite of a D'Angelo's steak-and-cheese sub. Half of it went in his mouth, the rest dripped onto white paper wrappings laid out on the table. "Fuckin' delicious. Want a bite?"

Lisa shook her head. "There's this thing called cholesterol, Frank. Have you heard of it?"

"You sound like my wife." DeMateo opened a can of Diet Dr Pepper and took a sip. "So?"

"Why didn't you tell me about Slattery when we talked last night?"

"I wasn't sure it was part of all this."

"And now you're sure?"

"You saw the wound path." When Lisa didn't respond, the Suffolk County D.A. put down his sandwich and wiped his fingers with a napkin. "You want me to get the M.E. back in here?"

She shook her head. He raised his arms like he'd done all he could.

"So it's Scales?" she said.

DeMateo started counting off reasons on his fingers. "He knew Patterson. He keeps newspaper clippings on Rosie Tallent under his fucking bed. We're pretty sure he put a couple of nails through this mick's hand the day before he was found dead. He runs a book that generates a shitload of cash. And someone with a shitload of cash is moving dope through Brighton. A shitload of it. And, oh yeah, he popped Curtis Jordan."

"Maybe he's killing them for fun."

"I'm sure he's having a hell of a time. Doesn't matter a damn bit to me. Let's take a walk."

DeMateo dropped the leavings of his lunch in the trash and led the way across the hall to a long, low room with a stone floor and cinder-block walls. Another attendant, this one a woman, was waiting.

"Where is he?" DeMateo said.

The room was dominated by two refrigerated boxes, each featuring three rows of silver doors with black handles. The attendant walked down to one of the drawers and slid it open. DeMateo and Lisa took a look at the corpse lying loose on a tray with two holes in his chest.

"What's this?" Lisa said.

"John Doe. Found him in a room at the Royal Hotel. No wallet, rings, watch, money."

"What name did he register under?"

"That's not clear. The manager at the Royal says he came in alone, paid cash, and took the room for the morning. Blah, blah, fucking blah. It's the Royal. You know the drill."

"So you're thinking he's a john?"

"Course he's a john."

Lisa touched one of the bullet holes with a gloved finger. "Wounds are less than an inch apart. Pretty good shooting for a hooker."

"So maybe it was her pimp."

"Pretty good shooting for a pimp."

DeMateo nodded at the attendant, who rolled the drawer shut. "Boston homicide says they'll have an ID within twenty-four hours. Come on."

They walked back across the hall to the autopsy room. The attendant there was finished with Slattery's chest and had moved on to sewing up the skull, lips, and one formerly working eye. He whistled softly to himself as he stitched.

"Let me guess," Lisa said. "You want me to handle the John Doe?"

"I need someone who can carry the ball."

"While you stay on Patterson?"

"Patterson's going to the task force. Tomorrow they'll pull warrants for Scales's apartment. I wouldn't be surprised if there's an arrest by the end of the day."

"What about Kevin?"

"All due respect, the relationship's finished. It was finished once you planted the wire."

"All due respect, my personal life's none of your goddamn business."

DeMateo held up his hands. "Fine. If he pulled the trigger on Jordan . . ."

"He didn't."

"Then he should be good."

"You won't use him to pressure Scales?"

"Didn't say that. Listen, I'm not in a position to be cutting deals. For you or anyone else." Her boss rolled his wrist and checked his watch. "I've got an appointment. Take another day. Then everything gets turned over to the task force."

"And I'm out?"

"This isn't the right case for you, Lisa. Never was. Besides, you've got the John Doe to keep you busy. And after him, plenty more."

She couldn't help but notice the grin stuck in his voice and stared at a sharp point between his shoulder blades as he walked away. The attendant finished up his needlework on Slattery and followed DeMateo out. Then it was just Lisa, face pressed to the glass, watching as her dreams were slowly strangled. She was about to leave when the attendant poked his head back in. "You've got someone here to see you."

Lisa didn't respond. The attendant took a tentative step into the room.

"Ma'am?"

"Yes."

"You've got someone here to see you."

"I heard you the first time. No one knows I'm here."

"She says she called your office and they told her where you were."

"What's her name?"

The attendant told her. Lisa felt her head snap up.

"And she's here now?"

"Yes, ma'am."

"All right. Put her next door. I'm sorry, what's your name?"

"Steven, ma'am. Steven Sutcliffe."

Lisa pulled out a legal pad and scribbled a few, furious lines. "Steven, do me a favor. Get me everything your office has on these cases. Physical records, electronic. Every scrap of information you guys have generated. Plus whatever you have on Slattery."

"That might be a lot of paper. Do you want it sent to your office?"

"Actually, I'd like to take a look at all of it right here. Today. Can we do that?"

"I'll set up a room. How about Mr. DeMateo?"

"It'll just be me, thanks."

The attendant left. Lisa gathered up her files and gave it five long minutes. Then she walked down the hall and into a small consulting room.

"We've never met, but I feel like I know you."

"Me, too." Bridget Pearce smiled and offered her hand.

36

DENNIS "LOLLIPOPS" Lombardo drove big cars—what his boss liked to call "breathers." For this job it was a Delta 88 finished in two tones of brown. Wide seats, plenty of leg room, and a deep, quiet trunk. He took a sip of his coffee and turned up the radio. Duke Ellington's "Take the A Train" popped and swelled until it filled the car. Lollipops liked to listen to old stuff, '40s and '50s swing and jazz. Scratchy as hell, but so was he. Besides, who was there to tell him otherwise? A squad car pulled up to the intersection, pausing at a red light before blowing through it and taking off down the block. Fuckers. Lollipops turned over the engine, feeling the Rocket V8 rumble through the steel frame and up into the soles of his shoes. He cruised the block and parked in a new spot with a different view of the same apartment. He'd been sitting in front of Bobby Scales's building since five A.M. It was now almost four in the afternoon. They'd told him Scales was a creature of habit. In bed early, up early. Real routine guy. But no one had been in or out of the place all day. Which was why Lollipops was pretty sure Scales had already skipped. Which meant he was gonna be someone else's problem. Lollipops didn't give a damn. He'd get paid. Not as much as if he were bringing back a body, but he'd get paid. It was the phone call that sucked. People skills his wife called it. She told him he needed to develop some. As usual, she was right.

Lollipops took another sip of coffee and thought about the last time he'd been to Boston. The job was an old man who lived alone in an apartment in the South End. Lollipops waited in an alley at night, across the street in the blowing snow and cold. The front porch was a sheet of ice so he knew the old man would take his time getting across. Lollipops crept from the alley as he pulled out his keys, hit the first step as he turned the lock, and pushed in as the door opened. He tied the old man to a kitchen chair. Lollipops never listened to any of the stupid talk—*you got the wrong guy, this is all a mistake, I can make it worth your while*—but this guy didn't do any of that. He just sat there, hands pegged behind his back, mouthing small, chopped-up words without ever making a sound. Lollipops found a Bible in a drawer and read aloud from John's prologue.

"In the beginning was the Word, and the Word was with God, and the Word was God . . ."

When he'd finished, he untied the man's hands and let him write a letter to his daughter. He wanted to go quick and begged for a bullet in the head. Lollipops knew he couldn't do that. Walls like paper, too much noise. He asked the old-timer a couple of questions about the daughter. The old man was explaining how if she stood just right and put a hand on her hip she could have been her mother when Lollipops came up from behind and strangled him with a dog leash. Not great, but under the circumstances, not bad either. The Duke had been replaced by Glenn Miller's "In the Mood." Lollipops closed his eyes and tapped his fingers against the wide, wooden steering wheel, losing himself in the shimmy and sway of the music. He dreamed of lying in bed with his wife and daughter when she was young. Lollipops would drape his arm across his little girl, allowing his fingers to brush his wife's cheek and hair as she slept. He'd settle his feet against the warmth of their dog at the foot of the bed, feeling the pup's ribs rise and fall, allowing himself to melt into the interconnectedness of life all around him. The snap of his cell phone jarred him awake. That was the thing about Providence. Either way, the call was gonna get made. Lollipops waited for the fourth ring before picking up.

"I think he's skipped."

He held the phone away from his ear while a string of invectives poured out like raw sewage from the other end of the line. People skills, my ass. Sometimes people just needed to get shot in the head, no one more than the jag-offs he worked for. Across the street, a skin-and-bones black kid wearing a Yankees hat scraped out of an alley and stared up at the windows of Scales's apartment. Lollipops felt a tiny pump of adrenaline. He pulled the slender twenty-two from under the front seat and laid it against his thigh. The asshole at the other end of the line finally paused for a breath.

"I might have something. Lemme call you back."

Lollipops flipped his phone shut. The kid crossed the street, pausing at the entrance to Scales's building. Lollipops cracked the door and put a foot on the pavement, gun in his right hand, hand stuffed in his pocket. The kid moved away from the entrance, drifting down the block like a ripple of wood smoke before slipping around a corner. Lollipops buttoned his coat and walked over to the building. The door was ajar. He shouldered his way in and was halfway up the stairs when he heard the squeak of canvas and leather. The kid with the Yankees hat stood just inside the door. He was eating Underwood deviled ham from a can with his fingers.

"I like to put it between a couple pieces of bread." Lollipops eased down a step as he spoke. The kid dropped the tin can and pulled out a heavy black gun. Lollipops could see the sun on the right side of the kid's face and a fever circling in the yellow of his eyes. The kid didn't understand the weight of taking a human life. But he'd killed before, and he liked it.

"You know how to use that thing?" Lollipops said.

"You about to find out, nigga." The kid held the gun stiff in his hand. Lollipops watched the skinny finger on the trigger.

"Maybe you're looking for the guy who lives here? If so, we can help each other."

The kid grinned like that was the funniest thing he'd heard in a while. At that moment, Lollipops knew the kid was gonna shoot him, right in the chest. Just for the fuck of it. Then God sent a breeze. Lollipops felt it in his face and tasted it on his tongue. At the same time, the sun dropped behind some clouds, and the old wooden door cracked on its hinges. It was this last turn of the wheel that caused the kid to flinch, dipping his gaze for an eternal second to see who might be behind him. Lollipops pulled the twenty-two and shot the kid in one motion, kicking the door closed with his foot and catching the kid before he hit the ground. His eyes were like mirrored glass, smart-ass smile still stuck on his face.

"Fuck." Lollipops dragged the kid under the stairs and laid him down gently. Then he went back outside for the roll of plastic he kept in the trunk.

37

TWENTY-EIGHT YEARS had come and gone since Bridget first watched Peggy Quinlan suck a dick. These days Peggy taught CCD on Sundays, railing at any teenager dumb enough to listen about the virtues of abstinence and the perils that befall those who indulge. But there she was in the fall of '74, tucked underneath a canopy of trees in the heart of Indian Rock, taking Eddie Evans right down to the root. Bridget was all of eleven when she lay on the tar paper roof of 8 Champney and watched, then wrote about Peggy. Now, she sat in the same spot and stared at the page of printed words, a collection of lumpy letters that looked more like finger painting, all of it smudged and a little off center. Bridget smiled at the memory of Eddie's cum shot, a leonine spurt of white that caught both her and Peggy by surprise. Bridget recalled nearly rolling off the edge of the roof and hearing a titter of laughter below as Peggy fell backward into a pillow of dead leaves and put her hand over her mouth, amazed at what it had wrought. Bridget flipped forward in her notebook. There were more pages devoted to Peggy. Not all with Eddie. In fact, he barely lasted six months before being replaced by a backup cornerback on the high school football team. Then, a baseball pitcher. A drummer. And, finally, the accounting major turned actuary who went to Bentley. Peggy had paid for Bridget's silence—twenty bucks a week, right up until the day she married the actuary. Folks in Brighton wondered why fourteen-year-old Bridget Pearce stood up in Peggy's wedding. But Bridget wanted to wear a fancy dress and get her picture taken in the worst way. And Peggy thought that was a fine idea.

Bridget closed the notebook and returned it to its place in the strongbox her grandmother had once kept on a shelf in a china cabinet. She thought about her conversation with Kevin's girlfriend. The inviting smile, the way she touched the back of Bridget's hand, the lilt of her voice that bubbled and ran like a string of perfectly struck notes on a piano. Even in the fucking morgue. Bridget was quite sure her brother never stood a chance.

There was a stirring below. Bridget dropped flat, the tar paper again cool and sticky at the same time on her face. A branch broke with a snap that sounded like a gunshot. She raised her head until the bottom of her chin was level with the parapet wall. Bobby Scales poked his head out from behind an outcropping of granite. A warm shiver coursed through her, curling her spine and loosening her loins. Bridget pulled out a fresh notebook and watched. A half hour later, Bobby left. Bridget scribbled away for another five minutes and reread what she'd written before flipping the notebook shut. Then she found a spot against the building, in the shade of what was left of the chimney, and slipped a hand down her jeans, feeling the stickiness there. It took all of ten minutes. When she was done, she picked up the notebook and put it back with the others—an even dozen, spanning more than a quarter century. She stared at her tomes lined up in a neat row, then sealed up the strongbox behind some loose bricks. It was stupid to leave them all up here, but old habits die hard. And sometimes not at all. She climbed down off the roof and circled the block.

———

The air was heavy with the smell of earth. Huge trees, knuckled trunks of wood topped by nodding heads of green, looked down on her as she'd so often looked down on them. And she could feel their judgment. Anxious to get out from under, Bridget climbed up on a shelf of rippled limestone and got her bearings. She had a pretty good idea why Bobby had been sniffing around Indian Rock but wanted to see for herself. Up ahead was a clearing, dominated by a large boulder. It sharpened to a narrow point, with a fissure that ran up its face and formed a cleft at the very top. This was the spot where she'd seen him. Bridget was sure of it. She climbed down and began to thread her way forward. All around her, wet light licked at the new leaves. Bridget quickened her pace. She never saw the root, erupting out of the ground like a web of gnarled, gray fingers, grabbing at her ankle and dragging her down into the mire.

"Fuck." Bridget rolled onto her back and sat up. He was squatting on the very top of the rock, balanced like some ancient totem, legs pulled up under his chin, arms wrapped around his knees. Bridget felt herself blush and scrambled to her feet. "You scared the hell out of me."

"We need to talk."

"About what?"

"Sit down."

Bridget remained standing. Bobby Scales's eyes never left her. "I need to disappear for a while."

"What do you mean 'disappear'?"

"Exactly that. For a month. Maybe more."

"Why are you telling me?"

"I want you to keep an eye on the business while I'm gone."

"I don't collect, Bobby."

"Finn will take care of that. You just make sure the money gets where it's supposed to."

"Don't I always?"

Bobby didn't nod yes or no. Didn't move a muscle. Bridget wondered what he knew about her and Finn.

"Are you afraid to be alone with me?" he said.

"Should I be?"

"No one knows we're down here." He smiled and it was like a terrible flash of lightning.

"You need something else?"

"A favor."

Bridget snorted. "What else is new?" She picked up a sharp stone, tossing it from hand to hand, testing its weight.

"The thing between us was a mistake, Bridget."

"You think that's what I'm talking about? Don't flatter yourself." She fired the stone at a squirrel, nearly catching him in the flank as he scuttled up the side of a tree.

"Will you help?"

"When he cut me, you were the one who did something about it."

"That was a long time ago."

"I'm just saying. That's why I'll help. Nothin' else."

"Okay."

"What are they after?"

"The Curtis Jordan thing. And two others."

"Others?"

"Two women. The cops will come around, take apart my apartment, nose around Joey's."

"They'll try to get us talking."

"So talk. You don't know anything anyway. Just don't leave any of the paperwork around."

"I'm good at hiding things."

"You think I don't know that?"

Bridget felt a thrill, soaked in equal parts lust and fear. Her whole life she'd been the watcher. Or had she?

"After a month or two, things will settle down and I should be back. If not, do what you want." Bobby's voice trailed off.

"You ain't coming back."

He swung his eyes across. "What makes you say that?"

"I know about the produce market. They say someone's coming up from Providence. Might already be here."

"I'll straighten it out."

"Don't go back to your place."

His fingers twitched.

She inched a little closer. "I can help, Bobby. I mean really help."

"No, you can't."

"Yes, I can. And the beauty of it is, no one ever has to know."

He tipped his head a fraction, as if he'd heard a soft, round note in the distance. "What are we talking about?"

———

After she left, Bobby remained where he was, perfectly balanced, staring hard at the roofline of 8 Champney, wondering about everything Bridget Pearce saw and everything Bridget Pearce knew. There was a rustle behind him, and Finn stepped into the clearing.

"Where is she?" Bobby said.

"Waiting for the bus."

"What do you think?"

Finn shrugged. "She's a devious cunt." He leaned his weight back against a flat slab of rock, stomach stretched tight against a blue Boston Red Sox fleece. Bobby watched the red B heave up and down as Finn panted in the heavy air. The hike through the woods had taxed him.

"What is it?" Finn said, itchy under Bobby's gaze. Bobby jumped down off his perch, prowling the edge of the clearing as he spoke.

"You ever get the rest of the money that Irishman owed us?"

"Sorry, B. I never got the chance."

"What are the cops saying?"

"He got stuck in the gut or chest or something. They found him behind the Winship."

"You said you drank up the Corrib with those guys?"

Finn pawed at the ground with the toe of his shoe. "A little bit, sure."

"But you're not going in there tonight?"

"Why the fuck would I go in there?"

"Good. Go home. Grab an early night in bed. And stay away from Bridget."

"Bridget?"

Bobby stopped pacing. "You think she's skimming off the book?"

"Bridget? Fuck, no."

"I know you're banging her, Finn."

"*Was* banging her."

"Come here."

Finn made a meal of shuffling closer but hardly moved at all.

"Come here." Bobby grabbed him by the thick shank of muscle between his shoulder and neck. Finn winced and dropped to a knee.

"Fuck, that hurts."

"Look at me."

Finn looked up and found a gun tickling his cheek. "How long we known each other, B?" His eyes were wide and swimming with broken blood vessels.

"Is that all you got to trade?" Bobby slid the gun down so it was under Finn's chin. "Take it."

Finn wrapped his lips around the barrel and waited for whatever was next.

"I know what you did, Finn." His friend tried to speak, but Bobby held up a finger. "Now, I need to know if you're solid."

Finn nodded once.

"You understand what that means?"

Another nod. Bobby ground the barrel in until it hit the soft back of his throat. Finn never broke eye contact, unblinkingly offering his life in the hope he'd be allowed to keep it. The moment hung on a hook, then Bobby put the gun away and helped his friend to his feet. "Go home and stay there. I'll swing by later if I get the chance."

Bobby half listened while Finn mumbled his apologies and promised to do better. Bobby patted him on the back, then gave him a hug, and sent him on his way back through the woods. Finn looked a little shook, but probably not as much as Bobby would have liked. That might wind up costing Finn his life, but it was so hard to tell. When it was quiet again, Bobby followed Finn out, a gym bag hanging from the fingers of his right hand. Six minutes later, he was standing on the roof of 8 Champney, enjoying the view. He squatted down and zipped open the bag, pulling out the nickel-plated nine with the black grip. Next came the thirty-eight he'd used to kill Curtis Jordan. He laid down both guns, side by side, and looked at them. Bobby didn't have a lot of time, not if Providence had already sent its man. But he didn't need a lot of time. And whatever happened after that, happened. He reached into his bag again for a beige envelope thick with photographs and dealt them out like a run of playing cards. Rosie Tallent and Sandra Patterson were the first two, then two more. Chrissy McNabb and Seamus Slattery. All of them, except for Patterson, the fucking dregs of Brighton. Bobby hung his head between his shoulders and studied the images. There was one picture missing from his collection. One person who was still breathing. And that was a distinction that wouldn't last for long. Bobby stalked the roof's perimeter, then walked back to front. When he was satisfied, he got to work.

38

A SKINNY guard with food in his mustache unlocked the door to Kevin's cell and motioned for him to follow. They put him in a small holding room with a table and two chairs. The Middlesex cops hadn't booked him. No prints. Just took him to a lockup in Cambridge and dumped him in the cell. That was almost seven hours ago. Kevin heard the scrape of metal as someone turned a key. Lisa Mignot walked in and sat across from him.

"Aren't you out of your jurisdiction?"

"The sheriff owed me a favor."

"You want to tell me what I'm doing here? Or should we discuss it in the context of the lawsuit I'm gonna file."

"You're not going to be suing anybody, Kevin."

"Why's that?"

Lisa measured out a long breath before answering. "I stashed you here for two reasons. First, I didn't want DeMateo to pick you up for questioning and parade you around downtown. Second, I wanted to let you know your friend's gonna be arrested on the Patterson thing."

"You told them about the reservoir?"

"Hell, no."

"Then what?"

"They have links between Scales and Patterson. Links between Scales and Curtis Jordan. The gun will tie in Rosie Tallent."

"It's all circumstantial."

"You ever hear of an Irishman named Seamus Slattery?"

"Why?"

"He turned up dead last night behind a grammar school in Brighton. Stabbed in the chest. Coroner says around eight or nine P.M."

"So what?"

"Scales and Slattery had some history. The feeling is Slattery might have owed him money."

"Bookies don't usually kill people who owe them money."

"DeMateo's gotten pretty comfortable with the idea your buddy's involved in a lot more than gambling. By the way, what time did you hook up with Scales last night?"

"Around eleven."

"No idea where he was earlier?"

The image of the bandage on Bobby's hand flashed through Kevin's head. "No."

Sounds from the hallway. Iron scraping iron. The whine of a hinge as a door swung open and shut. Somewhere, someone swore. Laughter.

"Was Slattery done like the others?" Kevin said.

"No ligature. No gunshot. But there is something. The margins and angles on the Slattery wound were identical to Patterson and Tallent."

"Same knife?"

"We think so. The M.E. also was able to map out the actual wound paths. We couldn't do much with Tallent, but in both

Slattery and Patterson it appears there was a nearly identical flaw at the very end of the blade. At first we thought the tip might have broken off during one of the attacks, but I went back through the M.E.'s files this afternoon and couldn't find anything."

"What were you looking for?"

"Sometimes if a knife breaks during an assault, it will show up in x-rays. In this case, it would have been a tiny piece of metal that looked like an inverted 'v.'" Lisa held her fingers about a quarter inch apart.

"But you didn't find anything?"

"I looked at all the x-rays we had. Nothing."

"What does that mean?"

"It means the case against your friend isn't perfect, but it's more than enough to get things rolling."

"Why are you telling me all this?"

"I used you. I used our relationship. And I'm sorry for that."

"You can keep the apology."

"Fair enough, but tell me how that helps you? Or your friend?"

"So it's business?"

"Either way, he's going down, Kevin. I'm just trying to make it a little easier all around."

He could smell her skin, still fragrant, still compelling even now as she sat across the table and bargained away his friend's life. "Bobby needs a day."

"Do you know where he is?"

Kevin shook his head.

"Can you find him?"

"I don't know."

She held up a finger. "One day. If he runs, they'll arrest you on the Jordan thing and march you past all your buddies in the media. Believe what you want, but I don't want to see that happen." Lisa pulled out her key to the apartment in Beacon Hill and put it on the table. "I moved my stuff out this morning."

Kevin stared at the key, a crooked reminder of all that was dead and all that was dying, then pressed it into a pocket. Lisa climbed wearily to her feet.

"Come on. Let's get you out of here before my boss finds you."

"Can I get a look at the autopsy files you were talking about?"

"They won't help."

"I'd still like a look."

"I've got copies in the car."

———

Lisa was parked on the street. She pulled a brown binder from the backseat wrapped tight with several rubber bands and gave it to Kevin. After he left, she clicked her nails on the steering wheel and thought about her final throw of the dice, wondering if she'd made a mistake giving him the files. And if maybe she wasn't being played herself. Fuck it. Lisa was all about Lisa. She knew that now, clear and hard as the painted eyes that looked back at her in the rearview mirror. So why did she feel like opening the door and getting sick in the gutter? She took out her phone and punched in the number for Bridget Pearce.

39

THE SHELF was still heavy with Hemingway and Steinbeck, the kitchen had all its pots and pans, and the Red Sox schedule was taped to the wall. But Bobby was gone as fuck. Just like he'd promised. Kevin walked over to Bobby's desk and opened a drawer. Inside was the usual—pens, pencils, rubber bands, a handful of old bills. Kevin could almost hear his friend chuckling as he pulled open the rest of the drawers, then ran his hands underneath the desk and down the back and sides, looking for anything that might be taped there and knowing there was nothing to be found. He rummaged through the kitchen drawers and Bobby's only closet, then returned to the books, shaking them out one at a time before cracking open the trunk under the bed. Kevin was on his hands and knees tugging at a loose floorboard when the barrel of a gun nuzzled his ear.

"He kept something down there, but it's empty now. Get up."

Kevin got to his feet. Someone gave him a shove in the back and he stumbled across the room.

"I found a rag and half-empty bottle of bleach on the counter. Sit down."

Kevin took a seat at Bobby's kitchen table. The man with the gun walked over to the windows and pulled down the shades. Danny DeVito. He was a dead ringer, except instead of crazy *Taxi* eyebrows this guy just had crazy eyes—amber with traces of current and a little bit of the end of the world running through them.

"Why do you suppose your friend . . . he is your friend, right?"

Kevin nodded.

"Why do you suppose he had out the bleach?"

"I don't know."

The man leaned neatly against the window frame, holding the gun across his wrist like it was an extension of his hand. "I might wipe down the place with bleach if I didn't want anyone to know I'd been here. But this is your buddy's apartment, which leaves one other possibility."

"What's that?"

"He killed someone here."

"I doubt it."

"You want some coffee? One thing he left behind was the coffee."

"No, thanks."

The man stuck the gun in his belt and rummaged around, whistling some sort of old jazz tune as he found filters, measured out coffee, and filled Bobby's machine with water. He stopped at the bookshelf and pulled out an album—Bach's mass in B-minor.

"The most perfect music ever written," Kevin said.

The man looked up from reading the back cover. "Your buddy tell you that?"

"He did."

"Yeah, well, he's right. Except it's composed, not written. Bach composed."

"I think that's what he said."

The man grunted and put the album back where he'd found it. He didn't seem concerned that Kevin might make a dash for the door. When the coffee was ready, he poured himself a cup in a chipped mug and took a seat at the table. "It's not bad. You sure you don't want some?"

Kevin shook his head.

"Suit yourself. So what were you looking for?"

"The police are gonna search this place tomorrow. I wanted to see if there was anything here . . ."

"Fucking with the cops. I like it." The man showed a quick grin full of thick, white teeth. "What do they want with Scales?" It was the first time he'd mentioned Bobby by name, and the sound rang like a hammer striking stone.

"They think he killed some people."

"People?"

"Yeah."

"My theory with the bleach doesn't look so stupid after all."

"Bobby's not a killer."

"What's your name?"

"Kevin."

"Kevin, that's the first lie you've told me. Tell me another and I shoot you in the knee. Tell me a third and I put one in your head. Then I wrap you up in plastic and stick you in the back of my car. You want to walk over to the window with me and see my car?"

"No."

"It's got a big fucking trunk."

"I believe you."

"So we understand each other?" The man studied Kevin like a butcher might study a cut of meat.

"Yes."

"Tell the truth and I'll be on my way. Maybe I find your friend, maybe I don't. To be honest, it makes no difference to me."

Kevin wasn't sure why, but he believed the man and felt himself relax a fraction. "I was looking for a gun. Thirty-eight caliber. Maybe a knife."

The man nodded. "My name's Lollipops, by the way. Don't ask why."

"I wasn't gonna."

"Good. I already searched the place. No gun. There's some knives in the kitchen. You wanna take a look, go ahead."

"I already did."

"Why would your friend leave a gun or a knife behind?"

"He wouldn't."

"But the search made you feel good."

Kevin flicked his shoulders. "I guess."

"Maybe there was something else you were looking for?"

"I'm an investigative reporter. Going on fishing expeditions is pretty much what we do."

"Who do you work for?"

"The *Globe*."

"Cops interested in you as well?"

"Probably. That doesn't matter."

"Of course it matters." Lollipops took another sip of coffee and waited for the story he somehow knew was coming.

"Bobby saved my life when we were kids."

"How'd he do that?"

"He killed a man."

"And now you want to make everything square?"

"You don't understand."

"Enlighten me."

"I was fifteen and the guy killed my grandmother. Cut her open and left her on the floor of her apartment. I went after him and Bobby followed."

"He wound up doing the killing?"

"I pushed when I shouldn't have and the dominoes just started falling."

"Tides shifted, lives changed. Your buddy became what he became. Shakespeare already wrote the fucking play." Lollipops slipped the gun from his belt and placed it flat on the table. "I'm sixty-three years old. Killed almost two hundred men, mostly for money. I came here to kill your pal. And if I find him, that's what I'm gonna do. You know why?"

"Cuz someone's paying you."

"We don't push dominoes. We are dominoes. Me, you, Bobby Scales. We get pushed, we fall, and there's not a damn lot any of us can do about it."

"I don't believe that."

"It doesn't matter what you believe. It doesn't matter what you choose, or what you think you're choosing. The dominoes are gonna fall like they fall. People live, people die. And we all go kicking and screaming, even the ones who don't say a word. Now leave and don't come back. Otherwise, I drop you in the trunk."

Lollipops got up and opened the door. Kevin wanted to stay, but his feet carried him into the hallway, then down the stairs. He walked numbly across the street and slid behind the wheel of his car. The passenger's door opened and Gemele Harper got in beside him. She pointed straight ahead.

"Drive."

———

From the high window, Lollipops watched the two figures in the front seat of the car. He hadn't been able to see who climbed in but hoped it was a woman. He hoped they were talking about getting on a plane. Somewhere warm. Drinks at sunset by the pool, late breakfasts, long lunches, walks on the beach. He hoped for all of that but read something different in the reporter's face. Something Lollipops knew all too well. Brake lights flickered and the Volvo pulled away from the curb in a soft prowl. Lollipops took down the tag number, then let the shade drop. The kid with the Yankees hat was wrapped in plastic and stashed in the tub. Lollipops would have to wait until dark to move him. The professional unbuttoned his coat and sat down again at the table, sipping at his coffee and enjoying the peace and quiet.

40

GEMELE WALKED through Fidelis like it was her backyard, taking the same crooked path to the same brick building Kevin had visited two days prior. They passed through the empty lobby and up two flights. Kevin counted footsteps as they went.

"Where are we headed?"

She stopped at an apartment and opened the door. The room had a single window with a table and two chairs beneath it. Kevin walked in and felt the walls exhale. He rubbed the heel of his hand against his forehead and thought about blood pooling and soaking, filling dark cracks in the linoleum floor.

"Sit down." Gemele swung the door shut and took a seat—her neat, sturdy figure limned in a final rush of sunlight pouring through the window. Kevin sat across from her.

"We could have met at Electric Avenue."

She shook her head. "This is better. This was the apartment Curtis died in."

"You knew Curtis Jordan?"

"He was my uncle."

He searched her face, eyes older than age, smile creased like worn leather.

"You wanna hear about it?"

Kevin nodded.

"It was the fall of '75. I was fourteen and lived across the hall. My moms had gone out."

"No kidding."

"Police talked to me. I told 'em I saw nothing, but that wasn't true. I heard a big bang. Two or three in a row. When you live in Fidelis, you get used to the bangs."

"And what did you do?"

"What we always did. Got away from the doors and windows, hid under the bed. There was a lot of running, then it was quiet. After a couple of minutes, I went to the door and stuck my head out. That's when I saw this skinny white boy come out of Curtis's apartment. About my age. Eyes big and round as dinner plates."

Kevin studied the curve of her mouth as she spoke, the high cut of cheekbone and slightly turned-up nose. His mind subtracted years and added braids, ones with pink and white bows in them. And then he was there, standing in the hallway, face-to-face with fourteen-year-old Gemele Harper.

"When did you know?" he said.

"First time you showed up at our door and wanted to investigate James's case. You got pretty eyes, Kevin. Nice and soft. Women gonna remember them."

"Yeah?"

"Sure. I knew you were the white boy I saw that day."

"And you didn't care?"

"You wanted to help James. That was enough for me. Besides, when you came out of this apartment, you didn't have no gun in your hands so I knew you didn't shoot Curtis."

"You heard about the cop that was killed the other day? Black woman?"

"Saw it on TV."

"The gun that was used in that crime was also used to kill your uncle."

Something naked moved in her face. "Guns floating all over the place. Don't mean nothing."

"If you gave a statement in Curtis's murder, you're probably gonna be questioned again."

"You worried I'm gonna talk? Tell 'em I saw you?"

"Did I say that?"

"Uncle Curtis used to have a guy, only job was to take care of the cash. He'd set up right here in this room with an ironing board. Iron twenty-dollar bills all goddamn day. Then we'd stack 'em and wrap 'em. Bundles of twenties rubber-banded in plastic grocery bags." She got up and walked behind Kevin, to the spot where Curtis Jordan was sitting when he caught two slugs in the chest. "Curtis stored the bags right here." Gemele pointed to the ceiling above her. "He'd give me a twenty every time I went up. But the money wasn't for climbing into the ceiling."

"It was for keeping your mouth shut."

She circled back and sat down again.

"What's going on, Gemele?"

"You know James loved you."

"What's going on?"

"I run the show here. All the dope in and out. James was in it before me. And before that, Curtis."

"I don't believe you."

"Rosie used to work for James. Everyone in the projects worked for James. And now they work for me."

"What about Electric Avenue?"

"Living simple keeps me off the radar."

"And your kids don't know what you do."

She leaned forward, small, hard hands planted on small, hard knees. "They're gonna have a life, Kevin. A real life. You don't like it, then fuck you, too. Now, you gotta leave. And don't come back."

"A cop was killed, Gemele. There'll be others, asking more questions. Harder questions."

"You were there. If anyone knows who shot Curtis, it's you."

"Is that why you brought me here? Just to warn me off?"

"I sent a kid looking for you."

"He never found me."

She raked her lips with her sharp teeth and clenched and unclenched her fists.

"Say what you need to say, Gemele."

"Then you leave?"

"Then I leave."

"I know about your grandmother. I know Curtis robbed her. And I know he killed her."

"Everyone in the neighborhood knew that."

"My uncle got his information from a white kid. Older than me, desperate for a bag. Told Curtis where your grandmother kept her money, the hours she worked, all that stuff. I was here when he told Curtis. Right here in this apartment."

"You got a name?"

She shook her head. "Lemme finish. The people who killed your cop are pushing dope into the suburbs. Causing a lot of problems. Lot of people getting smoked. But you probably already heard all about that?"

Kevin nodded.

"Whoever's running that show keeps a low profile. They do that cuz they're smart like me."

"So you don't know who they are?"

"No, but I know who they're gonna hit next. Yesterday I saw his picture. Been a couple of decades but I damn straight recognized the face."

Outside, the sun was all but gone and Kevin could just make out a pale moon bathed in a pink froth of sky. He pulled a photo from his pocket. It was the snap of himself, Bobby, and Finn in the bleachers at Fenway. Gemele studied it without touching it.

"You a smart boy, Kevin."

"How smart?"

"I'll tell you cuz it was your grandmother and cuz you deserve to know." She tapped the photo with a finger. "That's him right there. The one who told Curtis where your gram kept her money. The one who's gonna get clipped himself. Real fucking soon, too."

Kevin held up the photo in the first flush of evening and stared at the smiling face of Finn McDermott.

41

KEVIN DROVE back to his apartment and sat in his living room, thinking about Finn and whether he deserved to die. And whether the bloodlust of killing someone hadn't been what Kevin had wanted all along. Around midnight, he thought about the snub-nosed revolver. He'd gotten it from a Boston detective named Barry Fitzpatrick. One night Kevin was drinking in a Dorchester bar called the Eire when Fitzpatrick came in and sat down beside him. He was lean, with a heavy Adam's apple and blue stubble providing cover for pitted cheeks. When he spoke, he kept his head down and his voice low. Kevin found himself leaning forward on his stool and still only catching every other word. Fitzpatrick wanted to talk about a feature Kevin had written on a young female detective who'd been shot and killed in the line of duty. The detective had been Fitzpatrick's partner and he carried her death in worn eyes and the tired rag of a smile he flashed whenever he mentioned her name. Six months after their drink, Fitzpatrick would put his service weapon in his mouth and pull the trigger. That night, however, it was just talk. And booze. Their first drink became three. Three became five and a round of shots. Pretty soon they were closing the place. Kevin was feeling it and decided to grab a cab home. Fitzpatrick seemed none the worse for wear and insisted on giving him a lift. Fitzgerald parked in front of a hydrant on Cambridge Street. Before Kevin could get out, the detective reached across and pulled the snub-nosed from his glovie. He said it was a throwaway. Unregistered. Cold. Something to keep in the apartment just in case.

Kevin found the piece wrapped in a towel on a shelf in his bedroom closet. He took it back to the living room and laid it down on the coffee table. Kevin drank a beer, two beers, stood under a hot shower, and slept for three hours with the gun beside his bed. He woke at three thirty and went for a drive along the river, rolling down the back windows and letting the cold air blow across his scalp. The steering wheel moved smoothly under his hands, the car knowing what turns to make and where it needed to go. He pulled quietly to the curb and killed the engine. Then he called Mo Stanley.

"What time is it?"

"Four thirty, five."

"In the morning? Fuck, Kevin."

"You got a pen?"

"What?"

"Get a pen."

He listened as she hunted around, then came back on the line. "What?"

"Take down this name. Curtis Jordan. J-O-R-D-A-N."

"Got it. Who is he?"

"He was a drug dealer. Lived in Fidelis Way. Shot and killed in nineteen seventy-five."

"And?"

"He ties into the Patterson thing. Tallent, as well. I've written it all up. Everything I know. Even more that I don't."

"Why would you do that, Kevin?"

"Just wanted to get it down on paper. I e-mailed a copy to you at the newsroom. Don't trust anyone on it. Especially the D.A.'s office."

"Your girlfriend *works* for the D.A."

"Just keep it to yourself."

"Where are you, Kev?"

"In my car. In front of my apartment." He looked out his windshield at Finn McDermott's building, stuck on an ugly corner a half block from Brighton Center.

"You been to bed?"

"I caught a couple of hours."

"What's going on? And why should I care about Curtis Jordan?"

"Read what I wrote. Then we'll talk."

"Let's talk now."

"Later, Mo."

"You're scaring me a little."

"Go back to bed. I'll call you."

He cut the line and turned off his phone. A bird jumped on a wire. A rat hopped out from behind a Dumpster and scooted across an alley. Kevin checked the snub-nosed for the third time to make sure it was loaded and thought about Finn in Tar Park, touching Kevin's shoulder, offering condolences about his grandmother. He stuffed the gun in his pocket and reached for the door handle.

———

The lobby of Finn's building smelled like Fidelis. Seemed about right. Kevin walked up a flight of stairs and knocked lightly on the door to 2B. The hair on his arms lifted as the door swung open. Kevin took out the gun.

"Finn. Hey, you here?" His voice rang off the flat walls and boomed and echoed in his ears. He walked through the living room, taking note of a framed picture of Bobby Orr flying through the air as the B's won the Cup. Beside it was a photo of Finn standing outside Fenway with Luis Tiant. They both had cigars stuck in their mouths. A coffee table was littered with empty beer bottles. Nearby two full ones were taking a bath in a cooler full of half-melted ice. Kevin sat on a stool in the kitchen and stared at his gun on the counter, listening to his blood cool and thinking about a twenty-two pressed to the forehead of a dead man, the pop it made and the way the smallest of sounds can echo up and down the corridors of a person's life. He stuffed the snub-nosed back in his pocket and walked down the hall to Finn's bedroom. His sheets were in a tumble and there was a blue condom wrapper crumpled on the floor. The rest of the room was curtained in shadow. Kevin was turning to leave when he heard a soft thump. He crossed over to the room's only window. It let out onto a fire escape that overlooked an alley of blank brick walls. Finn hadn't left town. At least not in the conventional sense. He was on the fire escape, hanging from a rope by the neck, staring blindly through a black tangle of iron at eternity and beyond. Outside a siren whooped once and a police car rolled up to the mouth of the alley, sealing off the exit. Kevin took a final look at Finn's bare feet, spinning slowly in the pink and blue light. Then he turned and ran.

42

Today was her tenth birthday. No one had gotten her a cake. No one sent her a card. And that was just how she wanted it. Bridget sat in her bedroom, listening to the slop of soap and water coming from the bathroom, bright bubbles of laughter floating and popping all around her. She waited for the noise to subside before lazing across the hall and stopping in the doorway. Colleen sat in the tub, seven years old, giggling and unashamed of her nakedness. A breeze blew in through an open door, furrowing the milky green water and carrying the smell of smoke. Mom was out on the back porch, sneaking an afternoon cig. Bridget swung the bathroom door closed and knelt by the tub. Colleen grabbed for a rubber boat floating just out of reach. Bridget pushed it back to her. Colleen ducked the boat under the water and laughed as it resurfaced. Bridget played with a lock of her sister's hair, then slipped her fingers around the back of her neck, jamming her under the water until her forehead scraped bottom. At first Colleen thought it was some sort of game. Stupid Colleen. Then she realized it wasn't and tried to fight back, squirming and sliding along the bottom of the tub before slipping out of Bridget's soapy grip and managing a single, suds-filled scream. Footsteps pounded down the hall and their mother was there, filling *the doorway, staring at Bridget, who was sitting on the toilet as Colleen wailed. Maybe she was afraid to ask. Maybe she was just ashamed. Shame had always been Mom's strong suit. Either way, nothing was ever said. Nothing done. Until the day they decided to teach Bridget a lesson.*

She tugged a comb through her hair, watching in the mirror as the teeth dug straight rows across her scalp. The bedroom was achingly hot. She walked over to a window and cracked it, letting the fresh air wash over her face, inhaling it in tiny sips. A full-length mirror hung on the back of her closet door. Bridget took off her clothes piece by piece until she was naked in front of the glass. The puckered scar ran in a thick diagonal across her back, from left shoulder to right hip. Bridget twisted in the mirror and traced it with her eye. They'd burned her that winter—the winter of her tenth year—with a pot of hot coffee. She remembered it, black and scalding, a waterfall of pain that beat her to the floor where she curled up in a ball and screamed inside her head, never offering more than a mutter for public consumption. Her mother had pulled the nightgown off her back, taking sheets of flesh with it. Her father loomed in the background, eyes sweating and staring until she looked at him and he turned away. Someone found a stick of soft butter to rub across her back, already cooked with blisters. Bridget just lay there, withered like a still-born rotting away in an old woman's womb. She'd done it on purpose. Her mother. Bridget was certain of it. As for her father, he was there for the pain. And any morsel would do. Flesh and limb. Even one's own child. Bridget knew. Her brain was tuned to the same radio station that had played nonstop inside her father's head so of course she knew. And even understood.

She pulled a silk shirt she'd bought at Filene's off a hanger. The blouse was followed by a pair of black linen pants and flats. Up on the shelf of the closet was her old copy of *Gray's Anatomy*. The diagrams in it were covered with pencil mark slashes and childhood doodles. Bridget ran her fingers across a few of the creased pages, closed the book, and hid it at the back of the closet. She sat down again in front of the dresser mirror, piling up her hair with her hands, then holding up a pair of teardrop earrings, turning this way and that to see how they splashed in the light. It was her time now. Hers and Bobby's. They'd live here, in the house on Champney. Take over the first two floors and rent out the top. Or maybe they'd just keep the entire place for themselves. Bobby would have to disappear for a while. There wasn't much way around that. Or was there? The truth was anything could be arranged. At the end of the day, all you needed was a plan and the stomach for it. Bridget put on the earrings and stood up, giving her clothes a final brush in the mirror. Then she left the stifling space of her room, hurrying out of the apartment and up the back stairs to her appointment on the roof.

43

KEVIN HOPPED a fence that ran behind Finn's building. He could feel the police all around him and knew he had to keep moving. Three fences and two alleys later, he surfaced on Sparhawk Street. A couple of schoolgirls gave him a hard look that told him he didn't belong on this block and they sure as fuck knew it. Kevin kept walking until he'd circled back to his car. He slid behind the wheel and watched in the rearview mirror as a cop rerouted early morning traffic in front of Finn's place. A black sedan bumped over the curb and onto the sidewalk. Frank DeMateo jumped out from behind the wheel. Lisa slipped out of the passenger's side. She had sunglasses scooted up on her forehead and dropped them over her eyes as she scanned the block. Kevin pulled into the stream of cars. In his mirror, Lisa walked up the steps and disappeared inside.

———

She trailed DeMateo up the stairs, then hung back and watched as he ordered people around. Lisa had been surprised when her boss asked her to tag along. Maybe it was a going-away present.

Maybe he was trying to cover his ass if things went sideways. Finn McDermott had always been on the periphery of the investigation. Now he stood front and center—either as a killer who took his own life or yet another victim. DeMateo disappeared into the apartment's bedroom for a few minutes, then came out again. He motioned for her to move into the hallway. They found a quiet spot near the stairwell.

"They just cut him down," DeMateo said. He looked nervous. Lisa's instincts told her the less she said, the better.

"And?"

"Who knows? Could be suicide. Could be he was drugged and hoisted up there. Could be he was already dead when someone put a rope around his neck. Toxicology should help."

"Do they have a time of death?"

"Six to eight hours ago. I've got a woman downstairs says she saw a man leaving the apartment last night. We're gonna show her Scales's picture."

"You want me to handle that?"

"I'll do it. You stay here and keep an eye on things. The fucking press hasn't put this together yet, but it's just a matter of time."

DeMateo disappeared down the stairs, cell phone stuck to his ear. Lisa wandered back to the doorway and looked in. She counted three uniforms, a couple of plainclothes detectives, the coroner's people running in and out, and a forensics team. Everyone was doing their job. No one was giving her a second look. For the third time that morning she punched in Kevin's number and, for the third time, got his voice mail. Lisa slid the phone back in her pocket and thought about the dead man in the next room. *And the very real possibility she might go to jail for it.* A young black detective named Floyd McKinnon yelled her name and walked out of the bathroom holding a thirty-eight-caliber revolver by the trigger guard. McKinnon told her they'd found it secured to the underside of the tub. And they weren't done. Lisa felt her heart turn over as she took a quick look at the gun, noting the gray tape on the grip. She ordered McKinnon to bag it and walked into the bathroom just as one of the detectives pried up a couple of loose floorboards. Lisa pulled out a flashlight and knelt by the hole in the floor.

"What do we got?"

The detective crouched over the hole was a Dorchester guy named Billy Neelon. She'd worked with him before and knew he liked to take his time with a crime scene. Usually Lisa was fine with that. Not this morning.

"Let me get a few more shots before you move it," Neelon said.

"How many have you taken?"

"Maybe a half dozen."

"Two minutes."

Lisa watched while Neelon snapped away. Jammed into the bottom of the hole was a black Nike backpack. When he was done, she reached in with a gloved hand and pulled it out, taking a quick look to make sure there was nothing else in the hole. She opened the pack in the living room. Neelon moved around the table, snapping pictures as she worked. Another detective videotaped the scene, while a third took notes. The first thing Lisa found was a maroon-and-gold BC sweatshirt. There were smears of dried blood on the front and two cruel slashes in the side. Underneath the sweatshirt was a women's powder blue scarf and a winter hat. At the very bottom of the pack, she found a small leather change purse. Inside it were the driver's licenses of Sandra Patterson, Rosie Tallent, and Christine Flannery. Lisa took out her cell again and punched in her boss's number.

44

THE OLD-SCHOOL sign had gone dark, its neon letters staring out blindly over the intersection at North Beacon and Market like some modern-day Tiresias. Kevin pulled into an empty spot directly beneath the second "D." Lisa's autopsy files were still in the backseat. He grabbed them and headed into the Dunkin' Donuts, setting up at a table with a good view of the front door and close by the store's emergency exit. Outside a police car zipped past in a blur of color. Then another. A server wondered aloud what the Christ was going on and wandered over to the window for a better look. Kevin stirred some sugar in his coffee and saw Finn's face circling there. Part of him was glad he was dead. That part scared him, but there it was and he couldn't ignore it anymore. He took out his cell phone and dialed Lisa's number.

"Kevin, I've been trying to call you."

"You need to listen."

"All right."

"Is this being recorded?"

"I told you. That was a mistake."

"Is it being recorded?"

"No."

He didn't believe her but didn't think it really mattered. "I just left Finn McDermott's apartment."

"Hang on." There was a pause on the line, then she came back. "Where are you?"

"Never mind. I saw you and DeMateo pull up. Is it a suicide?"

"We don't know yet. Why were you here?"

"I found out Finn was hooked into the Curtis Jordan thing. I wanted to talk to him."

"We found the gun that killed Jordan in his apartment. At least we think it's the gun. We also found personal effects from Rosie Tallent and Sandra. I just got off the phone with DeMateo."

"So it's over?"

"We're not sure what it all means yet. If you were in this apartment, you need to come in and make a statement. And you need to do it before they find evidence you were here."

"Does Finn make sense?"

"Could be." Another slight, calculated pause. "Do you know where Bobby Scales is?"

"No."

"All right. Tell me where you're at and I'll have someone pick you up. Then we can go through it."

Kevin felt his stomach clench and the walls of the Dunkin' Donuts creep in about two feet on all sides. "Let's go through it now."

"I can't do that."

"Then I think I'll stay put."

"You're in a vulnerable position, Kevin. And I don't want to have this conversation over the phone."

His mind picked up the word *vulnerable* and turned it, watching how it caught and reflected light.

"Kevin? You still there?"

"Maybe you should try to explain. Then we'll see how things go."

"There's a decent chance McDermott's being framed."

"So you believe he was murdered?"

"We have a witness who says she saw Scales leaving his apartment last night."

"And you think I'm involved?"

"It's complicated, Kevin. Why don't you come in and we can talk. Just you and me . . ."

He cut the line and sat back in his chair. The phone buzzed. He turned it off. They were coming for him. They wanted Bobby, but they'd settle for him. And Lisa was leading the charge. He wondered if she had the ability to trace his call. Why not? His gaze caught the files she'd given him, stacked on the table next to his coffee. The reporter in him needed something to read. The rub of paper and ink under his fingers. Words scattered down the page in long, luxurious lines. Therapy for the broken mind. He unwound the rubber bands on the binder and opened it. The first thing he found was a summary report on Seamus Slattery's autopsy. Kevin's eyes skipped down to the description of the fatal injury.

The stab wound is diagonally oriented between the 5th and 6th ribs on the left side of the chest and measures approximately 1/2 inch in length. Inferiorly there is a squared-off end approximately 1/32 in length; superiorly the wound is tapered. Wound penetrates into the left pleural cavity, with an estimated depth of three to four inches. Wound pathway is irregular, perhaps indicating the tip of the weapon was broken off during the attack. X-rays, however, show no evidence of fragments.

He laid the report aside. What would they charge him with? Lisa was smart as fuck. She'd come up with something. Not that it mattered. He wouldn't say a word while Bobby was still out there. If he was arrested and wound up taking a deal, Kevin would provide a full statement detailing his role in the Curtis Jordan killing. It'd be the end of his career, his life as he knew it, and wouldn't help Bobby a damn bit. Still, Kevin felt good about that part of things. He took another sip of coffee and opened a second file. Staring back at him was a picture of his grandmother, crumpled in the hallway of her apartment, the late-afternoon sun of his youth filling the space around her with that perfect, sculpted light. He flipped the file shut and gazed out the window as a bus took on a handful of early morning commuters and chugged down the street. Another police car whipped past. Kevin didn't want to see any more but found himself opening the file again. Clipped to the death photo was his grandmother's autopsy report—a jumble of words and numbers that purported to catalog her essence and failed miserably. Underneath the report was a dusty gray sleeve with SAINT ELIZABETH'S HOSPITAL stamped in 1970s red block letters. Inside the sleeve, Kevin found a single x-ray. It was twenty-six years old and bore his sister's name. Kevin remembered Bridget returning from the hospital the morning after his grandmother died, white bandage taped to her side, cat's eyes staring out the front window as their mother cried blindly beside her. He held the x-ray up to the light and studied his sister's twelve-year-old ribs, lined up in a neat row like a rack of spring lamb you'd find at the butcher. Cozied between the fifth and sixth ribs, Kevin saw what he saw—a tiny white fleck, just like an inverted "v." Somewhere faintly, a penny dropped.

45

THE LADDER'S joints had popped and cracked, gray wood slivered and bleached nearly white from four decades of New England weather. Colleen reached for a rung and looked up at a square of tinted sky looking back. Slowly, she began to pull herself up.

Her sister was already there, bunkered in the layered shade of the trees that bordered the far side of the building, eyes peering over the roof's edge, blinking into the filtered light of the alley below.

"Bridget?"

She was wearing a gray cardigan, with black leather gloves, black pants, and winks of light at her ears.

"You look nice," Colleen said, but kept her distance. She'd been to the zoo before and knew the rules when visiting the lion cage. Bridget rose from her perch and circled closer.

"Why couldn't we meet in the house?" Colleen said.

Her sister thinned her lips. "Does it matter?"

"Sorry." The apology came tumbling out of her mouth before Colleen's brain had the time to process, never mind stop it.

Bridget gestured to the low wall that ran around the edge of the roof. "Let's sit for a second."

"I'm fine here, thanks."

"I know all about the Royal."

Colleen felt the quick heat in her face. Shame. Her mother's shame. Her grandmother's shame. Generations of women, buried in shame. Colleen bore it all as her own. And so it was. "That's none of your business."

Bridget took a seat on the wall and stared placidly at the turning light.

"I know *your* secrets," Colleen said, voice spitting with sudden and ancient venom. "What you've hidden up here. Everything else."

Bridget turned a fraction and blinked. "Really?" She patted the ledge. Colleen sidled closer, sniffing the air around her before taking a seat.

"Better?"

Colleen nodded and felt a throbbing, full in her throat. Almost shyly, Bridget reached across and touched her sleeve. "Do you think I'd actually do anything to harm you?"

"I hope not."

"I wouldn't. Couldn't." Bridget pulled out a shiny, gold derringer and placed it between them. "He was disrespecting you, Colleen. Disrespecting your marriage. So I took care of it."

Colleen lifted her eyes off the neat little gun that was suddenly part of her life and blinked away a hot tear. "When?"

"Yesterday. At the Royal. There'll be money for you and Conor. A new life."

"I talked to Bobby. Did he . . ."

"Fuck Bobby." Bridget smoothed her brow with a smile. "I

just need you to do one thing for me and then it's over. Can you do that?"

"Yes." Colleen's response drifted out into the silent space, turning into a thousand whispers in the hanging leaves of the trees.

"Good." In Bridget's left hand was a small spiral notepad. She ripped out a blank page. It made a dry, tearing sound and Colleen felt herself flinch.

"You've made mistakes, Colleen. Marrying him, buying the place in Newton, thinking you could make it all work."

"I lied to myself. I lied to everyone. I know that."

"Write me a single sentence. No details, no specifics. Just a sentence saying you're sorry."

"Seriously?"

"I know it sounds crazy, especially coming from me, but in some ways I think it'll help wipe the slate clean. Give us a reason to trust each other."

"And that's it?"

Bridget nodded. Colleen plucked the page from her hand, scribbled out a few lines and signed it.

I'm sorry for all the pain and hurt I've caused. All I can do is hope people forgive me, just as I forgive them.

Colleen Carson

"How's that?"

"Perfect." Bridget folded the page into a square and slipped it in her pocket. Then she stood up, Colleen now cleaving close. Morning air pushed up from below, prickling the skin on her arms and sending a delicious thrill through her bones.

"I remember coming up here when we were kids," Colleen whispered. "It was always your spot. Always, always, always."

Bridget held out her arm. Colleen tucked underneath it, head bending to her older sister's shoulder, Bridget's hand slipping to the small of her younger sister's back. From there, all it took was a nudge. Colleen teetered and tottered like a clown in the circus, painted eyes rolling, bright red mouth opening and closing, fingers grasping for purchase in the air. Bridget reached out to steady her sister and stuffed the note she'd just written in one oversized pocket. The shiny derringer in the other. Then she gave her a second push.

Colleen heard her heels rasp across the top of the wall before sliding away from the roof, down the slick face of the building. The fall took forever, dropping silently through alternate layers of light and shadow, looking up to see her sister staring down at her as if from the bottom of a deep shaft. The last thing Colleen remembered was the stick-on smile and a crooked set of fingers toddling good-bye. Then the back of her skull hit the pavement with a wicked crack and the movie cut to black. Colleen's body lay in the cooling shadows, hidden from a world she no longer inhabited, finally at rest.

46

THE LIVING room at 8 Champney looked like a stage, lights down, audience hushed, the final act about to unfold. Kevin called out Bridget's name and was greeted with crickets. He wasn't surprised and headed straight for the kitchen. It seemed even smaller than before, but maybe all the rooms seemed progressively smaller with each visit. One day he'd show up and the front door would open into the backyard, the entire apartment reduced to nothing more than a warped threshold of time and memory.

There were dishes in the sink and the faucet was dripping. Kevin turned it off. Beside the sink were three drawers. The middle one had always been the silverware drawer. Kevin pulled it open and found a mismatched collection of forks, knives, and spoons tangled up in a tray. He separated out the knives and took his time, examining each in turn. When he was done, he laid them out on the table. Somewhere a woman yelled and a door slammed. Kevin walked out to the back porch, deserted except for a yellow tomcat who blinked at him out of his one good eye. Kevin had the feeling he'd just missed someone and headed back into the apartment. To his left was the hallway. At the end of it, his parents' bedroom. It had always been off-limits when he was a kid. No one ever had to tell him. Kevin just knew. He pushed open the door and went in. Clothes stood like dead soldiers on hangers in the closet. He sat on the bed with one of his father's overcoats and ran his thumb along a rough seam, then buried his face in the fabric. It smelled like stale sweat and fear. And he hated it as much as he needed it. There was a sound, a groan of wood, and he looked up at the long light of morning staining the far wall. He remembered the only time his dad had ever comforted him. Kevin had been playing street hockey at the top of Champney where the street widened. The goal was marked by two boots, separated by the length of a hockey stick, and the Doors' "Light My Fire" was playing on a radio someone had stuck on the curb. He'd never seen his grandmother walking up Champney before and remembered her heavy black shoes and how the sight of them had parched his throat. She told him best she could—in bits and pieces the way those things always came out. His dog, a six-month-old streak named Jagger, had gotten loose. A garbage truck caught him in its teeth, snapping the pup's spine in three places. Kevin dropped his hockey stick and bolted, legs wild, arms pumping, trying to outrun death down the hill. The screen door, still in its youth, announced his arrival with a heavy slap against the wooden frame. A circle of faces were huddled around the kitchen table, staring out at him with tunneled eyes. There was muttering about blood and fractures and the look Jagger gave them when they put him down. "It was a blessing," someone told him in that condescending, knowing way people talk who've never loved anything in their lives except themselves. Kevin felt like putting his fist through a window, except he wasn't that way. And everyone knew it. He ran into his sisters' room and threw himself on the bed. The door creaked and a hand brushed his shoulder. His father's voice was suddenly in his ear. "We'll get another one," he whispered. Kevin never turned, never said a word. He was ten years old and not about to hand over the piece of himself his father coveted most. So he listened until the footsteps died away. And they never went to get another pup. And no one ever spoke of it again. And they lived, chained together by nothing but blood, yet chained together all the same.

Kevin hung the overcoat back on its hanger. The edge of a flat box peeked from under the bed. He pulled it out. Inside were a bunch of scuffed baseballs. Colleen's collection. Each was shellacked to protect it and dated with the teams and score written in his father's coiled black script. Kevin picked one up:

SEPTEMBER 12, 1975
City Semifinal
Brighton – 3
Charlestown – 2

He put the ball in the box and slipped it back under the bed. Then he left, closing the door behind him.

———

The knives he'd pulled out still lay in a row. Kevin stacked them neatly in the silverware drawer, then returned to the kitchen table, taking a seat and staring out a small window set over the sink. As a kid, he'd sat in the same spot with his mother when it was quiet in the early cusp of morning and the house was theirs. Kevin would eat breakfast while she shuffled around the room, a synchronized clock running in their heads that would tell them when it was time for him to go. He'd read whatever was put in front of him while he ate. Books, newspapers, the print off the back of the cereal box. Anything to feed his mind. When there was nothing to read, he'd memorize everything in the room—sixteen tiles across the ceiling one way; twenty-four, the other. Six magnets on the refrigerator door, except for a while when there were only five. Kettle on the stove, silver on top, charred on the bottom, black handle melted around the grip. Boxes of Cocoa Puffs, mac and cheese, pasta, sauce, and peanut butter in the first cabinet. Oreos, Lorna Doone cookies for tea, cans of Campbell soup, tuna, and deviled ham in the second. Plates, glasses, and cups in the third. Breadbox beside the toaster beside four containers, yellow tin stamped with blue flowers. Kevin's gaze stopped. There were only three containers on the counter. A space and a light patch on the wall where the fourth should be. He walked over to the containers, picking up each in turn and checking inside. Sugar, a bag of flour, a box of salt. He pulled across a chair and began to search the upper shelves. The missing container was in a small, dark hole above the refrigerator. Kevin brought it back to the table, his mouth dry as dirt, his heart fluttering like a small bird in his throat. Inside was a hard object wrapped in a white handkerchief. Kevin lifted it out and placed it on the table, unopened. There was a footfall on the back porch. He looked up, half expecting to see his grandmother standing in the doorway.

"Is this a bad time?" Father Lenihan said.

47

BU'S BOATHOUSE stood on a spit of land just where the Charles River bent before making its final run into the harbor and infinite ocean beyond. Bobby pulled the Toyota into a small lot and killed the engine. They watched as swatches of light switched and played across the city's skyline. Bobby was the first to speak.

"I come here sometimes."

"It's nice." Her voice sounded tight, like she was on a first date. Bobby glanced across. Bridget touched her left ear and dropped her head. Shy. Demure. Impossible.

"Let's get out for a second."

"You think that's a good idea?"

"Why not?"

Her features lit up at the challenge in his voice and she opened the door. He let her take the lead and walked on her right side, keeping the gym bag in his right hand.

"You ever been out on the river, Bridget?"

She shook her head.

"View's nice from here, but on the water it's something else. Sometimes, I'll paddle right down into the city, watch the sun hang over the buildings . . ."

"Feel the world is all yours."

"Exactly."

"I didn't know you had a boat."

"Just a little one." Bobby held a hand up to the cutting light and grinned. "You want to go out?"

———

Bobby knew one of the managers who let him keep the boat in a small shed next to the main boathouse. In return, Bobby took the kid's action, as well as that of his college pals. He snapped open the lock on the shed and dragged the boat onto the damp grass. The oars were inside, as well as four life jackets tucked under two wooden benches. A metal rail ran around the perimeter, ending at an oarlock on either side.

The water looked dark against the riverbank. Bobby pushed the boat down the incline and stepped in as it floated out. He picked up an oar and pulled the boat close until it was tight to the shore. Bridget took a seat on one of the benches. Bobby dug the wooden blade into the soft mud and pushed. Once, twice, and the river's current took hold. Bobby sat across from Bridget, fitted the oars into the locks, and began to pull. Five or six strokes took them into the middle of the river. The current eased and the air around them grew still.

"Are the crews out?"

Bobby shook his head. "You mind if we just drift?"

"I love to drift."

Underneath one of the benches was a length of rope tied to a small anchor. Bobby dropped it over the side and felt the boat tug lightly against it. She turned away from him and touched her neck as the breeze freshened, kicking up a few waves and jostling the boat before dying away again.

"Have you talked to Kevin?"

She swiveled around, head on a silky pivot. "Why would I say anything to him? Is that what you brought me out here for?"

"I brought you out for the view."

Her eyes dipped to the satchel between his feet. "What's in the bag, Bobby?"

He opened it and pulled out a notebook. Her face didn't move.

"I found them on the roof at Champney," he said. "Read 'em all."

"Good."

Bobby ran his fingers across "Saint Andrew's Grammar School" written in Old English script across the cover. "You were maybe ten, twelve, when you started this one?"

"You mean the first?"

"I mean your grandmother."

Bridget took the notebook in her hands and skimmed a couple of pages before closing it. Her voice sounded like tires on wet gravel. "She was supposed to be working. Instead, the old bitch comes creeping up behind me and grabs my wrist. I only wanted to rob her, but I had the knife in my hand and just hit her with it. Then I heard the nigger on the stairs." She popped her fingers. "It all happened. Snap, snap, snap. He took one look, grabbed what he could, and ran like hell. All I had to do was cut myself. And I knew how to do that. Then I hid the knife and waited for them to find me."

"And you'd had a taste of killing?"

"It never really bothered me. And once I got older, I wanted money."

"When did you start stealing from me?"

"I didn't steal anything. I expanded your business. Our business. First, it was selling dope in the neighborhood. Penny-ante stuff. Then, we moved into the suburbs. That's when things got crazy. We're rich, Bobby. Me and you. Crazy rich."

He held up the notebook. "I count at least five dead, including Rosie Tallent and Sandra Patterson."

"Both business."

"Chrissy McNabb?"

"Junkie whore. Thought she could squeeze me cuz we went to school together."

"Slattery?"

"More scum. He figured out we were running dope and thought you were involved. Was headed to the police when I asked if he wanted to smoke a bone."

"And what did Finn ever do to you?" For the first time, Bobby saw something close to surprise flit across the flat angles of her face.

"How did you know about that?"

Bobby thought about his childhood friend, throwing a line off a boat somewhere in the Gulf of Mexico. He'd always told Finn he'd visit. And every time had been a lie. "I stopped by his place last night. Must have just missed you."

"Don't look so sad. He sold you out for a piece of ass. And he was getting ready to take over the book once you skipped town. But now you can stay."

"How's that?"

"I let it slip to Kevin's girlfriend that Finn might be running the drug operation. They'll find evidence in his apartment linking him to all the murders."

"What kind of evidence?"

"I didn't give them everything, but there's enough. Articles of clothing. Driver's licenses. The gun that killed Jordan."

"Finn told you where it was buried?"

"Of course he did." She paused, lingering over her final piece of information like a last bite of pie. "I know about Colleen as well."

Bobby felt something tear inside. "Colleen's got nothing to do with this."

"Two nights ago she found the thirty-eight and brought it to your apartment. Her Prince Charming. Gonna solve all her problems with hubby. I wondered what you'd do. Then yesterday I watched you put it back on the roof. That's when I knew for sure you were on board."

Bobby stared at the slick, sliding scales of the river and the slope of the bordering bank, naked and running into the falling light. Beyond was Boston and the rest of the world, slightly askew and spinning silently on its axis. "So what's next?"

Bridget's eyes glowed pale green as she warmed to the task.

48

KEVIN LOOKED at the handkerchief spread out on the front seat of his car and the knife he'd found wrapped inside it. It had a black handle with a nick at the very tip of the blade that made a perfect "v." Beside the knife was Kevin's cell phone. Lisa was on speaker.

"Are you sure?"

"Blade's a half-inch wide. Small nick at the very top. What looks like bloodstains near the handle. It's the knife." Kevin took a left off Soldiers Field Road and crossed to the Cambridge side of the river. "There were really only two people who could have killed my grandmother. One was Curtis Jordan." He jumped on Memorial Drive and headed south. Up ahead the BU boathouse flickered in and out of the trees.

"Kevin?"

"The other was my sister. That's where I found the knife. In the house I grew up in."

"She was what, eleven or twelve at the time of your grandmother's death?"

"I saw an old x-ray of the wound she suffered in the file you gave me. There's a piece of metal lodged in her ribs. Looks just like a tiny 'v.' And then I found the knife in our house. Now, how could that be?"

"She stabbed herself?"

"That's right. She killed my grandmother, cut herself, and pinned it all on Jordan when he came walking through the door. Then she kept the knife . . ."

"Until she decided to kill again." A pause on the line. "But why the gun?"

"Bobby told me Bridget likes to collect things, especially people. Somehow she discovered where the gun was buried. Maybe through Finn, I don't know. She dug it up and used it in the Patterson and Tallent killings. If things ever got too hot, she could drop the piece wherever she wanted. Control the investigation and send it in whatever direction suited her. It's the power, the knowledge she could destroy someone's life on a whim. Bridget would love that."

"Where are you, Kevin?"

"She planted all that stuff in Finn's place. Then she led you by the nose to it."

"Where are you?"

Kevin eased around a bend, and the boathouse slid into view.

"I've got one more question before I go."

"Don't . . ."

"Shut up and listen. Bridget's x-ray. You knew what it showed. You knew my sister was the killer."

"I didn't."

"Fucking law review at Harvard Law School. Best prosecutor in the city. You don't miss that x-ray. You wanted me to find it. Hoped I'd go after her."

Kevin waited. Out on the river, a small boat slipped from behind a line of painted trees. There were two dark figures in it.

"It was your *sister*, Kevin. Yes, I wanted you to find it. And I wanted you to decide."

"Decide what, Lisa?"

"I don't know. Maybe talk to her. See if anyone else needed to be protected. Then I figured you'd come to me."

"I'd come to you and you'd make the arrest. And if I didn't come to you, you'd arrest her anyway and make your boss look like a fool for pulling in Bobby. Win, win for Lisa Mignot, our new district attorney."

"That wasn't my intent."

"Fuck your intent. I gotta go." He cut the line, climbed out of his car, and began to run. Kevin was halfway down the bank when both figures in the boat went into the water.

———

A dozen strokes and he was nearly there. The water felt oily on his skin. The boat looked larger and darker than it had from shore. Kevin swam the final few yards underwater and surfaced near the bow, hand gripping the gunwale, world tipping crazily as he climbed in. He saw the notebook first. The Old English script of Saint Andrew's Grammar School. Bridget's name in her slanted cursive. Then he noticed the anchor rope by the stern, stretched tight and dipping over the side. Kevin looked down into the water. His sister looked back. She was sitting a foot or two below the surface, the rope knotted around her neck, eyes wide and milky dead with the cold. Kevin dove in. It was only when he was submerged in the grit of the river that he could see the second body, circling toward the bottom. Bobby was floating facedown, hair spread in a halo around his head. Kevin grabbed him under the shoulders and pulled for the surface. He didn't have the strength to lift him into the boat, so he tied a life jacket around his waist and towed him back to shore. On the bank, Kevin pumped Bobby's chest, tilted back his head, and blew into his mouth. After a few seconds, he began to cough up black water, then rolled over and retched. Kevin squatted by his friend, pounding him on the back, not really knowing what else to do. Finally, Bobby rolled back, head lolling in the wash from the river.

"Where did you come from?" His voice was cut up into rough pieces that scratched and tore.

"Father Lenihan told me what you had planned. Said you laid it out when you took confession."

"She kept notebooks, Kev. Started with your grandmother."

"I know. I found the knife she used." Somewhere above them, Kevin heard a police siren stretch and scream.

"She walked me through it, but I didn't listen. Just waited for a chance to get the rope around her neck and put her down. Couldn't be no trial. Not for that."

Bobby was right. He was always right, even when he wasn't.

"No one's gonna blame you, Bobby."

"How about Curtis Jordan?"

"That was a long time ago. And you did it to save me."

"I did it cuz I thought he deserved it. And I was the only one smart enough to play judge and jury. The only one tough enough. Except I got it wrong."

The sirens were searching, growing louder one minute, fading to nothing the next.

"We'll get a lawyer."

"Nah, we won't." Bobby's pale eyes flashed and Kevin remembered the lean face of the mutt, poking its head out of a burlap bag for a final sniff of sun and breeze off the river.

"You came back here to bury your past, Kev. Thing is, you gotta kill it first."

"I'm not sure I can do that."

"Come on. We'll do it together." Bobby stood, scraping the mud off his clothes with his hands and wading into the water. Kevin followed, his legs making small ripples that arced out in perfect concentric circles before disappearing into the murk. When they were far enough from shore, Bobby gripped Kevin's arm and pulled him close. His words came in quick gasps.

"I'm gonna buck and fight and wanna come up. You hold my head down until I take a breath. You'll know when it's over."

"Bobby." Kevin's voice drifted out into the abyss, sucked down into whatever soundless place words went.

"One breath and then there's nothing."

"Yeah."

Bobby patted him on the shoulder and knelt so the water was chest deep, lips moving silently as he wet his fingers and blessed himself.

Ashes to ashes, dust to dust. Dust thou art and unto dust thou shall return.

He took a final look at the sky, brushed in immaculate strokes of orange and red as the sun finally lifted clear of the city. Then he touched his lips with his tongue, took a small inhale, and ducked his head beneath the surface. Kevin gripped the back of his neck and held it. Bobby was still at first, then fought just like he said he would, bucking once, then twice. Kevin screamed silently as Bobby thrashed, his life, in the end, reduced to little more than a string of bubbles. Kevin watched the bubbles pop and die, the world spinning like a mad top, a human life leaking away beneath his fingertips. Then he pulled his friend, his brother, his family from the dark, sucking well of water. He held him, kissed him, and swore at him. They swore at each other, at life, death, and everything in between. Kevin dragged Bobby back to the shore and laid him out on the bank, more dead than alive, but alive all the same. And then Kevin told Bobby his plan. It was the same plan they'd used twenty-six years earlier, except this time Bobby was the one who needed protecting and Kevin was ready to do his part.

———

Five minutes later, he slipped back into the river, sliding like an eel toward the boat. His teeth chattered with the cold as he took shelter under the bow then dove, untying the anchor rope that held his sister fast and watching her body spiral down until it was lost from sight. Kevin surfaced at the stern, wiping his eyes clear and looping an arm over the gunwale. The plan was simple. Bobby would disappear and Kevin would cut a deal with Lisa. He'd give her the knife if she forgot about Bobby . . . and Curtis Jordan. Kevin knew his ex well enough to know she'd jump at the chance to clear the Patterson murder. In her world, it was all that ever really mattered. Kevin looked over his shoulder at the far bank of the river. He could just make out Bobby standing there and waved him to his car. Bobby didn't move. On the Boston side of the river, a gas guzzler in two tones of brown had pulled off Storrow Drive at a service exit and made its way to a small parking area in the shadow of the BU Bridge. Lollipops got out wearing a long coat and carrying what looked like a rifle. Kevin dove again, surfacing in a screen of weeds near the edge of the bank. The killer had threaded a path along the river and nestled in a copse of trees about twenty feet away. He braced himself against the trunk of a small pine and raised the rifle, pressing his cheek against the wooden stock and sealing his eye to the scope. Across the water, Bobby dropped to his knees, arms spread as he tipped his face to the sky. Kevin crawled closer until he could see the second hand on Lollipops's watch and the blue burn of his beard. Lollipops moved his finger onto the trigger then stopped, taking his eye off the scope and squinting at his target. The professional had hesitated—an act with its own reason, a domino with its own destiny, a sin with its own consequence. Kevin unzipped his jacket pocket and pulled out the snub-nosed revolver. The gun was cold and hard and wet in his hands. He shook it once and held it in front of him. The river lapped all around and the soft mud squelched underneath as he shifted to get a better angle with the gun. He noticed the set of the killer's jaw and the crook of his arm as he dropped the rifle another fraction and rested his finger on the metal guard, studying his prey as Kevin studied his, alive now until Kevin pulled the trigger and then the man would be no more and everything else would remain and nothing would change, except for Kevin. For Kevin, everything would change. That was how Bobby said it would be, and if anyone knew, it'd be Bobby. Kevin steadied the gun with two hands and felt his heart thump against the riverbank until the two were one. A bird screamed overhead, flitting across the water and sailing into the trees. Kevin squeezed the trigger twice. Lollipops grunted in surprise, the rifle slipping from his hands, his bulk sliding down the bank until he came to rest a few feet away. He stared at Kevin along the plane of the gun barrel, eternity resting on his tongue and not a word escaping his lips. Kevin fired twice more, then pulled himself up, crawling across the skin of grass to where the body lay and dragging it into the river. Everything was easier in the water, Lollipops leaking crimson clouds of blood and staring blankly at the sky as Kevin steered him toward the boat. Halfway there, Kevin let the weight sink, watching the killer's mouth fill with water, then pushing down with his feet. The snub-nosed revolver followed, both trailing Kevin's sister to the bottom. By the time he reached the boat Bobby was gone, a wink of brake lights marking his passage as he disappearead down Memorial Drive. Kevin climbed over the gunwale and sat on the wooden bench, listening as the sirens returned, watching as a parade of blue flashers worked their way down both sides of the river. He slid the oars into their slots and started to pull, slowly and steadily, for shore.

49

HE SAT at his desk with the windows open, a fresh breeze running uphill and blowing through the apartment. The place was bare, walls scraped clean, everything he owned boxed up and shipped off to its new home. All that was left was a blue-and-white Nike bag he'd parked by his feet. And the FedEx package. He opened it and pulled out a manila envelope from the office of the Suffolk County District Attorney. *KEVIN* was written across the front in Lisa's beautiful cursive—cursive that was chock-full of the future, her future, if only everyone cooperated. It had taken all of three weeks for Lisa to take Frank DeMateo's job. At a hastily called press conference, he announced he was stepping down to spend more time with his family. In return for his abdication, Lisa quietly agreed to support him if he ever put together a run for attorney general. Of course, there was every chance she'd be his opposition, but that particular shiv would have to wait for another day to find its way into the Republican's ample back. For now, Lisa was calling the shots.

Kevin broke the seal on the envelope just as his phone rang. Lisa's name flashed up on caller ID. Kevin pulled out a thick sheaf of papers and began to pick through them. The first page covered the money and the business. They'd found nearly two million dollars spread across four bank accounts, all of them linked back to Bridget. Between the cab office and the cellar of the apartment in J.P., another quarter million in cash and product—cocaine, heroin, hashish.

Kevin turned to the second page. A list of Bridget's dead.

Finn McDermott. The person she kept closest and someone to take the blame when things went south.

Rosie Tallent. Tasked by James Harper to find out who was cutting into Fidelis's drug trade. Asked the wrong questions and paid with her life. It was Harper who'd eventually be convicted of Rosie's murder—not part of Bridget's plan but still ironic as hell.

Sandra Patterson. The one that counted. Lisa's office took a statement from one of Bridget's rank-and-file couriers, a student at BC who had a bad feeling about Sandra and passed his suspicions up the food chain where, the D.A. surmised, they came to Bridget's attention.

Chrissy McNabb. Bridget's grade-school classmate and a good customer. Did she make the wrong remark to her school pal? Rely on that old connection a little too heavily? In the end, it didn't really matter. She was dead all the same.

Seamus Slattery. An Irishman whose one good eye turned out to be too big for his stomach.

Scott and Colleen Carson. A manager at the Royal identified Bridget as the woman who'd knocked on Scott's hotel room door. Scott had been pushing dope for Bridget and thus a loose end that needed tying up. As for Colleen, Lisa assumed Bridget was going to frame her for Scott's murder but still hadn't figured out why Colleen had written the note they'd found in her pocket. Kevin could have helped with that. More than anything his baby sister had always wanted Bridget's approval and would do anything for it, right up until the moment Bridget threw her off a roof.

The phone rang, two, three, four more times. Kevin turned to the last item in the package, a set of pages stapled together and covered by a clear plastic cover. Bridget's autopsy report.

The official cause of death was at the top of page two. SUICIDE. No mention of the rope marks around Bridget's neck. No mention of Lollipops's body, pulled out of the water by a police boat in the dead of night after the camera crews had left and the river had gone dark. No mention of Bobby. And no mention anywhere of Curtis Jordan. Damn the accountants. The books were being balanced, then closed for good. Better for the new D.A., better all around.

Kevin collected the paperwork and slid it back in the FedEx sleeve, setting it on the desk between his hands. The phone had stopped ringing. Downstairs, Mo Stanley was waiting patiently in a car packed for Chicago. He zipped open his bag and shoved the FedEx package inside. At the bottom of the bag were the dozen or so notebooks Bridget had kept detailing her crimes, including how she killed her grandmother. Kevin's grandmother. At the very bottom of the bag was a loaded thirty-eight with gray tape wrapped around the grip. A final gift from his ex. The one with the killer smile. She sure as hell didn't want it and probably figured he'd take care of it as well as anyone. He pulled out the gun and held it in his hands. It was the alpha and the omega. The beginning and the end. For Kevin they'd always be one and the same. He jammed the piece back in his bag, closed the windows in the apartment, and left. The phone started ringing again until it stopped. Then, it was quiet.

Acknowledgments

If my bones are Chicago, my blood is Boston, and specifically Brighton. It's where I grew up, a place most of my family still calls home, and, like any childhood neighborhood, an integral part of who I am. It was a lot of fun returning to those streets and setting this novel there. Hope you enjoy it.

Thanks to my editor, Zachary Wagman, who believed in this book from the beginning and pushed to make it all it could be. Thanks to his boss, Dan Halpern, as well as all the folks at Ecco who have been so passionate and worked so hard to get this book into the hands of readers. Thanks also to my agent, David Gernert, and my early readers, Garnett Kilberg Cohen from Columbia College in Chicago and Patrick Sviokla. Thanks to my family and friends in Boston, Chicago, and all points in between.

Finally, thanks to my wife, Mary Frances, for her unending patience and support. Love you.

About the Author

MICHAEL HARVEY'S six previous novels include *The Chicago Way* and *The Governor's Wife*. He's also a journalist and documentarian whose work has won multiple news Emmys, two Primetime Emmy nominations, and an Academy Award nomination. Raised in Boston, he now resides in Chicago.